Titles by Sofie Kelly

WHISKERS AND LIES

A MAGICAL CATS MYSTERY

SOFIE KELLY

BERKLEY PRIME CRIME
New York

BERKLEY PRIME CRIME
Published by Berkley
An imprint of Penguin Random House LLC
penguinrandomhouse.com

Copyright © 2022 by Penguin Random House LLC
Excerpt from *The Whole Cat and Caboodle* by Sofie Ryan
copyright © 2014 by Darlene Ryan

ISBN: 9780593200025

Berkley Prime Crime hardcover edition / September 2022
Berkley Prime Crime mass-market edition / September 2023

Printed in the United States of America

Book design by Kelly Lipovich

1

The grave was surrounded by a smooth expanse of green grass, the headstone perfectly centered at the head of a rectangle of freshly turned earth that marked the burial site.

"Too sad?" Georgia Tepper asked, a frown wrinkling the space between her eyebrows.

Ruby Blackthorne was standing beside me. Before I could say anything, she leaned forward, swiped a finger over the earth and popped it in her mouth. Then she grinned and shook her head. "As Goldilocks said to the three bears, 'Just right!'"

Since we were looking at a selection of cupcakes and not an actual grave and since the ground she'd just sampled was made of finely grated dark chocolate and not real dirt, I wasn't going to disagree with her.

Ruby plucked the headstone from the top of the cupcake, broke it in half, more or less, and offered one of the pieces to me. I took a bite. The cookie was delicious—chewy without being too soft and chocolatey but not too sweet.

"Number one, I agree with Ruby," I said. "All of the cupcakes are just right. And number two, is there any way I can add some of these headstone cookies to the order for the adults? Just the cookies? They're so good."

Georgia ducked her head and smiled. She wore her jet-black hair very short and looked like she was in her early twenties when she was in fact ten years older. She was a very talented baker, but she was still a little shy about compliments. "Of course you can. A dozen?"

"Better make it two dozen," Ruby said, tucking a strand of her purple-streaked hair behind one ear. She was wearing a pale-green T-shirt with a line drawing of a bunch of kale and the words *Kale Yeah!* on the front.

I did a quick mental count of the staff and everyone else who was helping with the Halloween party for the kids in the library's Reading Buddies program. Twelve cookies would *not* be enough for the adults. "Ruby's right. Make it two dozen."

The Reading Buddies Halloween Party was just as popular with the teens and adult mentors who helped out as it was with the children. And this year it was also a way to celebrate the success of our garden project.

For the past few months, the kids had been growing their own vegetables in raised boxes just outside the building. One Saturday morning a group of them had appeared in my office doorway to present me with the huge salad they had made for my lunch. Seeing their proud faces made all the work that had gone into the project worth it for me. And the salad was delicious!

Ruby was still eyeing the cupcake. "Maybe someone should try this one," she said. She glanced at Georgia. "Not that I think there's anything wrong with your baking."

"In the interest of quality control, I think you better," Georgia said, straight-faced.

I picked up a fork from the table and handed it to Ruby. "For quality control."

She took a bite of the chocolate cake and creamy frosting and immediately grinned.

Georgia smiled then as well, but she wasn't smiling at Ruby or at me. She was looking just beyond my right shoulder. I turned and saw Larry Taylor walking toward us. Georgia and Larry had been a couple for the past several months and I loved the way her face lit up whenever she was around him. The relationship wasn't just good for the two of them. Larry's father, my friend Harrison, had taken a liking to Georgia, and not just because he had a sweet tooth. The old man liked talking politics and Georgia always seemed to know what was going on in town. And I knew that Larry's brother, Harry, was happy about his younger sibling's relationship because now their father was focusing on someone else's love life other than Harry's.

Larry returned Georgia's smile then turned his attention to me as he came into the meeting room where we'd been sampling Georgia's baking. Larry Taylor was a big man with blond hair and green eyes. He wore a red-and-blue-plaid shirt with the sleeves rolled back and a zipper-front navy blue quilted vest.

"How were the cupcakes?" he asked.

"Delicious, of course," I said.

Ruby had just taken another bite of hers, but she nodded and gave Larry a thumbs-up.

I gestured at the long wooden table. "I had one of the chocolate spider cupcakes and half of a spice cake pumpkin-shaped cupcake, and if anyone asked me to pick which one was best, I would be stumped."

Larry grinned and patted his midsection. "I know the feeling."

Georgia's cheeks were tinged with pink once again at our praise. It wasn't that she lacked confidence in her skills. It was more that words of praise made her uncomfortable. She indicated a box on the table next to her purse. "Those are for the staff room."

"Thank you," I said. "You didn't have to do that. You've already put in so much effort on the cupcakes for the Halloween party."

"I wanted to," Georgia said. "You know how often Emmy is here, and you're all so good to her. That's just a small thank-you."

"Seeing her with a stack of books talking about manga with Levi or *Anne of Green Gables* with Mary makes my day. I've already made my pitch for her becoming the head librarian someday." Emmy was Georgia's daughter. She loved books.

"You should know the old man is already trying to sell Emmy on law school," Larry said.

"Why law school?" I asked.

He shrugged. "It looks like Elizabeth is getting more serious about actually applying to medical school. And Mariah is talking about studying engineering or becoming a mechanic."

Elizabeth was Larry and Harry's much younger sister. Mariah was Harry's daughter.

"He figures if he has a doctor, a mechanic and a lawyer in the family he has all the bases covered."

In the family. So it seemed that at least Harrison had long-term expectations for Georgia and Larry's relationship.

Ruby had demolished her cupcake. She licked the last bit of green icing off the back of her fork.

"Would you like the skeleton or the spider to take home?" Georgia asked her.

Ruby put both hands behind her head, linking her fingers together. "I don't know," she said.

"You could just go one potato, two potato," I teased.

She gave me a mock frown. "This is too serious a decision to decide by counting vegetables." She switched her attention to Georgia. "The skeleton is the marble cupcake, right?"

Georgia nodded. "It is."

"Then that's the one I'll take, thank you very much. Number one, I really like marble cake. It has chocolate and vanilla. And number two, that will leave the spider for Kathleen, which I know she really wants because she's kind of a chocolate freak."

I put one hand on my chest. "I prefer the term 'aficionado.' And thank you."

Ruby made a gesture like she was doffing her hat

and bowed. Then she reached for her camera, which was sitting on the table. "I just want to get a couple more photos," she said to Georgia. Ruby was taking pictures for a digital portfolio of Georgia's work.

I turned back to Larry. "Did you get all the measurements you needed?" I asked.

"I did," he said.

There was a wooden gazebo at the back of the library. In good weather we often held story time out there. Someone had been staging elaborate practical jokes in the gazebo—everything from fifteen bales of hay stacked in a precise formation to setting up an inflatable swimming pool and filling it with Jell-O. Black raspberry Jell-O to be specific.

So far, the prankster had managed to elude the security measures Larry and Harry had used to try and catch him or her. In fact, whomever it was seemed to have taken the summer and early fall off. I was hoping the stunts were over. Neither of the Taylors was convinced and Larry had a new, very small camera that he wanted to install just above the back loading dock doors. He was hoping to misdirect our culprit by putting up a second, larger dummy device. Larry was an electrician with an interest in pretty much anything technological and he'd built this newest camera himself.

"You didn't have to do that today," I said, "considering how it smells outside." Just before lunch a garbage truck had overturned and spilled most of its load on the street in front of the library.

He shrugged. "I played football in high school. You

want to smell something foul? Boys' locker room after a game." He gestured in the direction of the circulation desk. "That air cleaner seems to be helping. It's not bad in here."

"Your brother showed up with that about half an hour after the truck overturned. Otherwise we might have had to close."

Larry smiled. "Well, the truck's upright now and about to be towed away by the looks of things, and they'll soon have the rest of the garbage cleaned up. Do you know what happened?"

"Apparently the driver took the turn too fast, and then braked too fast when a pair of squirrels ran in front of him," I said. "I guess his load shifted and the truck went over. At least no one was hurt."

The building had shaken when the garbage truck tipped, and I was happy to see both the driver and his helper climb out of the passenger-side window of the cab. Nonetheless I'd made them both sit on the curb until the ambulance arrived.

"I should be able to get everything installed on Monday as long as the weather stays good," Larry said.

Before I could offer, once again, to at least reimburse him for the electronics, he raised a hand. "I know what you're going to say, and the library doesn't owe me a penny. As far as I'm concerned it's no different than the old man and that dang groundhog."

Harrison had been battling a cocky groundhog that had been eating from his garden all summer. He'd tried spraying a mix of garlic and hot peppers around the garden, he'd sprinkled Epsom salts on the ground and even planted lavender. The groundhog had not been deterred. In fact, it seemed to like the scent of the garlic and hot peppers.

"Is it still around?" I asked.

Larry nodded. "Oh yeah. I'm not making this up, I swear it's bowling with the pumpkins. It's a sneaky little bugger."

I laughed. "As far as the groundhog war goes, it seems to me the rodent is winning."

He smiled. "Elizabeth got the old man a Super Soaker water gun. The Taylors don't give up without a fight."

"I've noticed that," I said. "And for the record, there will be no sitting on the roof trying to nail our practical joker with a Super Soaker water gun."

"You don't seem to understand how a good feud works," he said, pointing a finger at me.

Ruby tapped me on the shoulder. She had finished taking photos and she was holding a small waxed paper bag with her cupcake. "I need to get over to the co-op store for my shift," she said.

I gave her a one-arm hug. "Thank you for being here. The party wouldn't be coming together so well without all your help."

She smiled. "Hey, anytime. You know I like the rug rats." She inclined her head in Georgia's direction and nudged Larry—whom she'd known since they were in school—with an elbow. "Don't mess this up," she stage-whispered. She gave me a wave and she was gone.

Larry pulled a hand over his hair. "The other night

Dad told me if I was stupid enough to blow things with Georgia that the family will really miss . . . me."

I glanced over at Georgia to see if she'd heard what Larry had just said. She was staring at something out in the main area of the library, clutching her phone in one hand, frozen in place so still she didn't seem to even be breathing. Larry immediately crossed over to her, putting a hand on her shoulder. "Hey, what's wrong?" he said.

Georgia shook her head very slightly, the movement almost imperceptible. I saw her struggle to swallow as though something had gotten stuck in her throat. I followed her gaze and saw a man and a woman, in their early seventies I guessed, coming toward us. I had seen the woman in the building when I'd arrived just before lunch. She was at least a couple of inches taller than my five-six, with soft curls of blond hair—no gray in sight. She wore tailored jeans, a crisp white button-down shirt topped with a simple black blazer and a black-and-white-plaid scarf at her neck. The only bit of color was her red flats. She was all cool, intimidating elegance. I remembered, when I'd seen her earlier, how she'd frowned at four-year-old Payton Weston, in line to check out three picture books and happily singing "The Wheels on the Bus" while she waited.

The man she was with was a bit taller, five-ten or so, dressed in black trousers, a medium-blue pullover sweater and a black leather jacket. His iron-gray hair was clipped short on the sides and a little longer on the top. Everything about the two of them said money.

Georgia still hadn't spoken. Her lips were pressed tightly together, and her eyes were locked on the couple. I saw her fumble for Larry's hand and, when she found it, grip it tightly.

"What is it?" Larry asked again.

"It's them," she said, and all at once I realized who the man and woman were. No wonder Georgia looked so stricken. This had to be her former in-laws, the people who had tried to take Emmy after the death of Georgia's husband, their son, Scott. This had to be Hugh and Margery Wyler.

I stepped in front of Georgia, blocking her view of the Wylers for a moment. "I can tell them to leave," I said. Georgia closed her eyes. Then she let out a shaky breath and looked directly at me. "No," she said. "I knew this day was coming. I've been waiting for it for the past three years." Her voice was stronger than I'd expected. *Georgia* was stronger than the frightened woman who had come to Mayville Heights to hide more than three years ago.

Out of the corner of my eye I saw recognition spread across Larry's face. "Kathleen, is that . . . ?" he began. He didn't finish the sentence because he didn't need to.

I nodded. "Yes. The man and woman out there are Georgia's former in-laws."

His expression hardened, the muscles along his jawline tightening. Georgia finally looked at him. "Don't," she said. "I can do this." She let go of Larry's hand and took a couple of steps forward. Her chin went up and she squared her shoulders.

The Wylers stopped just inside the doorway.

"Hello, Paige," Margery Wyler said. She actually smiled but there was no warmth in it.

Georgia had changed her name from Paige Wyler to Georgia Tepper when she and Emmy had gone on the run to hide from her husband's parents. Once she'd settled in Mayville Heights she'd made that name her legal one. It was the name she'd asked us all to use.

She eyed Margery for a long moment before she spoke. "My name is Georgia," she finally said. "What are you doing here?"

"We'd like to see our granddaughter, of course," Hugh Wyler said, using the same pleasant conversational tone he might have used to comment on the sunny fall day outside.

I thought about what I knew about the couple. The Wylers, it seemed, had never liked their daughter-in-law. Scott Wyler had died in a car accident when Emmy was only six months old. The Wylers had tried to wrestle custody away from their daughter-in-law, arguing, among other things, that they were better equipped financially and educationally to raise Emmy. When that didn't work and Georgia was unwilling to move in with them, they had tried to kidnap the child. Georgia had been arrested and charged with assault because she'd pushed Margery and threatened her with a kitchen knife when the latter had attempted to lure the toddler away from her mother. The charges had been dropped once the truth about what Margery Wyler had been trying to do came out. But thanks to the couple's money and connections, there had been no charges against the Wylers. Georgia, who was still Paige at that point, had grabbed her daughter and run, changing the child's name from Ani to Emmy. She'd been looking over her shoulder ever since.

Georgia was shaking her head before Hugh Wyler was finished speaking. "That is never going to happen," she said. Her voice was cool and matter-of-fact.

"We have a new attorney," he continued, as though her words had been in some language he didn't understand. "The law is more aware of the importance of the grandparent-grandchild relationship now. We don't want to go to court over visitation. We would rather work things out privately." He held out his hands as though he were offering her something.

There was a look of disdain in Georgia's eyes even as the hand she had behind her back was trembling. "There is nothing to work out," she said. "Nothing has changed. The two of you haven't changed. You forfeited the right to see your granddaughter a long time ago."

Hugh Wyler's mouth pulled into a hard, thin line and anger flashed in his eyes. His wife put a hand on his shoulder. "Please, Paige," she said, "all I want—all we want—is to know our granddaughter. It's what Scott would have wanted."

"When did you ever care about what Scott wanted?" Georgia asked. Her hand wasn't shaking anymore. It was pulled into a hard, tight fist. "All the two of you ever cared about was what you both wanted, or to be more specific, Margery, what you wanted, so why would you start caring now?"

Her former mother-in-law tried to speak, but Georgia closed the distance between them and talked over her. "I would be happy to go to court because when a judge hears what you tried to do, you will never, ever get to see my daughter. Your money and your connections don't work here." She held up one finger in what was clearly a warning. "Stay away from my child. Or I will cause you more pain than you can imagine."

"Is that a threat?" Hugh Wyler asked, his tone somewhat mocking.

Larry stepped between Georgia and the couple. "You need to leave now," he said.

"This is none of your business," Mr. Wyler said, a challenge clear in his voice and his eyes.

"If you push me, you'll find out just how hard I can push back," Georgia interjected, leaning around Larry and raising her voice slightly.

I stepped forward, moving around the coatrack to the right of the door and briefly touching Georgia's arm. I gave Larry a warning look that I hoped he understood as I moved in front of him. "This is a library," I said, keeping my voice and my words as neutral as possible. "This is not the place for this conversation."

"This is a private matter," Hugh Wyler replied, his tone condescending.

He seemed to be the type of person who didn't have a lot of experience with hearing no. I thought about my formidable mother, who had directed actors twice her size and with enough ego to spill off the stage. I was Thea Paulson's daughter, and I wasn't going to be intimidated by a bully.

"Yes, it is a private matter," I agreed, "and this is a *public* library." I put a little extra emphasis on the word "public." "I'm Kathleen Paulson. I run this library and I am asking you, respectfully, to go." I paused for a moment, keeping my eyes fixed on Hugh Wyler's face.

His wife put a hand on his arm. The sleeve of her black jacket slipped back. She was wearing a vintage Cartier Tank watch with a black leather strap and an ornate rectangular gold case on her right wrist. "I thought there was a chance that Paige would be reasonable," she said. "I can see that, sadly, I was wrong."

"I'll see you out," I said.

"There's no need for that," her husband replied.

Once again, I channeled my mother, straightened my spine and gestured in the direction of the circulation desk. "The main doors are this way."

I took a step forward and the Wylers were forced to move back. I led them to the front entrance. The smell from the garbage truck was much stronger there. Mr. Wyler made a sour face.

Mrs. Wyler didn't seem to notice the odor at all. She glanced at her husband as he put a hand to his face, frowned and then turned her attention to me. "She isn't who she pretends to be," she said. "You'll see."

They were gone before I had a chance to reply.

2

I stopped at the circulation desk to tell Susan that Georgia and I had a couple of things we still needed to take care of.

Susan had pushed her cat's-eye glasses up onto the top of her head and her topknot was listing a little to one side. I knew that she had seen me escort the Wylers to the front doors and was probably curious about what was going on but all she said was, "No problem. Mary's shelving right now and Levi will be here soon. We've got this." It had been a busy afternoon despite the smell outside. The building was over a hundred years old, but it had been beautifully renovated several years ago and a lot of people used the space now.

Levi was our part-time student. His wide-ranging reading interests and his friendly personality had made him a big hit with our patrons. Mary looked like—and was—a sweet older woman in her seasonal collection of cardigan sweaters. She was also state champion in kickboxing for her age group. And Susan, who had genius-level twin boys, was pretty much unflappable. I knew the three of them could handle anything that came up.

I went back to the meeting room. Larry was standing in front of Georgia, talking in a low voice, his hands on her shoulders. They both looked at me when I stepped back into the room.

"They're gone," I said.

"Are you sure?" Larry asked. His hair was a bit disheveled, as though he'd run his hands through it.

I nodded. "I am. I saw them get into a car in the parking lot and I watched them drive away."

"I have to get Emmy," Georgia said. She was squeezing her hands together so tightly her knuckles were white, the skin stretched taut over them.

Larry looked at his watch. "Emmy's still in class. She's safe. They can't get her."

She was already shaking her head. "You don't know what they're like. You don't know what they're capable of."

"Emmy's school won't let out for another half an hour," I said. "They're not going to let a stranger take her."

"You need to talk to Brady," Larry said. Brady Chapman had been Georgia's lawyer for a while now. He was good at what he did. He should be able to stop the Wylers.

"I can't do anything until I know Emmy is safe," Georgia said. I could see the fear in her eyes and hear the edge of panic in her voice.

Larry reached up and brushed a stray strand of

hair off her forehead. "I'll go pick Emmy up from school. You put me on the sign-out list, so it won't be a problem. I'll be there when the bell rings and I'll go right to her classroom and get her. I don't think your former in-laws would be stupid enough to go anywhere near the school, but I promise they would never get past me. You know how much I love that kid."

Georgia swallowed a couple of times. "Okay," she finally said.

"You can stay here, upstairs in my office," I said. "No one will know you're still in the building and you can call Brady."

She nodded and turned to Larry again. "The word of the day is 'dragon.' "

"Dragon," he repeated. "Got it." He kissed the top of her head and then he looked at me.

"I'll stay with her until you get back," I said in answer to his unspoken question.

"Thanks," he said. He grabbed his jacket from the coatrack by the door and was gone.

Georgia watched him head for the main doors. "Emmy and I have a code word. If anyone comes to pick her up and doesn't know the word, even if the person is on the approved pick-up list with the school, she knows not to go with them." She looked at me then. "I know it probably makes me sound like some kind of crazy person, but it's the only way to keep her safe."

My chest ached thinking about the kind of stress Georgia had been living with for most of Emmy's life. "You're not crazy. You're just being a mother."

We gathered up the forks and plates and took them, the rest of the cupcakes and Georgia's coat and purse upstairs. I put the cupcakes in the staff room and noticed that someone—probably Susan—had made a pot of coffee not that long ago. I poured a cup for myself and one for Georgia, added cream and sugar to both and went back to my office.

Georgia was standing behind my desk, looking out the window at the grass and the water beyond it.

I offered her one of the mugs. "Cream and sugar, right?"

She nodded. "Thanks," she said, taking the coffee from me. She took a sip and wrapped both hands around the big pottery mug. She seemed less frightened, more in control now. "I always knew this day was coming, you know, but now it's here it's hard not to panic."

I sat on the corner of my desk. "I get that," I said, "as much as I can. You're a great mom and there is a town full of people who will be happy to tell that to any judge or lawyer or social worker."

"Mayville Heights is home," Georgia said. "I can't imagine being anywhere else."

I took a sip of my coffee, searching for the right words to let her know that everyone who knew her would be on her side. "Nobody will let the Wylers hurt you or Emmy."

She looked out the window for a moment and then back at me. "Hugh and Margery have a lot of money and influence, Kathleen, and they've always used it to get what they want."

I thought about my neighbors, Rebecca and Everett Henderson. They had money and influence and neither one of them would ever use those things to try to take a child away from her mother. I also knew that they would do anything to help Georgia if they found out what was going on.

"Everyone loves Margery," Georgia said. "All they see is this wonderful, sweet person who puts on spectacular parties for charity. She wears that image like it's a costume." She held her mug with one hand and wrapped the other around herself as though she were cold.

"Eight days before the wedding she offered me money to not marry Scott." Her voice was flat and emotionless.

I shook my head. "That's horrible."

"I didn't tell him. It's not that he wouldn't have believed me. He knew his mother was manipulative. It's just that I couldn't bring myself to hurt him that way, to make him see just how low she'd sink." She took a breath and let it out slowly. "And no one else would have believed me. I mean, it was just my word against hers, but I swear it's the truth."

"I believe you," I said. Because my parents were seasoned actors adept at taking on someone else's personality, I was pretty good at sussing out subterfuge. Even though Georgia's reaction to the Wylers was very emotional, I didn't see any signs that she was lying. Nothing in her body language or her voice suggested she wasn't being truthful.

"Margery had planned Scott's whole life. He was

supposed to marry his college girlfriend, go to medical school so Margery could say 'my son the doctor' and have a son to carry on the family name. Instead he married me, became a teacher and we had Emmy."

"It sounds like a pretty good life to me."

Georgia nodded and gave me a sad smile. "It was a wonderful life. Even with all the turmoil Margery caused, we were happy. We were supposed to grow old together." Her eyes filled with tears and she blinked a couple of times. "Right after Emmy was born Scott decided we should move across the country and cut off contact with his parents because of the way they had treated me and reacted to Emmy's birth. I talked him out of it. I thought with a little time the baby would win Margery over, at least a bit, and if she changed her mind then Hugh would go along. But Margery couldn't get past her belief that Scott had made a mistake in marrying me."

She cleared her throat and her voice was softer when she spoke again. "I talked him out of having the life he wanted. I was wrong. Maybe if we'd left he'd still be alive."

"You were trying to find the good in your husband's mother. That doesn't make you a bad wife. It makes you a pretty good person."

There was a tap on my office door then. Larry had arrived with Emmy. Georgia wrapped her daughter in a hug. "Are you done with your meeting?" Emmy asked.

"We are," Georgia said.

Emmy looked at me. "Hi, Kathleen," she said. "Did

you like my mom's cupcakes?" She was tall for her age with chin-length blond hair with a blue streak in the front courtesy of Ruby. Emmy was in fifth grade but tended to choose books a couple of years beyond her grade level.

"They were delicious as usual," I said. "I think my favorite is the spider."

"Well, yeah, because it's all chocolate."

"Exactly," I said, wrinkling my nose at her. "Do you want to come out with me to check on the lettuce in the cold frames?" The Reading Buddies kids were growing lettuce and radishes in the cold frames Harry Taylor had built at the side of the building.

"Can I?" Emmy asked, turning to look at her mother.

Georgia nodded. "Go ahead."

"Can we pick some of the lettuce?" Emmy asked as we started down the stairs.

"Harry says we need to wait another week." I scanned the main floor of the library just in case the Wylers had come back. There was no sign of them.

She shrugged. "Okay."

We looked at all the lettuce—there were three varieties—and decided it was all doing well. Emmy was kneeling down next to me. She brushed her hair back out of her face. "You know a lot of things because of your job, right?" she asked.

"I do," I said, wondering what was on her mind.

"Can a woman propose to a man? I think it's okay because my mother and my teacher both say girls can do anything boys can do and Harrison says they can do more than boys because they have babies, too."

I stifled a smile because that sounded so much like the old man. "I agree with all three of them," I said, standing up and pulling Emmy to her feet. "I don't know of any reason a woman can't propose to a man."

"Some of my friends say it's not the right way to do things."

We started walking toward the main door. "Well, a man being the one who does the asking is a tradition that goes back a long way and some people like tradition. Who are you planning on marrying?"

Emmy laughed. "I'm ten. I'm not getting married until I'm really old, maybe thirty."

I nodded. "Sounds like a good plan."

"What I want to do is propose to Larry. I want him to marry my mom and be my dad."

I suddenly had a lump in my throat. I swallowed a couple of times. "It doesn't work that way," I said.

Emmy frowned up at me. "Why? My real dad . . ." She stopped. "I mean my biological dad died when I was a baby and from all the things my mom has told me about him, he wouldn't be mad."

I kicked a rock and sent it skittering along the walkway. "From everything I've heard about him I agree with you, but you can't propose to Larry."

"So what you said before about a woman being allowed to propose to a man isn't true after all."

She had stopped walking and her hands were on her hips.

It struck me that the child was scary smart.

"No," I said. "It is true, which means it would be

okay for your mom to ask Larry to marry her, if it's what she wanted and if she thought it's what he wanted."

"But because I'm a kid I can't do it."

I nodded. "Yes."

She made a face. "Well, that sucks."

"Some things in life do," I agreed.

We went back up to my office. Georgia seemed better now that Emmy was close by.

"We're going over to Brady's office right now," she said quietly, while Emmy told Larry about the lettuce. "Thank you for everything. Thank you for being my friend."

"If you need anything, call me. Please," I said.

Georgia nodded, and then to my surprise she wrapped me in a hug. She wasn't a demonstrative person and I felt that lump back in my throat again.

As I drove home at the end of the day I couldn't help thinking about Georgia. I wondered how the meeting with Brady had gone. I wondered if the Wylers were still in town.

Hercules was waiting for me, sitting on the top step by the back door. The little tuxedo cat had his left paw on something brown and knobby and had a decidedly smug look on his face.

"Have you been fighting with the grackle again?" I asked. He and one of the large black birds—or maybe it was several of them for all I knew—had been having regular skirmishes over the backyard for quite some time now. Hercules managed to snag the occasional grackle feather and the bird managed to swipe the occasional sardine cracker. Their battles seemed to me to be mostly posturing.

"Mrrr," he said, wrinkling his nose. I leaned down to see what was under his paw. He immediately pulled his treasure a little closer to his body. The cat wasn't very good at sharing.

"Just let me see," I said. He gave me a glare and I glared right back at him. Reluctantly, he lifted his paw. His find was a brown rubber wishbone.

"Where did you get that?" I asked.

He looked skyward and then looked at me, all green-eyed innocence.

"No, it did not just fall out of the sky."

He continued to stare at me without blinking.

I looked around the yard. "Does that belong to Fifi?" I asked.

His response was to set his paw back on the toy. Hercules was very much a finders-keepers kind of cat, unless what had been found by someone else belonged to him.

Fifi was my next-door neighbor's dog. The name suggested a small bundle of fur with attitude, when in fact the dog was a German shepherd–sized mixed breed that hid whenever he saw Hercules or his brother, Owen. Yes, *he*.

"That has to go back to the Justasons' yard," I said. I had no doubt that Hercules had been nosing around over there, probably while Fifi hid around the side of the house. Dogs were not the cat's favorite creatures, and this was the first one he had ever encountered that was afraid of him.

He bent down and picked up the rubber wishbone in his mouth and then eyed the back door, a glint of defiance in his eyes.

"Don't even think about it," I warned.

He took a step toward the door.

I felt a little like the captain of a pirate ship whose crew was about to mutiny. Time to pull out my cutlass. "I wonder if Fifi likes sardine crackers."

Hercules froze but he didn't set the toy down.

"Maybe I'll walk over after supper for a visit," I continued.

Several seconds passed. Then he set the wishbone down, gave a disgruntled murp and walked through the door into the porch. Walked through as in he went directly through the solid door without waiting for me to unlock or open it. That was because Hercules wasn't exactly an ordinary cat. He could pass through solid objects like doors and walls without any problem whatsoever. I had no idea how or why and it wasn't the sort of thing I felt I could ask anyone.

Owen, his brother, didn't have the same skill. Owen's talent was the ability to become invisible at will, which generally meant at a time most inconvenient for me. The only person who knew about the boys' abilities was Marcus.

Detective Marcus Gordon was not the kind of person who believed in things that didn't have a rational, logical explanation. He was a just-the-facts police detective, albeit a very cute one. Ever since I'd told him

about Owen and Hercules—and his own cat, Micah—
and convinced him I wasn't having some kind of mental breakdown, he'd been trying to find an explanation
for what all three of them could do. (Like Owen, Micah could vanish whenever she felt like it.) Marcus
requested just about every physics book the library
system had and he still had no answers. I didn't think
there were any. Some things just defied explanation.

I let myself into the porch. I discovered Hercules
had already made his way into the kitchen when I
unlocked the back door. He was sitting over by the
refrigerator with his back to the rest of the room and
to me. I was on ignore.

I changed from my work clothes to a red sweater
and jeans. Hercules continued to act as though I
wasn't in the room. I'd managed to leave the library a
little early. Susan was taking care of locking up the
building so I had time to grab some supper before I
met Marcus. I fed both cats and heated up a bowl of
chili for myself. I worked late on Friday nights and
usually took a supper break, but two of our ancient
computers had decided to stop working at once and it
had taken all of my supper break and all of my limited
computer skills to get them running again. Luckily
our new computers—the result of a very successful
fund-raising campaign—were arriving soon.

After he'd finished eating, Owen made his way
over to me, looking at his brother and then at me,
cocking his head to one side.

"We're having philosophical differences."

"Mrrr," he said. He took a couple of swipes at his

face with a paw. If things didn't affect him directly, Owen, like most cats, wasn't interested.

I cleared the table and when I turned around again, he was sitting on my chair washing his face a little more thoroughly. "How was your day?" I asked.

"Merow," he said, without missing a pass of his paw. Translation: "Fine."

I ran the water in the sink for the dishes and wiped the table. Owen paused his grooming routine to meow softly again. *How was your day?*

I told him all about Georgia and her former in-laws showing up at the library. Even though Hercules was ignoring me I saw one ear move, which told me he was listening as well. I talked to Owen and Hercules a lot. Part of it was just a way for me to sort out my own thoughts by hearing them out loud. But a small part of me was certain that they understood what I was saying, as outlandish as that sounded. When I was finished, Owen jumped down to the floor and made his way over to where my messenger bag—containing my laptop—was hanging on a hook next to my jacket. He looked at the bag and then at me. Both cats often helped me with my online research, not a fact I shared with anyone else.

"You're right, we should see what we can find out about the Wylers," I said. I checked the kitchen clock. "But not right now. I'm meeting Marcus in a little while. Tomorrow."

I gave him two sardine crackers and left two in Hercules's dish. He had wandered off somewhere, still full of righteous cat indignation.

                                *   *   *

It was a beautiful night, so I decided to walk down the
hill. Marcus had worked even later than I had so we
were meeting for dessert at the St. James Hotel and
then going to a screening of *Gaslight* at the Stratton
Theatre. I loved old movies, and Marcus had never
seen this one. As we walked through the lobby, I spotted Margery Wyler talking to a middle-aged man. He
wore dark pants and an olive-green Henley sweater. I
couldn't see his face, but the set of his shoulders and
the way his hands were punctuating his words suggested that he wasn't happy with Mrs. Wyler.

"Do you know those people?" Marcus asked as he
opened the door to the hotel's restaurant.

"I know her," I said. "Well, I kind of know her."

He raised an eyebrow. "I sense a story."

I nodded. "A complicated one."

We found a table near the windows. Our waiter,
Lena, was a friend of Levi's. She had been in the library several times. She liked old movies and hard
science-fiction novels. I suspected she also liked Levi.

"If you're here for dessert I recommend the apple
galette with vanilla whipped cream instead of ice
cream," she said.

"That's what we came to try," I said.

She smiled. "Word is getting around."

I ordered a glass of wine, and since Marcus was
driving he ordered coffee. After Lena brought our
drinks, I told Marcus about Georgia's in-laws and

their efforts to see Emmy. "I know there are two sides to every story, but I can't help siding with Georgia."

"You know her," he said, tracing a finger around the rim of his coffee cup. "And it sounds as though the Wylers didn't make a good impression."

"They didn't," I said. "I didn't see any genuine emotion from Mrs. Wyler except for her comment to me when I walked them out."

He reached across the small table and put his hand over mine. "Brady is a good lawyer. And Georgia has a lot of friends in town."

"And from what she told me, the Wylers have a lot of money."

"Money can't get you everything you want," Marcus said as Lena came toward us carrying a large tray.

The galette was as good as everyone had said it would be and Lena was right about the vanilla whipped cream being perfect with it. As we ate Marcus and I talked about spending the holiday season in Boston with my family. I was eager to see them all, but I wasn't sure Marcus really understood what he was getting himself into.

"Mom and Dad have a performance on New Year's Eve," I warned him, "and since they both pretty much live their parts I can promise it's going to be chaotic. Plus, Ethan will be performing with his band and Sara should be working on her latest film." My brother was a musician and my sister was a makeup artist and filmmaker.

Marcus took a drink of his coffee and smiled. "I'm

looking forward to seeing your family doing the things that make them happy. And I know it makes *you* happy to see them. I don't care how crazy it gets."

"I need to ask Lena how they make the vanilla whipped cream," I said.

Marcus looked confused at the sudden change in the conversation. "Why? Do you want to make some?"

I nodded. "I do, for you when you have to eat your words."

He laughed. "So will Rebecca and Maggie look after Owen and Hercules while we're in Boston?"

I swirled a bite of apple and pastry through the whipped cream and ate it before I answered. "They already offered. What are you going to do about Micah?"

Micah was a small ginger tabby. Like Hercules and Owen, she had come from Wisteria Hill, the old Henderson estate just outside of town.

"Roma and Eddie have offered to take care of her." He smiled. "You know, we still have to introduce Micah to Owen and Hercules one of these days."

"I know," I said. "I need to talk to Roma and get some advice on the best way to go about that."

"You're stalling," he said, pointing at me with his fork. "Talk to Roma the next time you see her."

"I will," I said. "I promise."

"So everything is settled for the holidays. Nothing is going to go wrong. We're spending Christmas and New Year's in Boston. I promise it will be special."

I set down my fork and studied him across the table. "How can you be a police officer and still be such a positive person?"

He shrugged. "I don't know. I've seen people do some horribly despicable things, but I've also seen acts of incredible sacrifice and bravery. In the end, I just think there are more good people in the world than there are bad ones."

I was waiting for Marcus to pay our bill when Denny Albrecht came in carrying a bottle of champagne. I knew Denny slightly from my friend Maggie's yoga class. He smiled when he caught sight of me.

"Are you working here?" I asked.

He nodded. "I'm bartending on Friday and Saturday nights. I don't know if you heard my good news. I got into nursing school."

I smiled at him. "I'm so happy to hear that."

"Thank you for all the books you got for me to study for my PAX exam," he said.

"I'm glad they helped."

He held up the bottle he was holding. "I better get this over to the table—newly engaged couple. It was good to see you."

"You too, Denny," I said. "Good luck."

Marcus and I decided to park his SUV at the library and walk over to the theater. The street was clean and there was no sign of the mess that had been there earlier in the day.

The movie was a bit late starting so it was after eleven when we stepped outside. *Gaslight* was one of my favorite classic movies and I was happy to have been able to see it again on the big screen.

It was a beautiful, not-too-cool night, with the stars

a sparkling canopy overhead. We headed in the direction of the library. As we walked, I told Marcus about Larry's latest plan to catch the practical joker.

"I thought you felt whoever it is was done," Marcus said. "He or she has been quiet for weeks now."

"I do. Harry and Larry disagree. And I think Larry's pride is still smarting over our joker finding his last security camera and disabling it so easily. You know the Taylors all have the same stubborn streak as Harrison."

"So where exactly is he going to set up the camera?" Marcus asked.

"On one side of the loading dock door and not too high up because I don't want whoever the culprit is to be climbing around on the roof." We were almost at the library. I tugged at his hand. "C'mon, I'll show you."

We cut across the grass to the back of the building. Marcus saw it first. "Kathleen," he said, pointing at the gazebo.

"Crap on toast," I muttered. I had jinxed myself with all my talk about how I thought our merry prankster was done. What looked like a centaur without a head stood in the middle of the gazebo. "Whoever this is seems to have a sense of humor," I said to Marcus. "Half man, half horse, no head. It's a headless horse/man."

The back end of the horse/man looked to be some part of a lawn ornament. It wasn't as big as a real horse, but it looked close to pony size. The front section seemed to be from a mannequin with the head detached. It was dressed in breeches, a ruffled white shirt and a huge black cape. I thought that the clothes looked like something I'd seen in a production at the high school. As much as these stunts were a mess to clean up, I was also taken by the person's creativity. As practical jokes went, these were pretty benign.

"Do you have to call this in?" I asked Marcus. "Technically is it even vandalism?"

"How about we check the gazebo and the building just to make sure nothing's been damaged?" he said.

I nodded. "All right." I made a wide circuit around the gazebo, but aside from the headless horse/man it looked just the same as it had when I'd left work. I glanced down along the riverbank hoping that somehow I'd catch sight of whoever had set this whole thing up. The library had closed at eight and it was nearly eleven thirty now. Whoever it was couldn't have been gone that long.

I didn't see anyone in any direction along the shoreline. It was still and silent in both directions. Then something caught my eye in the grass a few feet ahead of where I was standing. I walked over and picked it up.

It was a driver's license. It belonged to Margery Wyler.

3

I looked around. There was no sign of Mrs. Wyler. How had her driver's license ended up behind the library? I felt uneasy. This didn't make sense.

I walked back to Marcus. My face must have given me away. "What's wrong?" he asked.

I held out Mrs. Wyler's license.

He took it from me and studied it for a moment. He looked up at me. "Hang on, isn't this Georgia's former mother-in-law?"

I nodded. "It is. I don't like this."

"Let's take a look around," Marcus said.

We started moving along the embankment. I had gone over the side once myself, on the stretch of the Riverwalk across from the St. James Hotel, and I knew how dangerous the rocky shoreline could be. I gave an involuntary shiver at the memory. If Mrs. Wyler had fallen, we needed to find her fast.

"You're sure you didn't see anyone before you found that license?" Marcus asked.

"I'm positive. There was no sign of anyone in either direction." It was a clear night and the moon was almost full. I didn't see how I could have missed Margery Wyler or anyone else if they had been anywhere nearby.

Marcus was using the flashlight app on his phone to give us more light. There was some scraggly brush—alder, high bush cranberry and dogwood for the most part—in some areas close to the edge and he swept it with his free arm but there was no sign of anyone.

I concentrated on scanning the ground below the embankment all the way out to the water's edge. The moonlight glinted off the water and I could see out into it a good eight to ten feet. There was no sign of a person, and no indication that the water had been disturbed.

"I don't see anyone," I said.

Marcus raked a hand through his dark hair. "Be careful. Don't get too close to the edge."

I stopped for a moment, closed my eyes and listened intently, hoping to hear something, but other than the night sounds there was nothing.

When I opened my eyes again Marcus was standing beside me. "This isn't working," he said. "I need to call this in. I should have done it sooner. We need more light. We need more people searching."

"I know," I said. I took one small step closer to the edge of the bank and looked up along the waterline. I tried not to search for anything, just let my eyes pick up whatever was there. And then I saw something up ahead on the gravel shore between the bottom of the embankment and the water's edge. I wasn't sure what it was. Was it a person? Maybe. I leaned sideways and almost lost my balance.

Marcus grabbed my arm.

"There's something up ahead," I told him, pointing at the shape on the ground. "See? Right there at the edge of the water."

"I see it," he said.

I looked at him. "It could be a person, couldn't it?"

"Maybe," he said. "I need to get down there and find out, and we need some help." He pulled out his phone again.

I knew that there was a makeshift path down to the water somewhere just ahead. I remembered Harry Taylor telling me that he thought it was the way the practical joker had been traveling. Harry had said the path was just on the other side of a large rocky out-cropping. If that was a person lying down there, maybe injured, every minute mattered. I started along the grass, looking for some sign of the path.

And there, just ahead, where the embankment curved, I found it. I didn't wait for Marcus. I started to make my way down the precipice, grabbing rocks and exposed tree roots to keep from falling.

Marcus appeared above me. "It's definitely a person," I said. I slipped a bit on some loose rocks but put out both hands and managed to stop my slide.

"Are you all right?" he called down to me.

"I'm fine." I moved a little to the right and more loose rocks skittered down to the shoreline, but the ground felt more stable.

It was slow going but I finally made it to the bottom. I picked my way over to what I could now see was a woman's body sprawled on the rocks. She was lying half on her back, her head half-turned, and she wasn't moving. The going was slippery. The rocks were wet and many of them had a slimy coating of some kind, algae I guessed.

Marcus was right behind me. He felt for a pulse at the woman's neck and shook his head. "I'll do chest compressions," he said. "Can you do the breathing?"

I nodded. "I can."

He caught the woman by her shoulders and pulled the top half of her body sideways so it was off the rocks and more on the flatter, gravel shore. Marcus immediately started chest compressions as I moved to the other side of her head to start breathing for her. I brushed a clump of wet hair off of the woman's face. It was Margery Wyler.

I felt the taste of something sour at the back of my throat. I swallowed it down and started mouth-to-mouth, concentrating only on the rhythm of the rescue breathing, willing Mrs. Wyler to breathe, to move, to be alive. Her body was still warm. At one point I glanced at Marcus, who wordlessly shook his head. Margery Wyler's heart wasn't beating. She wasn't breathing. But we both kept on trying to somehow bring her back.

At some point I heard sirens and soon after there were voices and lights sweeping along the riverbank. Marcus stood up, waved his arms and yelled, "Down here!" before resuming chest compressions.

I wanted Margery Wyler to breathe and her heart to beat, but deep down I had known that the woman was dead before we even began working on her.

Finally, someone put a hand on my shoulder. "We've got this," a voice said. The paramedic was someone I didn't know—tall, close-cropped hair, maybe around thirty.

I straightened up. "She's not breathing on her own," I told him.

"Okay," he said. He moved into my space and I took a couple of steps backward. My pants were wet from the knees down and my shoes were soaked. A damp clump of hair hung in my face. I tucked it behind one ear and then folded my arms over my midsection. It was cold so close to the water.

Marcus was talking to two uniformed officers, gesturing with both hands, in full cop mode now. I looked down at Margery Wyler's body. It was easy to see that she was dead. Her body was limp and with the extra light I could see how pale and waxy her skin was. She was wearing the same shirt she'd had on at the library with a rose-colored sweater instead of the black blazer. There was a gash on the right side of her head and what looked like blood matted in her hair. Her right arm was lying at her side, the wrist and the palm of her hand streaked with dirt. I noticed that she was clutching something in her other hand. A piece of fabric. A yellow scarf. She hadn't been wearing that earlier, either.

Marcus made his way over to me. "Are you okay?" he asked.

"I'm fine," I said. "I scraped my hand but it's nothing serious. What about you? Are you all right?"

"Mostly, I'm just wet." He glanced over at Margery Wyler's body. "Are you certain that this is Georgia's former mother-in-law?"

I nodded as my stomach seemed to do a somersault. "I'm positive. I was face-to-face with her just a few hours ago."

Marcus raked a hand back through his hair. "She's wearing the same clothes she had on when you pointed her out in the hotel lobby."

I thought about Margery Wyler's husband. He hadn't made a very favorable impression on me any more than his wife had, but now he'd lost his son and his wife. It seemed like too much to expect one person to bear.

"Can you stay just a bit longer?" Marcus said.

"Of course," I said. I stepped off to the side and tried to stay out of the way as everyone else did their jobs. An officer marked off the area with crime scene tape. Another used lights to check the shoreline in both directions. The wind was coming in and I knew Marcus would want to find any evidence before it was lifted away by the resultant waves. A basket stretcher was brought down and Margery Wyler's body was loaded onto it. With the assistance of several police officers and a couple of rope lines, the stretcher made its way up to the top of the embankment. Once it was safely at the top Marcus came over to me again.

"An officer is going to take you home. I don't know how long I'm going to be but I promise I'll call you in the morning."

I nodded and reached over and gave his hand a squeeze.

It turned out to be easier to climb back up the embankment than it had been to get down. Having the rope to grab on to helped in a couple of places.

"Stay safe," I told Marcus once we were safely at the top.

"Always," he said.

The officer who was taking me home explained that his cruiser was in the library lot, and we headed in that direction. I didn't look back.

When I stepped into the kitchen at home, Hercules was just coming in from the living room. I kicked off my shoes by the door, padded over to the table in my dirty wet socks and dropped onto a chair.

My hands were streaked with dirt and who knew what else. The fleshy outside of both of them was scraped pretty much raw. There was blood on my jacket and my sweater. Mud and bits of rock clung to my pants.

I exhaled slowly and stared up at the ceiling for a moment. I knew I needed to wash my hands and clean the abrasions, but I was drained. The count from the rescue breathing kept running in the back of my head. I heard a soft murp and looked down to see Hercules at my feet, looking at me with concern. "I'm all right," I said, but he didn't seem convinced.

I shrugged out of my jacket and peeled off my sweater. I went over to the kitchen sink in my white cotton T-shirt and wet pants and washed my hands well. The raw skin stung a little when the soap and water hit it.

Hercules watched while I put bread in the toaster and warmed milk for hot chocolate. I went down the basement stairs and fished a pair of pajama pants from the laundry basket. I took off my wet trousers and left them on the floor.

Once I was settled at the table with peanut butter toast and hot chocolate—comfort food—Hercules launched himself onto my lap. He nuzzled my chin and I stroked his fur with one hand and picked up my mug with the other. After I'd taken a long drink, I set the hot chocolate on the table and broke off a tiny bit of toast. "Don't tell Roma," I said as he ate it from my hand. "This is a onetime thing."

Roma was one of my closest friends and vet to both cats. I was trying very hard to follow her instructions to feed them cat food, not people food.

Hercules put his paw on my hand and I wondered if that was the cat version of a pinkie swear.

I told Hercules about finding Margery Wyler's body; how it seemed that she had fallen over the embankment. "I can't believe she's really dead," I said. "Just a few hours ago the woman was at the library trying to bully Georgia." This had to be the end of any effort to get visitation with Emmy.

Hercules gave a loud and indignant meow. He loved Georgia. She had made cat-shaped kitty treats as part of a fund-raiser for the new animal shelter earlier in the fall. The boys had been her taste testers.

"Relax," I said. "Georgia had nothing to do with

what happened. It was an accident. It was dark and the area was unfamiliar to Mrs. Wyler. She probably just got too close to the edge and lost her balance."

That seemed to satisfy the cat. He eyed my plate and I swiped a finger over a dab of peanut butter on it and held it out to him. He happily licked it off.

What happened to Margery Wyler was just an accident, nothing more, I told myself even as a knot tightened in my chest. The fact that she'd died in Mayville Heights just hours after she'd found Georgia and her granddaughter was just a coincidence. Coincidences did happen.

But I couldn't help thinking of a quote attributed to baseball player Yogi Berra: "That's too coincidental to be a coincidence."

4

Marcus called while I was starting the coffee the next morning. Owen and Hercules both listened to my side of the conversation with open curiosity. Or maybe they were just wondering if the call would delay their breakfast.

"You're all right?" he asked.

"I'm fine," I said. "I have a few scrapes but nothing serious. I still feel a little overwhelmed at everything that happened. Are you okay?"

He yawned then. "Sorry. It was a late night but I'm good. Like you I have a few scrapes and bruises but nothing serious."

I leaned against the counter. "Have you talked to Georgia yet?"

"No. I spoke to Brady and I'm guessing he let her know what happened. I'm hoping to talk to her sometime this morning. I did talk to Mr. Wyler last night."

"I'm guessing he told you a different version of the conflict with Georgia," I said.

"I can't tell you that," he said. Which basically meant *yes*, I knew.

"So what happens now?" The two furballs at my feet seemed very interested in that question as well. Hercules had raised a paw as though he had something he wanted to add to the conversation.

"Margery Wyler's body is at the medical examiner's office and the autopsy will be done later today. After I see Brady I'll stop by the library. I need to ask you a few questions."

"I'll be there," I said.

"Thanks," he said. "Did you figure out what you're going to do about your headless horse/man?"

I made a face. "I forgot all about it. I'll have to call Harry."

Marcus suddenly seemed to be fumbling with his phone. "Hey, are you still there?" I asked.

"I'm here," he said after another few seconds of garbled sounds. "And Micah says hello."

I laughed. "Tell her hello back and give her a scratch for me."

"I will," he said. "I better get going. I'll see you later."

I ended the call and Hercules immediately meowed at me. "There's nothing to report," I said. "Marcus is still talking to people. The autopsy is sometime later today."

Owen looked from Hercules to me. He wrinkled his whiskers in what looked like confusion.

"I'm sorry," I said. "You don't know what happened. Remember I told you that Georgia's former

in-laws, the Wylers, showed up at the library yesterday? They wanted to see Emmy." I remembered the
look on Georgia's face when she told them she'd be
happy to go to court and tell a judge what they'd done
to her.

I pushed away from the counter. I needed a cup of
coffee. "Last night Mrs. Wyler must have gone for a
walk. Somehow she went over the embankment down
beyond the library where it gets really steep." I took a
breath and let it out as I remembered Margery Wyler
sprawled on the wet rocks. "She's dead."

Owen exchanged a look with his brother. More
than once I'd wondered if the two of them had some
kind of ability to communicate with each other. It
seemed ridiculously far-fetched until I remembered
that one cat could walk through walls and the other
could disappear.

I poured my coffee and added cream and sugar
while Hercules waited patiently and Owen made a
sound a lot like an impatient sigh. Then I finished getting their food and set their bowls in the usual place
next to the refrigerator.

Owen noticed my hand. He sniffed at the patch of
raw skin, which had scabbed over and really didn't
hurt much anymore. He looked up at me and meowed.

"I'm fine," I said. "I swear it barely hurts and I'll put
on a bandage before work." That seemed to satisfy
him. I gave the top of his head a little scratch. "Thank
you for your concern," I added.

I grabbed an egg from the refrigerator and went

to start my own breakfast, wondering if dog people talked to their animals the same way cat people did.

Once I'd made my egg, bacon and tomato sandwich and eaten a couple of bites, I called Harry. I knew he was an early riser.

"I heard what happened last night," he said. "You and Marcus are both okay?"

"Just a few scrapes," I said. "Nothing serious. Do you know how Georgia is?"

"Pretty much how you'd expect."

"The last twenty-four hours have been a nightmare." I rubbed my left knee. It was a bit sore, probably from kneeling on the rocks.

"Georgia's a good mom and she makes Larry happy. Plus, she gives as good as she gets from the old man. She doesn't deserve any of this."

"No, she doesn't," I said. "But Brady Chapman's a good lawyer. He'll sort it out."

"Let's hope so," Harry said. "You know, what happened last night shouldn't have happened. It's time the town came up with a plan to deal with that stretch of shoreline. It's not safe and we've all gotten complacent. I'm going to try to get it on the agenda for the next town meeting."

I nodded even though he couldn't see me. "I'll help in any way I can."

"Good to know," he said. "And that's enough of me getting on my soap box. You called for a reason. What do you need?"

I explained that the practical joker was back.

He made a frustrated sound. "I knew this wasn't over but I was starting to hope I'd be wrong. Larry told me about his plan to put up the cameras Monday. We only missed whoever it is by a few days."

"We'll get them next time."

"I'd rather there isn't a next time but I don't seem to be having much luck in making that happen. So what was it this time? Another pool full of Jell-O?"

"A headless horse/man."

"You mean like *The Legend of Sleepy Hollow*."

"Crossed with a centaur from Greek mythology."

"Halloween is coming up soon. I guess we shouldn't be surprised. I'll call Larry and remind him about the cameras."

"Larry has a lot on his plate at the moment," I said. "The cameras can wait."

"He likes to keep busy. But I'll tell him what you said. I'll see you down at the library."

I finished breakfast and got ready for work. I gave each cat a scratch and told them both to stay out of trouble. They each gave me an innocent stare.

The rubber wishbone was still on the back steps. I picked it up and walked next door to the Justasons'. Mike Justason was loading boxes into the back of his truck.

"This belongs to Fifi," I said. "I'm sorry. Hercules swiped it."

Mike smiled and took the toy. "It's no problem. Fifi seems to like chewing on my shoes better."

I laughed and told him to have a good day.

*   *   *

When I got to the library I decided to walk around and have a look at the horse/man in the light of day. I found Susan standing in front of the gazebo. She turned and smiled as I came across the grass.

"I take it you've seen this," she said. She had a shrimp cocktail fork and a bamboo skewer in her updo.

"I have," I said.

"I was kind of hoping the pool full of Jell-O might come back."

"You and the squirrels both."

Susan grinned. "You think they were same two squirrels that caused the accident yesterday?"

"I know this is going to sound crazy but I do. The driver said one of the squirrels had a stubby tail. I remember Harry said the same thing about one of the two that was in the pool."

"You know, squirrels are very intelligent."

"Squirrels are just rats with fuzzy tails and better PR," I said.

She laughed and moved a little closer to the horse/ man. "Do you have any idea who's doing this?"

I shook my head. "At first I wondered if it might be Mariah."

Susan swung around to look at me, eyes wide. "Harry's Mariah?"

"I know at first glance it doesn't make sense, but she's smart and creative and she butts heads with her dad, so maybe she just wanted to aggravate him a little. But I don't think she'd keep it up this long."

"I thought for a while that maybe it was Will Red-fern," Susan said.

I stared at her. "Will Redfern?" Redfern had been the contractor on the library renovations. His work had been less than stellar.

Susan nodded. "I heard he was in Red Wing for a while back in the spring. Then I realized it couldn't have been Will or any of the guys who worked for him. All of these stunts?" She gestured with one hand. "Way more work than those guys would have put in."

I laughed. The truth was she was right.

"I heard about Georgia's ex-mother-in-law. That was her and her husband you walked out yesterday, wasn't it?"

"It was," I said. "Bridget doesn't miss anything, does she?" Bridget Lowe was the publisher of the area newspaper, the *Mayville Heights Chronicle*. She always seemed to know what was going on.

"No, she doesn't," Susan said, "but in this case my source isn't the paper. It's Eric. One of the police offi-cers came in for coffee just as he was getting ready to close and said someone had fallen over the embank-ment down beyond the library." Susan's husband, Eric, owned Eric's Place, one of my favorite places to eat in town.

"The odd thing is I saw Margery Wyler walking in that direction last evening," she continued. "When Eric told me what happened I figured it had to be her who fell. No one who's from here would be wandering around down there."

"Do you remember what time that was?" I asked.

Susan nudged her glasses up her nose. "Based on what time I got home I'd say it was eight thirty, give or take." She frowned. "Why?"

"I think it's something Marcus would want to know. He's probably putting together a timeline for Margery Wyler's last few hours."

"Wait a minute. Wasn't her death an accident?"

"It doesn't mean the police don't still have to do their due diligence. Tourists usually don't walk out that way. Maybe Mrs. Wyler got confused or lost."

"Good point," she said.

"Marcus is stopping by sometime this morning."

"I'll talk to him," she said.

We headed inside. I dropped my things in my office and cleared the book drop. Susan made coffee and brought me a cup.

"I don't mean to be unfeeling," she said, "but does Margery Wyler's death make things better or worse for Georgia?"

I picked a bit of cat hair off the sleeve of my sweater. "I'm not sure."

Larry showed up about ten minutes after we opened. He looked tired.

"Hey, Kathleen," he said. "Harry called me. I brought the cameras, although it's kind of like locking the barn door after the horses have gotten out."

"You don't have to do this right now," I said. "Go be with Georgia."

"They're at Abigail's. I think I might have been hovering. She told me to go do some work."

"Is she all right? I know this can't be easy for her."

He made a face. "She's keeping it together for Emmy but she's upset. She wanted the Wylers to leave her and Emmy alone. She didn't want either of them dead."

"If she needs a break, Emmy can come spend some time with me. Owen and Hercules love her."

Larry smiled. "Thanks. We may take you up on that. You probably know that Marcus wants to talk to Georgia."

I nodded. "That's just a formality. Margery Wyler's death was just a very sad accident."

"The Wylers had no business coming here, but people don't always make good choices. And speaking of questionable choices, I'll go get these cameras up."

"Thanks," I said.

As Larry was heading out, Harry came in. I walked over to him.

"I just took a look at your headless centaur. How in the heck did someone get that thing into the gazebo without anyone noticing?"

I shrugged. "I'm guessing mostly good luck. I think you're right that whoever it is brings everything from the direction of the old warehouses. Susan reminded me anyone who lives here generally stays away from that whole area because the embankment *is* steep. And tourists don't end up down there because there's no proper walkway and really nothing to see. So aside from the occasional couple in love looking for some privacy, there isn't anyone around at night."

"That makes sense," Harry said. "I'm going to see if the police department will throw their support behind fencing off that area or at least putting up signs."

"I'm pretty sure you'll have Marcus's support."

"I'll take whatever I can get," he said. He gestured toward the back of the building. "I'll go get started on taking that thing apart."

Harry left and I walked over to the circulation desk, where Susan was sorting books from the book return. "Is Harry going to dismantle the headless horse/ man?" she asked. The cocktail fork in her hair was listing to the right.

I nodded. "As soon as he's done helping Larry."

"Could we keep him?" she blurted.

"I think Harry's family would notice he's missing," I said with a smile.

Susan rolled her eyes. "Ha, ha. I mean could we keep the headless horse/man? He'd make a great decoration for the Halloween party."

I looked around. "Assuming we could get it into the building—which is not a given—where would we put him?"

"I was thinking about setting it up outside, near the front entrance, maybe with lights."

I narrowed my gaze. "You're serious."

She nodded, which made her topknot bounce and the cocktail fork slip sideways a little more. "Yes. Well, as serious as I get. And I know you're thinking, won't that just encourage the prankster?"

"Actually, I was wondering where we'd plug in the lights."

"Also important," Susan said.

I held up a finger. "But you made a good point. Won't it encourage our practical joker?"

Susan smiled. "My boys tend to fall into the category of it's easier to get forgiveness than it is to get permission. Maybe that's how our practical joker thinks. If we use horse/man for Halloween we'll be sending a message that if he or she asks to do something in the gazebo maybe they'll get a yes."

"It can't work any worse than anything else we've tried. Let's do it."

"Yes!" Susan clapped her hands together and grinned.

"I'll go tell Harry to keep everything," I said. I started for the door and then stopped and looked back at her. "So how has this approach worked with the boys?" Susan's twins were scary smart. Genius-level smart.

"They did ask before they started working on a rocket last weekend."

"That's good."

Susan nodded. "But they didn't ask before they used Eric's Vitamix to make the rocket fuel."

I couldn't help laughing. These were the same two kids who had once managed to make pancake batter explode. I held up one hand. "I'm sorry," I said.

Susan was laughing, too. "It's okay," she said, "but just so you know, if Eric tells you about the blender, whatever you do, do not laugh." She emphasized the last three words by holding out her hands.

"I'll keep that in mind," I said.

I found Harry at the back of the building holding the ladder as Larry installed the decoy camera.

"Do you think we can put the horse/man in the storage area via the loading dock?" I asked.

"You want to keep the evidence?"

"Not exactly," I said. I explained Susan's idea.

"You think that will work?"

I glanced over at the gazebo for a moment. "Do I think it will prompt our jokester to come forward? Probably not. But the horse/man would be a great decoration for the party."

"There isn't enough room to keep that thing here," Harry said. He gestured at the loading dock door. "There just isn't enough space. Look, the whole thing isn't just wide, it's high."

I sighed and rubbed the back of my neck. I'd already been picturing the horse/man out by the front doors.

"We could bring down the trailer and take it out to your house," Larry said. "It would kind of be a hoot to drive that thing through town."

Harry nodded slowly. "Probably room in the old barn."

"I have a couple of big tarps to wrap the thing up in to keep it dry and keep the squirrels out," Larry added.

"That's a lot of trouble," I said.

Harry took off his Twins cap and smoothed down what little hair he had. "Not really," he said. "I've got lots of rope."

"Believe it or not, he's moved odder things in that trailer," Larry said.

"I'm thinking there's a story or two I need to hear," I teased.

Larry looked down at me and dipped his head in his brother's direction. "Later," he stage-whispered.

It was good to see that his mood had lightened. "I'm going to leave things in your very capable hands," I said.

As I headed back around the building, I heard Larry say something about putting lights inside the horse/man's neck.

I went back inside and told Susan I'd be up in my office. I sat at my desk with a fresh cup of coffee. When I checked my e-mail, I saw that Ruby had sent a couple of the photos she'd taken the day before. There was one of me eating a cupcake that made me laugh because I had frosting on my nose and my eyes looked like they were crossed. There was another photo of Georgia and me. I looked at it for a long moment and a buzzing sound filled my ears as though the room had been suddenly swarmed by a hive of bees.

I remembered Ruby taking the photo right after Georgia had arrived with the boxes of cupcakes. She was still wearing her coat. And her scarf.

A long, silky scarf in shades of yellow.

5

For a moment I just stared at the screen. *Don't jump to conclusions*, I reminded myself. Just because Margery Wyler had been clutching a yellow scarf in her hand didn't mean the scarf belonged to Georgia. There were probably lots of people in town who had yellow scarves. And lots more in this part of the state.

I looked at the image again. I had a scarf very similar to the one Georgia was wearing, only mine wasn't yellow, it was a pretty shade of medium blue. *My* scarf had been made by Ella King. Marcus had bought it for me. He'd thought I was kidding when I'd told him that Ella's fine stitchwork probably benefited from the skills she'd learned tying flies with Brady's dad, Burtis.

I shook my head. I wasn't going down this rabbit hole. Georgia owned a yellow scarf. Margery Wyler had been holding a yellow scarf. It was a coincidence. It had to be, because I just didn't believe that Georgia could have been there when Mrs. Wyler fell and not have helped her.

I knew how strong her dislike of the Wylers ran but walking away and leaving Margery Wyler to die just wasn't something I believed Georgia would have done. She was a good person. She was kind. She did the right thing.

I rubbed the space between my eyebrows with two fingers. "Headache?" a voice asked. I looked up. Marcus was standing in the doorway.

"Hi," I said. I got to my feet and walked around the desk to give him a kiss. "I need to show you something."

He frowned, but all he said was, "All right."

I reached across my desk and turned the computer around so he could see the photo of Georgia and me. "Ruby took that yesterday. Georgia is wearing a scarf that looks like the one Margery Wyler had in her hand."

He glanced at the photo. "It does." He didn't seem surprised.

"You already knew."

He nodded. He looked tired. There were dark circles under his eyes and he'd missed a tiny spot on the left side of his jaw when he'd shaved.

"Have you talked to Georgia?" I asked.

"I have," he said.

"And you can't tell me what she said."

"You know I can't."

I reached over and plucked a bit of cat hair from the arm of his jacket. "You didn't arrest her," I said, "because if you had you would have told me that first thing."

"No, I didn't arrest her, or anyone else for that matter."

I smiled. "I'll take that as a good sign." I sat on the edge of my desk. "Did you see Susan when you came in?" I asked.

Marcus nodded. "I did, and she told me about seeing Margery Wyler last night."

"I thought you'd probably be trying to figure out where she was and what she did before she fell."

He pulled a hand back through his hair. "I'm not telling you anything you probably haven't already figured out; there's about two hours that we haven't accounted for from the time you and I saw Mrs. Wyler to the time we found her body."

"So what's next?"

"We keep investigating. Susan saw Mrs. Wyler. Chances are so did someone else. It was a Friday night."

I picked up a pen that was on the edge of my desk and turned it over in my fingers. "Marcus, her death was an accident, wasn't it?"

"My job is to collect the evidence," he said. He looked past me out the window.

"It's also your job to follow the evidence to decide if a crime has been committed."

He stuffed his hands in his pockets. "I'm sorry, Kathleen. We can't have this conversation."

I opened my mouth to argue, and then closed it again. I didn't really know Margery Wyler but that didn't mean her death didn't sadden me. Once again, I thought of the words the poet John Donne had written four hundred years ago: *Any man's death diminishes me, because I am involved in mankind.* I knew that Marcus always felt a responsibility toward every victim he encountered. Georgia was my friend. I wanted to make sure she was treated fairly. I wanted to stand up for her. But it was up to Marcus to make sure Margery Wyler was treated fairly even though she was dead. It was his job to stand up for her.

"I'm sorry," I said. "I know you're just doing your job. You said on the phone that you needed to talk to me."

"I just have a few questions."

I reached over, grabbed his hand and gave it a squeeze. "Go ahead."

He squeezed back before he let my hand go. "Do you know what time we got to the library?"

"It was just a couple of minutes before eleven thirty. I remember checking the time." I looked down at my watch. "I'm one of the few people who still wears an actual watch, according to Levi."

He glanced over at the window again. "When you were looking around to see if you could see any sign of your practical joker, are you sure you didn't see anyone?"

"I'm positive," I said. "I looked in both directions. There was no sign of anyone."

Marcus nodded. "What did you see when you got down by the water?"

I thought for a moment, trying to be as precise as I could. "The wind was moving in. I knew it was definitely a person lying on the rocks and not a pile of debris."

"How did you know?"

I flashed to Margery Wyler's body. "I saw her leg." And she hadn't moved or made a sound. I realized that on some level I'd known she was dead.

"Did you know it was Mrs. Wyler?" Marcus asked.

I shook my head. "Not until we were starting CPR."

"Did you notice anything about the body?"

"It was . . . on her back. One arm was close against her body. Her clothing was intact. There were injuries to her head, mostly from the rocks and the fall, I assume. She had the scarf in one hand."

He exhaled slowly. "Okay," he said. "Is there anything else you think might be important?"

"I didn't see any footprints. It doesn't mean there weren't any, because the waves made by the wind could have washed them away, or if anyone else had been there they could have just walked in the water. For the record, I didn't see anyone. But I was focused on getting down the embankment and getting to whoever was lying there. I could have missed something . . . or someone." I pushed away from the desk and stood up. "What happens now?"

"Like I said, we keep gathering evidence." He looked at his own watch. "I have to go. Are we still on for supper?"

"Absolutely. I have to get groceries, among other things, but I should be out around four thirty."

Marcus leaned forward and kissed my cheek. "I'll see you then."

He left and I reached across my desk for my coffee. It was cold. I shut off the computer and went to get a fresh cup. I stood in the middle of the staff room with my coffee. Marcus's questions had me thinking about Margery Wyler's body. There was something about it that felt off, but I couldn't figure out what it was. I thought about first spotting the body and then realizing it was actually a person and not a tarp that had just washed up on the shore. I remembered watching the paramedics at work but I still couldn't figure out what was causing that unsettled feeling.

I finished my coffee and left the mug in the sink. Then I went back downstairs. Susan was sorting through a box of Halloween decorations. "Thanks for talking to Marcus," I said. "Do you know if Larry is still around?"

"He went to go get some kind of screw or something that he needed a little while ago but he's probably back by now," she said.

I gestured over my shoulder. "I just need to talk to him for a second," I said. "I'll be right back."

"No problem." I started for the front doors.

"Hey, Kathleen," Susan called after me, "do you care what the bulletin board looks like as far as Halloween goes? How scary is too scary?"

I turned to look at her. Susan was one of the most positive people I knew. She always managed to find the joy in life. "To steal from the late Mrs. Patrick Campbell, as long as it doesn't frighten the horses it's fine by me."

Susan put one hand over her heart. "I promise not to traumatize any member of the equine family."

I couldn't help laughing. "Then what more could I ask for?"

I walked around the building and found Larry staring up at the side of the loading dock door. He raised one hand when he spotted me. "Harry's gone to get the trailer," he said.

It took a second for me to realize that he meant for our centaur without a head. I'd almost forgotten all about that. "Great," I said. "I know it's none of my business and you can tell me that, but were you with Georgia last night?"

His eyes narrowed. "Do you know something I don't?"

I frowned. "What do you mean?"

"Marcus asked me that same question."

"He's just looking to cross all the t's and dot all the i's. And I'm trying to figure out how Margery Wyler ended up at this end of town in the first place. Georgia doesn't live in this neighborhood and I would have thought that Mrs. Wyler would try to see her again. She didn't strike me as the kind of person who gave up easily."

Larry was holding a small set of pliers and he opened and closed them a couple of times. "We had planned to have supper at Eric's, but after all the upset, Georgia just wanted to go home, soak in her bathtub and go to bed early." He looked up at me. "Mrs. Wyler's death was just a horrible accident, wasn't it?"

"I think so," I said.

Larry looked troubled and shook his head. "That's

not the answer I wanna hear. Kathleen, you were there. C'mon, tell me that woman fell by accident."

I hesitated and the moment seemed to go on too long. "I don't know," I finally said.

Larry swore and looked away for a moment. "I should have lied," he muttered.

"What do you mean, you should have lied?" I asked. "Lied about what?"

His mouth worked before any words came out. "I should have told Marcus that Georgia and I were together," he said, a defiant edge to his voice. "I was alone all night out in the shop working on a second camera. No one would have known."

"Lying to the police wouldn't solve anything." As soon as I'd spoken I realized how self-righteous I sounded.

"It would make sure that Georgia wasn't a suspect in Mrs. Wyler's death."

"Hang on a minute," I said, holding up one hand. "No one has said anything about Margery Wyler having been murdered."

"Really?" Larry retorted. "Because you couldn't say for certain her death was an accident."

I struggled to keep the frustration I was feeling out of my voice. "No, I can't. But that's because I'm not a doctor or the medical examiner. She could have slipped and fallen, yes. She probably did, but she also could have had a heart attack and fallen over the side of the embankment. Or had a dizzy spell or a seizure or a brain aneurysm." I took a slow breath and let it out even more slowly. "The autopsy is sometime today. Let the police do their job and don't look for trouble. It already knows where you live."

Larry looked down at the pair of pliers he was still holding then back up at me. "I'm sorry," he said. "I didn't mean to take out my frustration on you."

"I'm sorry, too," I said. "It's none of my business where Georgia was last night. I'm going to let you get back to work." I went back inside and relieved Susan at the front desk. The rest of the morning was busy and I managed to keep my mind off of Margery Wyler for the most part.

Harry and Larry got the horse/man out of the gazebo and into the trailer. When the library closed at one o'clock, I went out to make sure there had been no damage done to the gazebo. Everything was fine. One thing the practical joker wasn't was destructive.

I wondered what exactly he or she was up to. To me it felt like a bid for attention. I glanced over at the shoreline, and before I could decide if it was a good or bad idea, I was walking over to where we'd found Margery Wyler.

The trail down to the water was blocked off. There were two police sawhorses in place and a concrete buffer. I looked around, trying to figure out where and how Mrs. Wyler could have fallen. There was a large boulder, easily close to five feet high, just before the top of the path. I looked back toward the library and, due to the curve of the land and the slight dip that I'd never really noticed before, discovered I couldn't see the building at all.

I noticed what looked like a fallen log—maybe a big piece of driftwood someone had dragged up from the shore below—lying next to the rock. The end of it seemed to be stuffed with pinecones. It was a squirrel cache. Maybe it belonged to one of the squirrels that had been in the pool with the Jell-O.

I noticed a torn scrap of paper among the cones. I fished it out and smoothed it flat. The paper was covered with what looked to be mathematical calculations, written in tiny, squared-off writing. The paper didn't look like it had been out there very long. Could Mrs. Wyler have dropped it? Could someone else? Was it important or just a bit of garbage?

I had no answers.

6

I got groceries on the way home and spent the afternoon doing laundry and cleaning, with Hercules and Owen taking turns grumbling about freshly washed floors getting in the way of them wandering around the house at will. About four thirty I drove out to Marcus's house for supper. It was unseasonably warm for mid-October and he had decided to grill. "It'll be the last time for this year," he'd said.

"This is the third time you've said it's the last time," I teased. "I think you'll be out here doing the turkey on Thanksgiving."

Marcus took his grilling very seriously. He used a selection of different marinades and barbeque sauces. I was happy to curl up on the swing on his back deck with Micah next to me and watch him make chicken and vegetables for our supper and occasionally talk to himself.

"Could we agree not to talk about Georgia and the Wylers for the night?" he asked.

"Yes," I said, "but first I need to show you something." I pulled out the scrap of paper I'd found and explained how I came to have it. "It doesn't seem to be faded or weathered at all." I handed it to him and he looked at the writing on the front before turning the paper over to look at the back side. Micah craned her neck as though she was trying to see as well.

"I don't think I found some important piece of evidence," I said. "I just didn't want to keep this to myself in case it did mean something."

He tucked the bit of paper in his pocket. "It probably has nothing to do with Mrs. Wyler's death. Anyone could have dropped it, including the other police officers, or the paramedics or even someone who was nosy enough or morbid enough to walk down and take a look at a place where someone died, but thanks for giving it to me."

He sat down next to me on the swing and reached over to stroke Micah's fur. She made a happy little murp sound. "Have you given any more thought to introducing her to Owen and Hercules?" he asked.

"I haven't talked to Roma yet and I really want to. Owen and Hercules are very spoiled—mostly my doing, but some of it from Maggie and Rebecca and you."

"I don't spoil them," he protested. He was trying to look chagrined but couldn't quite pull it off.

I folded my arms over my chest while Micah cocked her head to one side. "Of course you don't. It's just a coincidence that every time we have pizza Owen has pepperoni breath."

"I can neither confirm nor deny the whole pepperoni

breath thing, but I can remind you that Micah is pretty strong willed herself."

"Mrrr," she said as if in agreement.

"And since all three cats come from Wisteria Hill and all three have the same skills, they might get along just fine."

I leaned my face close to the cat, who had moved onto my lap. "You're the girl here and I'm counting on you to be the mature one," I stage-whispered. "I'm sorry, but you know how boys can be."

Marcus was back at the grill. "I can hear you two, you know."

Micah gave me a look and I had the feeling that she had somehow understood every bit of the conversation.

Marcus had an early-morning training session with Brady and the girls' high school hockey team, so we made it an early night. Sunday morning I met Maggie and Roma down at Eric's Place for brunch. Mags and Roma were my closest friends in Mayville Heights. They were pretty much total opposites. Maggie had curly blond hair she kept cropped close to her head and beautiful green eyes. She was an artist as well as a yoga and tai chi instructor, and she was a very spiritual person. She'd been involved with Brady for quite a while now but insisted they weren't a couple. Roma, on the other hand, was a veterinarian. She had glossy dark hair and dark eyes and she was married to former hockey player Crazy Eddie Sweeney. Maggie had indirectly been responsible for the two of them get-

ting together—a combination of a life-sized mannequin of Eddie and a lot of small-town gossip and
rumors.

Roma was already at Eric's when I got there. She
stood up and hugged me when I joined her at a table
in the front window. "I heard about what happened
to Georgia's former mother-in-law. You're all right?"

"I'm fine," I said. I held out my left hand. It already
looked a lot better than it had the day before. "See?
Nothing serious."

"Something needs to be done about that stretch of
shoreline," Roma said as we sat down.

Over at the counter, Claire, my favorite waitress,
held up the coffeepot and raised her eyebrows. She
knew me well. I nodded.

"Harry said the same thing," I said to Roma.

"Harry said the same thing about what?" Maggie
had arrived. She slipped out of her jacket, tucking a
pair of fingerless gloves into one of the pockets.

"He thinks it's time we did something about the
embankment that runs down past the library," Roma
said.

Maggie nodded. "Harry's right." She sat next to me
and immediately looked me over. "You're sure you
didn't get hurt?" she asked.

"I didn't," I said. "Just a few scrapes on my hand.
That's it."

She smiled and leaned against me for a moment.
"I'm really glad to hear that."

Claire joined us then. She set a little teapot in front
of Maggie, who wasn't a coffee drinker, and then she

filled my cup and topped up Roma's. "Are you ready to order?" she asked.

"Breakfast sandwiches?" Roma asked, raising an eyebrow.

Maggie and I both nodded.

Claire smiled. "It shouldn't be too long," she said. She headed back to the kitchen.

Maggie was already going through the little ritual she followed with respect to her tea. Roma added a splash more milk to her coffee and took a sip, nodding her head with satisfaction. She looked across the table at me. "Is Georgia all right?" she asked.

"As far as I know," I said, stirring my own coffee. "She's been staying with Abigail."

"I hate that it took Georgia's former mother-in-law dying for anyone to realize something needs to be done about that drop-off," Roma said. "What was she doing walking along there? Does Marcus know?"

I shrugged. "If he does, he hasn't said."

Maggie lifted the lid of her teapot and peered inside. "I saw her. At least I think it was her."

"You saw Mrs. Wyler?" I said. "Where?"

"At the co-op store. It was fairly late in the afternoon. She was about your height with blond hair. She was wearing a white shirt, jeans and a black blazer with a black-and-white scarf. And red flats."

"That was Margery Wyler."

"She was looking around and she asked Nic about the Riverwalk, how far it went in either direction and if she could get down to the water's edge. He told her she'd have to go down by the marina to get close to the water. The embankment was too high across the street from where we were and it just got higher as you got closer to the library." She stirred her tea and then gestured with the spoon as though she'd just thought of something else. "She said she liked to walk and I remember thinking not in those shoes she was wearing. Maybe she went for a walk after supper and just got too close to the edge."

"We need signs," Roma said, tucking her hair behind an ear. "The Riverwalk pretty much ends at the library. At least a sign telling people to turn around would be better than nothing. Does Harry have an actual plan?"

I traced the rim of my mug with one finger. "He didn't say."

"When I was a kid the town tossed around the idea of using a backhoe to grade the embankment," Maggie said, "but nothing ever came of it."

"They could do that to reduce how steep the embankment is and then plant vegetation to stabilize the soil," I said. "Or use geomats or maybe terrace the whole thing. There are geomats that biodegrade over time, which gives plants time to get established."

Maggie and Roma were both looking at me, smiling.

"What?" I said.

"I'd like to climb into your brain and look around," Roma said. "I always picture it looking like a huge library with shelves full of all the things you know."

Maggie nodded with enthusiasm. "Like the British Museum Reading Room, the original one before they turned it into exhibition space."

"With that gorgeous domed ceiling," Roma added.

"My head's not that big," I said.

Maggie took a sip of her tea. "It's dimensionally transcendental."

I frowned at her. "It's what?"

"I can't believe you don't know that. Your brain is like a TARDIS, you know, from *Doctor Who*. On the outside it looks like a police call box from the sixties but it's a lot bigger on the inside because the inside and the outside exist in separate dimensions."

Roma was nodding. "That would explain why you know so many things. Your brain is so much larger than an ordinary one."

Luckily Claire arrived then with our sandwiches. Once we all had our food, I changed the subject away from my giant head by asking Roma how the cats were. I had a soft spot for the feral cat colony that lived out at Wisteria Hill. Roma had recently moved them from the old carriage house they had lived in for years to a smaller building that Eddie had built just for the cats.

"They're all doing well," Roma said. "Smokey is starting to slow down a little. I've noticed that sometimes when Eddie is working on something outside Smokey will be lying somewhere nearby. I think he likes the company."

My throat got tight for a moment. Smokey was the oldest cat of the group. He looked like a grizzled old prizefighter and I knew it was going to break my heart just a little when we lost him.

*   *   *

After we finished eating we decided to walk over to the Sunday market. Roma wanted some of the Jam Lady's apple butter and Maggie was looking for apple spice donuts, which were Brady's favorite. I wanted pumpkins for the library.

Maggie had stopped to tie her shoe. "Are you doing jack-o'-lanterns?" she asked.

"No," I said. "It's too warm inside. They start getting fuzzy about day three. I was thinking about getting some of those terra-cotta pumpkins I told you about seeing at that flea market, decorating them and mixing in some real ones."

"The real ones could be used for pies after Halloween," Roma said.

"Eddie Sweeney's pies?" I asked. Not only could Eddie fly like the wind on a pair of skates, it turned out he was a pretty good baker.

Roma smiled. "I think that could be arranged."

I knew from experience that it would take Roma a long time to decide whether she wanted apple butter, marmalade or jam and in the end she'd probably choose all three. I left her and Maggie debating which apple butter from which combination of apples was the best.

I noticed Ella King had a booth with her scarves, hats and mittens. She waved when she caught sight of me and I walked over to say hello.

"How's Taylor?" I asked. Ella's daughter was away

at college. She'd been in the tai chi class Maggie taught and we all missed her.

"She's doing well so far," Ella said. "She likes her roommate and her professors."

"Please tell her I miss seeing her in class. My Cloud Hands have gone downhill since she left."

Ella laughed. "I will."

"Could you answer a scarf question for me?" I asked. "I've been thinking about buying one for my friend Lise, back in Boston, for Christmas."

"Silk or knitted?"

"Silk," I said. "I have one and I wear it a lot."

"I've noticed," Ella said with a smile. "So, what's your question?"

I had been set to ask her if Georgia had bought a yellow scarf from her but I couldn't get the words out. The question suddenly felt disloyal. "Each one really is one of a kind?" I said instead.

She reached over and slipped one of the scarves from the wooden rack where it was displayed. It was a mix of soft shades of rose and lavender. "No two are alike, partly because of the randomness of the dying process, and partly because of the color mixing."

"I like this one," I said, reaching out to touch one corner of the fabric.

"I'd be happy to sell it to you," Ella said, "but if you really want to give your friend something she'll wear a lot, take a bit of time to think about her favorite colors. What colors does she wear? What colors have you seen in her home? I'm always here on Sunday and there are more scarves at the co-op store—or at least there will be on Wednesday. They sold out a few days ago. And if you don't see anything that feels just right let me know and I can custom-make something for you."

"I will," I said. "Thanks, Ella."

She went to help a woman who was looking at hats and I turned to go back to Roma and Maggie, when someone tapped me on the shoulder. I swung around to find Georgia standing there.

"Hi," she said. She had her hands jammed in her pockets and she looked a little awkward and uncertain.

"Hi," I said. "I'm so glad to see you. Are you all right?"

"Yes," she said, nodding her head.

"And Emmy?"

Georgia pointed several booths away to where Emmy was picking out donuts with Larry. "She's fine." Emmy caught sight of me then and waved enthusiastically and I waved back. "I've been able to keep most of what's happened away from her, but Brady thinks I need to tell her about the Wylers before someone at school does."

"Brady's a good lawyer and a good person," I said.

Georgia nodded. "I'm learning that." She cleared her throat. "Larry told me that you asked where I was on Friday night."

I held up a hand. "And I shouldn't have. It was none of my business. I'm sorry."

She looked down at her feet for a moment then her eyes met mine again. "It kind of became your business when Hugh and Margery tried to ambush me at your library." She squared her shoulders. "The truth is I canceled with Larry because I was planning on taking Emmy and running again."

I hesitated and then put a hand on her arm for a moment. "I'm sorry you felt that was your only choice." I couldn't imagine how panicked Georgia must have felt to even consider going on the run a second time.

"I felt as though I was right back where I'd been when I first came here. I was afraid that the Wylers' power and influence would win them visitation and that Margery would find a way to take Emmy away from me." She shifted uncomfortably from one foot to the other. "I know it would have been a crappy thing to do to all the people who have welcomed me and tried to help me, but no one who hasn't been through it could understand the lengths Margery and Hugh would go to."

"What changed your mind?" I asked.

She smiled then. "Larry. And the rest of the Taylors. Abigail. Ruby. You. Mayville Heights is my home and more importantly it's Emmy's home. I'm done running. I don't know what's going to happen now but I'm going to stand my ground and fight back."

"No matter what happens, you won't be fighting alone," I said. I had to swallow down the sudden rush of emotion I felt.

Georgia nodded. "I know that. I do." She glanced over at Emmy and Larry. "I better go rescue Larry before my daughter talks him into two dozen donuts." She looked at me again. "It may sound strange coming from me, but thank you for trying to save Margery."

"I'm sorry we couldn't," I said.

She hugged me and headed back to Larry and her daughter while I walked over to rejoin Maggie and Roma. For the first time since Friday night I felt as though things were going to work out.

The next several days were busy. Ruby and I finalized plans for the party. Susan and I went through the boxes of Halloween decorations we had in the workroom. And we got word that the new public access computers would be arriving at the beginning of November.

Our practical joker hadn't returned and I was crossing my fingers that the headless horse/man had been his or her last hurrah.

On Wednesday morning I was walking around the computer area with Harry discussing how we were going to set up the new computers, when Larry Taylor walked in. He came past the front desk and walked up to me.

"Why didn't you warn me?" he said. "I thought we were friends."

"Warn you about what?" I asked.

Harry stepped between us. "What's going on?"

Larry was still looking at me. "So you don't know?"

"No, I don't know," I said, frustration adding an edge to my voice.

"Just tell us what's going on," Harry said.

Larry pulled a hand over the back of his neck. "What's going on is Marcus just arrested Georgia for killing Margery Wyler."

7

I stared at him and I'm pretty sure my mouth hung open a little. "That doesn't make sense," I said. "Margery Wyler fell. It was an accident."

"Not according to the police," Larry said.

Marcus hadn't said anything about the case in the last couple of days. I'd assumed that meant nothing was happening.

"Kathleen, can you call Marcus and find out what's going on?" Harry asked.

I nodded. "Yes. My phone is up in my office. I'll be right back." I looked at Larry. "I give you my word I didn't know." His jaw tightened. He didn't say anything.

I called Marcus's cell, hoping that he'd answer and not let me go to voice mail. I stood in the middle of my office with one arm crossed over my midsection. I could see the river through my office window. The water looked cold and angry, which seemed to fit with how I felt.

He answered on the fourth ring. "I thought I'd probably hear from you. I only have a minute to talk."

"You arrested Georgia," I said.

"I did."

"Why didn't you tell me that Margery Wyler's death wasn't an accident? And why didn't you tell me Georgia was a suspect?"

"You know I couldn't," he said, his voice quiet. "I can't do anything that might jeopardize the case. You had to know both were a possibility."

I hadn't wanted them to be.

"I would have called you right after we arrested Georgia but I couldn't. Can you just trust that I know what I'm doing?"

There was a time when neither of us trusted the other, but those days were long past. I let out a slow exhale. "Of course I can."

"I have to go," he said. "I'll talk to you later. And just so you know, Brady is already with his client."

"Love you," I said.

"You too."

I put my phone back in my desk drawer, locked my office and went back downstairs. Harry and Larry were still waiting in the computer area. Harry was speaking quietly to his brother. I didn't need to hear what Harry was saying to know his words weren't doing anything to quell Larry's anger. Larry's body language told me that. He stood, feet apart, hands jammed into his pockets, and his face was flushed.

I walked up to them. "It's true," I said. "Georgia has been arrested."

"That was never in question," Larry said.

"Brady is with her."

"That's good," Harry said. "Do you know what will happen next?"

"A judge will hopefully set bail and if all goes well, Georgia will be home for supper."

Harry nodded.

"What about Emmy?" I asked. "She's not in school, is she?"

"She was making cinnamon rolls with Peggy and the old man when I left," Harry said. "She's fine."

The hard knot in my stomach loosened a little bit.

"How does bail work?" Larry said abruptly. He looked past me through the high, multipaned windows.

"A judge will decide the amount based on a number of things," I said. "How serious the crime was, does the person have a criminal record, do they have a job and ties to the community? After bail is set there are three choices. The defendant can stay in jail, if they or their family have money, they can pay the bail in full, or they can come to an agreement with a bail bondsman, which means paying him or her ten percent of whatever the bail is set at."

"What if you don't have the ten percent?" Harry asked. I suspected he was already trying to calculate what that ten percent might work out to.

"If you don't have the ten percent you can use something like a house or a vehicle as collateral, and the bail bondsman will loan you the money."

"We can work out any bail, then," Harry said.

"Push comes to shove we can use the house as collateral."

Larry shook his head. "I can't ask you to do that."

Harry took the tape measure he'd been holding on to since Larry walked in and put it in his pocket. "I didn't hear you ask," he said. "I offered."

"Brady can tell you the best person to deal with," I said.

Harry nodded. "Thanks."

I looked at Larry. "I am so sorry this happened, but like I said before, Brady is a good lawyer. He'll do everything he can to help Georgia." I hesitated. "And just because she's been arrested doesn't mean Marcus will stop digging for the truth."

Larry still had that stubborn set to his jaw. He finally looked at me. "You figure it out, Kathleen. You find the truth."

Harry stared at him, shock etched in the lines on his face. "What the hell are you saying?"

Larry turned his attention to his brother. "I'm saying that everyone in town knows that Kathleen is the reason we found Elizabeth. And she's the one who figured out who killed Mike Bishop."

"And both times she damn near paid with her life," Harry exclaimed. He shook his head. "No. That's not happening."

"Oh, so the old man gets Elizabeth and you get justice for the death of one of your best friends but Georgia is supposed to get nothing? And what about Emmy?" Larry was right in Harry's face, and I could feel the anger vibrating off his body.

"Stop," I said.

The first time they didn't hear me. "Stop," I said again, raising my voice enough that Mary over at the front desk turned to look at us. Both men looked at me then. "I get that you're angry," I said to Larry, "but it doesn't help Georgia one bit. So yell at me or curse me out or go outside and punch a tree, but get it together and be there for Georgia. And for Emmy. As far as figuring out what happened to Margery Wyler, Marcus won't stop looking for evidence just because Georgia has been arrested." I almost poked him in the chest with my finger but I stopped myself and just gestured with one hand instead. "And you should know that about him."

Larry's mouth moved but no words came out. I could see that he was angry, yes, but he was equally afraid, I realized. His skin had a gray cast and one hand was pulled into a fist so tight his knuckles were white while at the same time the entire hand trembled slightly.

My own anger dissipated like early-morning mist rising from the river. "And I will . . . see what I can find out. I'm not making any promises."

Larry raked a hand back through his hair, the same sort of gesture Marcus made when he was stressed. "I'm going over to the station to see what *I* can find out," he said.

"Let me know what you need," Harry said. "I meant what I said. We'll figure out the bail money."

Larry nodded. Then he was gone.

"Don't do this," Harry said as soon as his brother

was out the door. "I know you care about Georgia and Emmy and you're pretty much part of our family, but you don't owe anyone anything. You don't have to get involved."

I twisted my watch around my wrist. "I'm already involved. The Wylers showed up here, in my library. I climbed down that embankment in the dark, Harry. I helped Marcus do CPR on Mrs. Wyler. I saw what falling that distance did to her."

"And you almost got killed when you figured out who killed Mike Bishop. I don't want a repeat of that. You might not be so lucky the second time."

I took a deep breath and let it out. "You just said you were willing to put up your house to keep Georgia from having to stay in jail."

"We all care about her and Emmy."

"So do I," I said. "You're doing what you need to do and so am I."

He looked at me for a long, silent moment. "Is this one of those times when we're going to agree to disagree?" he asked at last.

"Yeah, I think so," I said.

Harry shook his head. "I always thought that line was pretty much a load of . . . fertilizer."

I laughed. "Me too."

"You do what you feel you have to," he said. "And try to stay safe while you're doing it."

We agreed we'd get together in a few days to figure out what needed to be done in the computer room.

Harry left and I walked over to the desk.

"You heard about Georgia," Mary said. She was

wearing one of her many Halloween sweaters. This one was pumpkin orange and covered with black cats all wearing witches' hats.

"I did," I said. "She didn't do this. She couldn't kill anyone."

Mary nudged her glasses up her nose. "I know she didn't kill that Wyler woman. Georgia's smart enough to do a better job than just shoving the woman off an embankment."

"Hang on. Are you saying you think Georgia *could* kill someone?"

Mary reached across the counter and patted my hand. "Someday when you and Detective Cutie have a child you'll understand that there isn't anything you wouldn't do for that child. My Bridget is a grown woman, perfectly capable of taking care of herself. But if someone threatened her, I would do anything to protect her. I would risk my own life, or anyone else's. You think Georgia would do anything less for Emmy?"

I thought about my own mother, who had once told a man who had hassled me that if he ever came near me again she would remove his head from his body, hollow it out and use it as a bowl for dip, all said in the same conversational tone she might have used to comment on the weather.

"Are you going to figure out what really happened?" Mary asked.

"I'm going to try."

"Good," she said.

8

Georgia went before a judge just after lunch. Her bail was set at three hundred and fifty thousand dollars. The prosecutor noted that Georgia had no family in town and was self-employed. She also reminded the judge that Georgia had run and changed her name rather than allow the Wylers to see their granddaughter. Brady countered by pointing out that Georgia had no family in town because she was an only child and her parents were dead, but she had created a circle of close friends who were just as much her family. Larry, his brother and Harrison were seated in the front row of the courtroom and Brady pointed them out. Georgia's bail was paid by someone who wanted to stay anonymous. I could think of several people who could have done that. Harrison Taylor was at the top of the list.

Harrison came to the library right after he left the courthouse. I came downstairs to find him having a conversation with Mary at the front desk. He was dressed in a dark suit with a crisp white shirt and a red striped tie.

"You look very handsome," I said, giving him a hug.

"I'd rather be in my old work pants," he said. "But needs must when the devil drives."

"Do you have time for a cup of tea?" I asked.

"I do if it's coffee."

I settled him in the smaller of our meeting rooms and got each of us a cup of coffee and one of Mary's cranberry muffins to split.

He took a sip of the coffee and gave a satisfied sigh. "You make a good cup of coffee, Kathleen," he said. "You know I love Elizabeth, but I have no intention of drinking that green tea she kept making me when she was here. Throw a handful of grass clippings in a cup of hot water and it would taste about the same—maybe better."

I rolled my eyes. Elizabeth was always trying to get her father to drink less coffee and not indulge his sweet tooth so much. "Green tea has antioxidants."

He gave a snort of derision. "So does coffee. Besides, a man needs a vice and as far as vices go, coffee is a pretty tame one. And by the way, I don't see you drinking any green tea."

"And I'm changing the subject now," I said. "Harry told me that Georgia is doing well, considering everything that happened. What about Emmy? Is she all right?"

Harrison nodded. "She stayed with Peggy while we all went to court. She knew something was up but she just rolled with it. Georgia and Larry are with her now explaining what's happened. So tell me that man of yours knows what he's doing."

I took a sip of my coffee. "He does. You know the kind of person Marcus is."

"That's what I'm counting on," he said.

I studied him over the top of my mug. "I heard the person who paid Georgia's bail wants to stay anonymous. Was it you?"

He broke the muffin in half and took a bite. "Well, if it was me, I wouldn't be likely to tell you, would I? But no, it wasn't me. I was all prepared to take care of the bail but someone beat me to it. Wasn't either of my boys. I'm thinking Rebecca and Everett."

I nodded. "It's the kind of thing they would do."

"Reason I stopped in is I'd be interested in hearing your opinion of Brady Chapman. Everything I hear says he's a good lawyer but I can't help wondering if he has enough experience for this case."

"Everything you've heard is true. Brady is a good lawyer. And he's smart enough to ask for help if he needs it. If I were in trouble I'd want Brady to represent me."

"Good to know," he said. "And you'll be sitting this one out."

"Are you asking or suggesting?" I said.

"Some of both, I guess." He set his cup down on the table. His blue eyes grew serious. "We came way too close to losing you this summer because you tangled with Mike Bishop's killer."

"I'm just going to ask a few questions, that's all.

You're the one who said I'm good at getting people to talk."

He reached over and laid his hand on mine. "Just keep it to talking. I'm planning on dancing at your wedding one of these days." He smiled. "And the two of you might want to get a move on. I'm not exactly a spring chicken anymore."

"You're not exactly an old rooster, either," I said. "And as for dancing at weddings, you could make an honest woman of Peggy."

He gave a snort of laughter. "Okay, missy," he said. "Now I'm the one who's going to change the subject. Emmy tells me you have a big Halloween party planned."

I told him about our plans, including the headless horse/man that Harry had stored in his barn.

"They used to have Halloween parties here when the boys were young," Harrison said. "I've got pictures somewhere. One year Harry was the shark from *Jaws*. Another time he was some kind of disco roller skater. Teased his hair and used half a can of his mother's hairspray."

I laughed, trying to picture Harry with the equivalent of a seventies perm. "I would love to see those pictures," I said.

He grinned. "I'll try to find them."

Peggy showed up then to collect him. I gave the old man a hug. "You be careful," he said, resting one hand against my cheek for a moment. "It means a lot that you want to help Georgia and Emmy, but I don't have it in me to lose you."

I was touched by his concern. I swallowed down the sudden lump at the back of my throat. "I'm not going anywhere," I said. "I promise."

The rest of the afternoon was quiet except for a trio of seventh-grade boys who showed up after school with an assignment on kinetic energy they had no clue how to get started on.

"What *is* kinetic energy?" I asked them. That got me three blank looks. I had a feeling they hadn't paid much attention in class. One of the boys was air drumming. "Noah has kinetic energy," I said.

One of the other two almost bounced out of his seat. "He's moving. Kinetic energy has something to do with moving!"

I nodded. "Exactly. Kinetic energy is the energy an object has because of its motion." I looked at the third boy. "Jacob, do you have a basketball stashed in the bushes out front?" I had a firm rule about balls and skateboards in my library.

Jacob ducked his head. "Maybe," he mumbled.

"Good," I said. "Let's go."

I stopped at the desk to get a small rubber ball I'd found in the book drop a couple of days ago. We trooped outside and Jacob retrieved his basketball.

"Okay, hold that in one hand," I told him. I handed him the smaller ball. "Hold this on top of the basketball. When I say 'go,' let go of both balls at the same time."

He nodded then all but rolled his eyes at his friends.

"What's going to happen when Jacob lets go of the balls?" I asked the other two.

"Duh, they're gonna bounce on the ground," Liam said.

Noah shook his head. "No. You're tricking us somehow."

I held up both hands. "No trick. Just kinetic energy." I looked at Jacob. "Ready?" I said.

"Sure."

"Okay, go."

Jacob let go of both balls at the same time. The basketball bounced on the pavement. The smaller ball hit the top of the larger one and bounced in the air.

That got me a dumbfounded look, a "Cool" and a "Whoa."

"What happened?" I asked. Jacob was chasing after his ball. "Both balls were moving so they had kinetic energy," he said over his shoulder.

I smiled at him. "Right. So why did the little ball go up in the air?"

Noah frowned. "It hit the bigger one."

I nodded. They were getting it. "What did it get when it hit the bigger ball?"

"Detention!" Liam said with a smirk.

"Quite possibly," I said. "What else?"

I saw the light dawn in Jacob's eyes. "It got some of the basketball's kinetic energy."

I loved watching people learn new things. I grinned. "My work on this planet is done for today."

I got home and found Hercules with a bone that I was pretty certain belonged to Fifi.

"This is not funny," I said sternly.

He put both paws on the rawhide dog bone and meowed indignantly.

I leaned down so my face was just inches from his. "You are aware that bone has been in Fifi's mouth, which means it's covered in dried dog slobber."

He lifted one paw and looked uncertainly at it.

I straightened up. "That thing stays out here. No dog slobber in my kitchen."

He made a huffy sound and flicked his tail at me. "Fine," I said. "I'll bring your supper out to you."

He glared at me. I folded my arms and stared back. This time he yielded first. He left the bone on the step and went inside with me, waiting, for once, for me to open all the doors. Once we were in the kitchen Hercules went to sit next to the refrigerator, making little grumbling sounds almost under his breath.

"Give me a minute," I said. I set my messenger bag on one of the kitchen chairs and put away my jacket and shoes. Hercules continued to sit by his food dishes, making a point of not looking in my direction.

Owen wandered in, walked over to where his brother was sitting and seemed surprised that the dishes were empty. He looked from Herc—who was still not acknowledging my presence—to me and gave an inquiring murp.

"Your brother and I are having a difference of opinion. Again," I said. "I'm going to change and then I'll get everyone's supper."

I went upstairs trailed by Owen. He rummaged in my closet while I changed into jeans and a long-sleeve T-shirt. One slipper came out of the closet.

"Thank you," I said. I looked around the bedroom. "Do you know where the other one is?"

His furry gray face peered around the closet door. "Merow," he said.

I narrowed my gaze at him. "It better not be downstairs in your stash." He looked affronted at the idea.

I checked the closet but the other slipper wasn't there. When I turned around Owen had one paw stretched under the bed.

"Is that where it is?" I asked. I crouched down for a look and spotted my missing slipper. I just managed to grab it. I sat on the floor, pulled bits of cat hair off each slipper and put them on. Then I gave Owen a kiss on the top of his head. "Thank you," I said.

We went back downstairs to find Hercules hadn't moved. He could hold a grudge for a long time. I put the water on to boil for spaghetti and got the cats food and water. I checked my phone to see if I had missed a call from Marcus, but I hadn't.

I cooked the spaghetti and warmed up some sauce I'd put in the fridge that morning from the freezer. Owen finished eating first and climbed onto my lap. I told him about Georgia being arrested.

Hercules ate the last bit of his food and went to the chair where I had set my messenger bag. He stood on his hind legs and put a front paw on the bag, meowing loudly.

"Yes, we will look up the Wylers," I said, "but I want to talk to Rebecca first to see what she might know."

Hercules dropped back to the floor and headed for the back door.

"We can wait a few minutes until I do the dishes," I said to the cat's retreating back.

He didn't even slow down. He walked directly through the door, the end of his tail disappearing with a faint pop.

"Or not," I said to Owen. He looked over my shoulder and I think he would have shrugged if he were capable of it.

I got to my feet and set him on the chair. We both knew that he was going to jump back up if I set him on the floor and it seemed like a good idea—at least for tonight—to eliminate that middle step. While I washed the dishes, I told Owen about the plans for the Halloween party and he at least pretended to listen, cocking his head to one side and making occasional murps.

I was just wiping out the sink when there was a tap on the door. I turned just as Marcus stepped into the kitchen. He looked tired. His tie was skewed to one side, he needed to shave and I could see he'd raked a hand through his hair several times.

"Hi," I said, crossing the floor to give him a hug and a kiss.

"My day just got better," he said.

Owen jumped off his chair. "Thank you," Marcus said, sitting down.

"Have you eaten?" I asked.

He shook his head. "But I'm going home to have a

shower and change because there are a couple more things I need to do at the station, so I'll get something then." He reached for my hand. "I just wanted to see you."

"How about a sandwich?" I said. "I have eggs and turkey bacon and some of Rebecca's honey-sunny bread."

"You don't need to wait on me," he began. Then he stopped. "Actually, that sounds great."

Owen meowed in agreement. I pointed a finger at him. "You already ate."

He gave me a wide-eyed look as if to say, *What does that have to do with anything?*

I gave Marcus's hand a squeeze and went to the fridge.

"I'm sorry I didn't tell you that Georgia was a suspect," he said. "I couldn't. The prosecutor has been calling me every day. The case is getting a lot of scrutiny behind the scenes. The decision to arrest Georgia was made very quickly and for what it's worth I argued against it. That being said, this isn't a frivolous arrest."

"Georgia said the Wylers have a lot of influence and connections," I said as I put a couple of strips of bacon in the pan.

Marcus propped an elbow on the table and leaned his head on his hand. "They do."

"Is Hugh Wyler still in town?" I asked.

He nodded. "And so is his lawyer."

"Do you think he'll keep trying to see Emmy?" I put two slices of Rebecca's bread in the toaster and broke an egg into a bowl.

He made a face. "I wish I could say no, but I think Georgia being arrested plays right into his hands. Brady thinks Wyler will try to get emergency custody of Emmy."

I closed my eyes for a moment. "Is there any way to stop him? Emmy doesn't even know the man."

"Wyler's lawyer will argue that's Georgia's fault because she kept Emmy away from them."

"They would know her if they hadn't tried to kidnap her from Georgia!"

Marcus got to his feet and put his arms around my shoulders. "Brady will figure it out," he said. "He's a good lawyer. I know he seems like a straight arrow but he has a bit of Burtis in him."

Burtis Chapman had once worked for the town bootlegger, who also happened to be Ruby's grandfather. Those days were long gone and Burtis was now a legitimate businessman. For the most part.

"Is that a good thing?" I asked.

Marcus kissed a spot just below my ear. "In this case, definitely."

He sat down again and I turned the bacon. I knew Marcus wouldn't have arrested Georgia without some kind of evidence. I'd been going over everything I'd seen the night Margery Wyler died. I thought I knew what that evidence was. "You think that Mrs. Wyler was pushed and fell backward."

Marcus sighed. "You know I can't tell you that."

"Bridget will be telling the world in the morning," I said.

He made a sour face. "Yes, she likely will."

"I've been thinking about the injuries to the back of Mrs. Wyler's head. Those wouldn't have happened if she had slipped and fallen because she would have fallen forward or maybe partly sideways. The chances of her falling backward on her own are slim, but falling backward does fit with being pushed."

I glanced at Marcus. He didn't say a word, but nothing in his body language suggested he disagreed. So far, I was on the right track. Now for the piece of evidence that tied my stomach in knots. "Margery had a yellow scarf in her hand. I saw it."

"She did," he said after a long moment.

"It belongs to Georgia. Which Ella told you when you showed the scarf to her." Surprise flashed across his face. I kept talking. "I'd told you that Ella learned to tie flies from Burtis and that's probably why she's so good at the fine detail on her scarves. You remembered that."

"Kathleen, I can't—"

I held up the tongs I'd been using to turn the bacon. "You can't talk about it. I know. That scarf incriminates Georgia because it's one of Ella's and they are all one of a kind but you have to have more than that." I looked over my shoulder at him. "You have to have another piece of evidence or a witness." I noticed how his eyes flicked away for a moment when I said "witness."

I finished his sandwich, poured him a glass of milk and then I sat at the table and Owen jumped onto my lap. "You have some kind of a witness, don't you," I said. I didn't even phrase the sentence as a question.

"Someone saw Margery Wyler arguing with a

woman that matches Georgia's description not that long before we found Mrs. Wyler's body. The witness heard Georgia called by name." He shrugged. "I'm sure the information will be in the paper in the morning, so I'm not giving away any secrets."

"So except for the scarf the evidence is circumstantial, and Brady could argue that Georgia dropped the scarf and Mrs. Wyler picked it up," I said.

Marcus looked at me across the table. "Don't get involved in this one," he said.

I'd gotten involved in the Gregor Easton case because for a while Marcus had considered me a possible suspect in the man's death. I'd been involved in some of his subsequent investigations because someone had asked for my help. As Harrison had pointed out, people did tend to tell me things. I think a lot of that had to do with the fact that I was a face they saw at the library all the time and not a police officer. A lot of people were naturally wary of the police I'd learned. Then again, not all police officers had Marcus Gordon's integrity.

"Why?" I said.

"Because I just have a bad feeling about this case and about some of the people who are involved." He shook his head. "Go ahead and laugh. I know usually I'm all about the facts and you're the one trusting your instincts. But I haven't given up on the investigation just because Georgia has been arrested. And I believe in the legal system. Let it work."

Marcus finished his sandwich in two more bites and snuck a tiny piece of egg to Owen when he thought I didn't see. "I'm sorry to eat and run," he said. "But I do need to go."

I gave him a hug. "I love you," I said.

He smiled. "We've come a long way from when we first met."

I gave him a mock glare. "You thought I was having an affair with Gregor Easton, who was more than twice my age."

"And you thought I was too rigid and never colored outside the lines."

I laughed. "I also thought you were cute. And then Maggie set us up to sit next to each other at the final concert of the music festival."

Marcus smiled. "I owe her for that." He kissed me. "I love you, too," he said. "I'll call you tomorrow and we can figure out the weekend."

"Sounds good," I said. He gave me one more kiss and he was gone.

I cleaned up while Owen sat on my chair and washed his face.

"Let's see if we can find your brother and then go talk to Rebecca," I said.

We stepped outside and I looked over into Rebecca's backyard. She was in her gazebo talking to Hercules. "It seems Hercules has already gone to talk to Rebecca."

She spotted me then and waved. Owen and I walked across the backyard and Rebecca came to meet us. She smiled down at the cat. "Hello, Owen," she said. He dipped his head to acknowledge her greeting and then went to see what his brother was doing.

"Oh, Kathleen, it's so nice to see you," she said, giving me a hug.

"I'm glad you're home," I said. "We missed you." Rebecca and Everett had gone to see his granddaughter, Ami.

"How is Ami?" I asked.

"Wonderful," Rebecca said. The two of them were very close. Even during all the years that Everett and Rebecca weren't part of each other's lives, Rebecca was always in Ami's.

"Come have a seat," she said. There was a round table and two chairs in the gazebo. In the warmer weather Everett often ate breakfast there, usually with Hercules for company. They shared bacon and conversation. It seemed the cat had some strong opinions on local politics.

Hercules was sitting on one of the chairs. I picked him up and set him on my lap. Rebecca took the other chair. "I heard about Georgia. It must have put Marcus in a difficult spot."

That was typical of Rebecca to think about Marcus as well as Georgia.

"There's still lots of digging to do and lots of questions to ask," I said. "Do you by any chance know anything about the Wylers?"

She shook her head. "I don't, other than what a search online would find you. But I think Lita might."

Lita was Everett's assistant and office manager.

"Lita hears a lot of things. And she's a very good judge of people," Rebecca added.

"I'll give her a call," I said. "Now tell me all about Ami."

She brought me up to date on Ami's classes and her new boyfriend. "He's a very nice young man but you know how Everett is. No one is good enough for his girl. Ami threatened to elope and get matching tattoos if he didn't lighten up."

I laughed. His granddaughter was the only person other than Rebecca and Lita who could challenge Everett that way.

"I'm glad I got to see you," I said. "I have to get home now and make some egg bites for breakfast."

"I'm making bread tomorrow," Rebecca said. "I'm experimenting with a couple of cheese bread recipes. I'll bring you half a loaf of each."

"Did I mention how much I like you being my neighbor?"

She laughed. "Maybe once or twice."

"Time to go," I told Hercules. He immediately went from sitting on my lap to sprawling across it while Owen, who had been nosing around the gazebo, totally ignored me. I picked up Hercules, who went totally limp like a bag of wet laundry.

"Oh, for heaven's sake," I muttered just as the cat lifted his head and looked past me at something. I turned to see what had caught his attention. Georgia was coming around the side of Rebecca's house.

9

A m I interrupting anything?" Georgia asked. She was wearing jeans, a deep-green hoodie and no makeup. She could have passed for a college student.

"No, you're not," I said, setting Hercules down. "How are you?"

She gave me a small smile. "I'm okay. Glad to be home." She turned to Rebecca. "That's why I'm here. I wanted to say thank you in person."

"For what?" Rebecca seemed confused.

"For paying my bail."

Rebecca smiled. "I didn't."

Georgia looked surprised.

"It's something Everett and I had decided we were going to do," Rebecca said, "but it turns out you didn't need us."

Georgia swallowed a couple of times. "Then I guess I'm saying thank you for believing in me."

Rebecca gave her hand a squeeze.

Georgia turned to me then. "I'm glad you're here," she said. "I was coming to see you next."

"What do you need?" I asked.

"I don't need anything," she said. "I wanted to let you know that nothing has changed with respect to the Halloween party. I'm still planning on doing the cupcakes for the kids." She paused. "I mean, unless you don't want me to."

"Of course I want you to," I said. I looked at Rebecca. "Georgia outdid herself on the designs for the Halloween cupcakes. She did an all-chocolate spider cupcake and a skeleton that's marble cake."

"Do you have a pumpkin design?" Rebecca asked.

Georgia nodded. "I do."

"If it's too short notice, I understand, but would you be able to do a Halloween order for me?" Rebecca asked. "Probably five dozen cupcakes or so. They're for the party at the senior center. I should have asked you sooner but Everett and I went to visit his granddaughter and things got away from me."

"I could do that," Georgia said.

Rebecca smiled. "Thank you for squeezing me in."

Georgia gave a wry smile. "I've had a few spaces open up in my schedule."

"That worked out well for me," Rebecca said. "If it's all right I'll stop by tomorrow so we can work out the details."

"Thanks to Ruby I have some photos of my Halloween cupcakes that I can show you," Georgia said.

"I'm looking forward to that," Rebecca said.

Georgia made a vague gesture over her shoulder. "I should get back to Emmy."

"You know where I am if you need anything," I said, giving her a hug.

She nodded. "I'll talk to you soon." She turned to Rebecca. "And I'll see you tomorrow." She headed around the side of the house and disappeared down the driveway.

I folded my arms and studied Rebecca. "I saw what you did," I said.

She gave me a blank look. "What do you mean?"

"Things do not get away from you, Rebecca Henderson. You are the most organized person I know. The extra work you just gave Georgia. Not only is it a vote of confidence in her, it will also help her keep busy, which is probably good right now." I gave her a hug. "Tell Everett that he has excellent taste in wives."

I leaned down and picked up Hercules, who decided once again to use passive resistance to show his displeasure at being taken home. It was like trying to carry a bag of water. "Let's go," I called to Owen.

He leaned around the entrance to the gazebo and looked at me, wrinkling his whiskers. "C'mon, let's go," I said again, making a "move along" gesture with one hand.

He yawned.

"In this lifetime, please."

Owen made his way over to me, stopping to stretch twice. I looked at Rebecca and shook my head. "Have a good night."

"You too," she said, struggling to stifle a smile.

Once we were halfway across the lawn Hercules gave up the whole resistance thing and scrambled to get down. I decided I was losing the battle and set him on the grass. I was expecting him to turn around and head back to Rebecca's but he sat down and began to wash his face.

Owen had gone ahead and was now at the back steps. He meowed loudly. It seemed I was taking too long. "I could have had fish," I said. "Lots of soothing bubbling water, maybe a little castle and some pretty rocks." I was talking to myself. Both cats were ignoring me.

I walked over to join Owen. He was on the small landing sniffing at the rawhide bone. He made a face.

"It belongs to Fifi," I said. "At least I assume it does." Owen jumped backward as though he'd suddenly discovered the bone was on fire.

I unlocked the door and led him into the porch, then looked around for Hercules. He was sitting on one of the Adirondack chairs. "Are you coming?" I asked.

He murped a no.

I opened the kitchen door, kicking off my Keds in the porch because they were dirty. I padded across the floor in my sock feet, grabbing my computer from my messenger bag. I warmed milk for hot chocolate and put the last piece of honey-sunny bread in the toaster for peanut butter toast.

Owen sat by the table and watched me. "This is part of my research process," I said as I spread peanut butter on the toasted bread.

He seemed to think for a moment. Then he went over to the cupboard where I kept the sardine crackers.

"You're a cat. You don't have a process," I told him.

He looked at my food and then he put a paw on the cupboard door.

I looked up at the ceiling. "What am I doing?" I asked the universe.

The universe had no answer. I got Owen two crackers. He meowed a thank-you.

I sat at the table, ate a bite of toast and turned on the laptop. I knew the Wylers were from Chicago. I decided to start with media sources in the city.

I had just pulled up an article on the *Venture Chicago* website, when I heard a loud meow. Hercules was at my feet. Owen had disappeared. Possibly literally. It seemed that his process was eating crackers but not actually doing anything else.

In the interest of fairness, I got up to get Herc two crackers and when I turned around again he had taken my chair and was staring at the computer screen. Somehow, he had brought up a different article from another site.

"I was reading something," I said. He kept staring at the screen as though I hadn't spoken. Not the first time. "Okay," I muttered. "I guess we're reading your article."

I gave Hercules a cracker and settled him on my lap. I knew from past experience that when his paw ended up on the keyboard more often than not it would take me to something useful. It almost seemed like he knew how to use the laptop. I sometimes wondered if he was watching Netflix while I was out.

I read the entire article Hercules had discovered and then looked up more information in a couple of newspaper databases. I was almost overwhelmed by what I'd learned about the Wylers and I wasn't sure how to put it all in perspective. I decided to call Lita instead of waiting until morning.

"I thought I might hear from you when I heard that Georgia had been arrested," Lita said.

"Rebecca said you could tell me more about her former in-laws. I've been online and I can't really wrap my mind over everything I've learned. Georgia said they had money and connections but from what I've read they have a lot more of both than I realized. Can you give me some perspective?"

"I can try," Lita said. "Hugh Wyler is a polarizing figure in the business world—and not just in Chicago. The man is pretty much worshipped by the people closest to him and loathed by the people who feel he betrayed them."

"What about Margery? I found very little about her online."

"Because that's the way she wants it, or so I've heard."

"What do you mean?" I asked.

"It's not common knowledge," Lita said, "but Margery had a pretty unstable childhood. Her mother was married multiple times and there wasn't much money in the times between those marriages."

Hercules shifted on my lap and craned his neck as though he were trying to listen in on the conversation—which I was pretty sure he was.

"I just assumed they both came from money," I said.

"Oh, no. Neither one of them was born with the proverbial silver spoon in their mouth. Once they'd made a little money Margery became charity royalty. She was a fixture on the fund-raising party circuit and if she loaned her name and her presence to a charitable event it was guaranteed to be a success."

Something about the way Lita said "success" twigged for me. "Define success."

"Yes, there's the kicker." I could hear her smile coming through the phone. "Margery's events always resulted in lots of publicity for the cause and all the right people in attendance, but the amount raised for the actual work of the charity was for the most part in the vicinity of only thirty percent. In my opinion the only time thirty percent is a decent number is if it's your batting average."

Hercules had given up trying to listen in and had leaned his head against my chest instead.

"From what I read, Mr. Wyler is involved in a number of lawsuits," I said.

"The Wylers use the court system the way other people use the self-checkout at Walmart," Lita said. "I know of three cases working their way through civil court right now."

"I read one article that seemed to suggest some of Mr. Wyler's business associates were not exactly reputable businessmen."

"That's because they're not," she said. "Hugh Wyler helped build his pharmaceutical company, Eptec, from the ground up, but he also did business with known criminals."

"Could any of his business associates have killed Margery?" I asked.

Lita took a moment before she answered. "In my experience, those kinds of people do their fighting through lawyers, but Hugh tended to make everything personal, so it's not impossible. Be careful, Kathleen. Hugh Wyler doesn't care about the money. It's just a way to keep score. He cares about being right and he will use that sense of righteous certitude to keep going long after anyone else would have the good sense to move on."

"This helps a lot," I said. "Thank you." We said good night and I ended the call. Nothing I had learned about Georgia's former in-laws made me like them any better, but I didn't feel as though I was any closer to figuring out who had pushed Margery Wyler to her death.

Burtis Chapman showed up at the library a little before ten the next morning. "A little bird told me you need some pumpkins," he said.

Brady's father was a large block of a man. His face was lined and weathered and his complexion ruddy from years of working outdoors. Burtis was very smart, although he had no education beyond high school. He could calculate down to the penny in his head what it would cost to put hardwood flooring in your house and discuss whatever books were at the top of the *New York Times* bestseller list. And he'd also once gotten drunk with Marcus's father at the bar at the St. James Hotel and the two of them had serenaded the other patrons with their version of "Sweet Home Alabama."

"Is the little bird's name Maggie?" I asked.

"Could be," he said, with a gleam in his brown eyes.

We went out to his truck, where he had several boxes of various-sized pumpkins on the backseat. "Take whatever you need."

"Are you sure?" I said.

"I'm either going to give you pumpkins or the squirrels are going to steal them and leave a mess all over my garden since Lita won't let me shoot the darn things anymore. It's just better for everyone if you take what you need."

"You were shooting squirrels?"

Burtis reached into the bed of the truck and pulled out a hot-pink-and-lime-green water cannon. "It kept the little buggers out of my corn. Harrison gave me the idea." He gave a snort of annoyance. "Lita claims getting hit with a blast of cold water was traumatizing the things. I offered to use warm water." He gave me a look. "Sometimes that woman does *not* have a sense of humor."

I bit the inside of my cheek so I wouldn't laugh.

In the end I chose a dozen pumpkins, four large and eight small ones. "Keep 'em somewhere cool like the basement," Burtis said. "And you know how to make them last once you set up your decorations."

"No," I said.

"Get yourself a can of paste floor wax." He narrowed his eyes at me. "You know the kind of thing I mean?"

I nodded. "My mother uses it on the floor in the butler's pantry. It's real linoleum."

Burtis gave a nod of approval. "Smart woman," he said. "Before you put your pumpkins out, put a layer of wax on each one and use a soft cloth and some elbow grease to polish it to a nice shine. Same way you'd do with your shoes. It keeps the pumpkins fresh a bit longer and keeps the squirrels at bay, too."

"I'll do that," I said. "Thanks. Last year by November first we had a pretty good colony of fruit flies by the front desk."

Burtis picked up three pumpkins with one hand. "You know how to make a fruit fly trap?" he asked.

"I made two. I couldn't figure out why they weren't working. Turns out Susan is pretty soft-hearted. She kept covering my traps with a piece of cardboard."

"She probably wouldn't be impressed with my squirrel story," he said.

I laughed. "Yeah, I'm pretty sure Susan would side with Lita."

We made short work of storing the pumpkins in a box in the basement. I walked Burtis back out to his truck. "I heard you and Marcus found that Wyler woman down on the rocks. I was sorry to hear he thinks Georgia Tepper had anything to do with that."

"You know Marcus," I said.

He gave me a long, appraising look. "Should I take that to mean he's still investigating?"

"I wouldn't tell you you're wrong," I said.

"Good," he said.

"And Georgia has Brady."

Burtis pulled off his ball cap, bent the rim between his huge hands and put it back on again. "I have faith in my boy. He's a damn fine lawyer."

I could hear the pride in his voice, and just like that something clicked into place for me.

"That's why you paid Georgia's bail," I said.

We had reached his truck and he jingled his keys in one hand. "That's a pretty far-fetched idea," he said.

"Doesn't mean it's not true."

"Doesn't mean you have to spread that all over town, either," he retorted.

"It doesn't," I agreed. I was touched by Burtis's show of faith in Brady. He really was a big softie deep down inside.

I gave him a hug. "You don't fool me," I said. "I know why Brady's such a good guy."

He shook his head. "And you are so full of it," he said, but he was smiling. "If you need more pumpkins, let me know. And I'll bring you some turnips next week."

"I'm looking forward to that," I said.

The rest of the day was busy. There were kids who needed help finding information for school projects and an order of books that was delivered earlier than expected. One of the computer monitors went on the fritz and it took three whacks on the side with the heel of my hand to get the blank half of the screen functional.

"I'm going to dance on top of the circulation desk in fishnets and feathers when the new computers are in place," Mary said after I'd gotten the monitor working again.

I put my hands on my hips and sighed. "That was how I was going to celebrate," I said, "but fine, I'll defer to you."

Mary, who had been trying to get me to try exotic dancing for quite a while now, just shook her head at me and laughed.

Marcus called mid-afternoon. "How about I pick you up after tai chi and we stop for chocolate pudding cake?" he asked.

"You know the way to my heart," I said.

As I pulled into the driveway after work, I spotted Mike Justason in his yard. I grabbed the rawhide bone from the back step and took it to him with another apology. "I don't know what's gotten into Hercules," I said.

"Don't worry about it," Mike said. "Considering the number of times my kids have desecrated a library book it will likely take a few dozen dog toys to even things out."

"I love that the boys are readers," I said, putting a hand on my chest. "It makes my librarian's heart happy."

"If they were just a little less enthusiastic with their love for books, I probably could have bought a yacht by now," Mike said with a wry smile.

When I got to the back steps, I saw Rebecca coming

across the yard with the bread she'd promised me. "Thank you," I said, taking the two half loaves from her.

"You are very welcome," she said. "I'm eager to hear what you think of each recipe. Everett is no help. He likes everything."

I had spaghetti again for supper with a slice from one of the loaves of bread. I thought I tasted Parmesan cheese but I wasn't sure. What I was sure of was that the bread was delicious. Owen wandered in, ate and headed for his basement lair. I knew if I went down later, I'd probably find him sitting in a laundry basket.

Hercules hung around as I did the dishes. I told him that Burtis was the one who paid Georgia's bail. I felt certain he wouldn't spread the information all over town.

"I didn't have time today to do any more digging into the Wylers," I said, "but given what Lita said, I think our next step is to find out more about those lawsuits."

Hercules gave a murp of approval for the plan and went out to the sunporch, for once waiting for me to open the door for him.

I got ready for tai chi and decided to walk down to class since Marcus was picking me up.

Maggie was standing by the window with her tea when I got there. "Burtis brought me pumpkins," I said. "Thank you for mentioning that I was looking for them."

"You're welcome," she said, "but I had an ulterior motive. He's been targeting the squirrels with that water gun he bought online and that doesn't make Lita very happy."

I laughed. "Yeah, he told me about the war he has going with them."

Maggie grinned. "I figured that since the squirrels once stole your coffee and Susan and Harry gave chase, you're probably on Burtis's side."

I held up my thumb and index finger about an inch apart. "Little bit," I said.

Maggie worked us hard and I was sweating by the time we finished. I wiped my forehead with my sleeve. I'd left my towel in my bag.

"Your Cloud Hands are getting better," Roma said.

I smiled at her. "You're lying, but I'll take it."

Marcus appeared in the doorway then. I changed my shoes and put on my hoodie and we headed over to Eric's. When we walked in, there was a man at the counter. As he turned around, it registered that he looked familiar to me.

I was right. It was Marcus's father, Elliot Gordon.

10

Marcus smiled. "I didn't expect to see you here, Dad," he said, giving his father a hug.

Like his son, Elliot Gordon was tall with broad shoulders and strong arms. They both also had great hair, although Elliot's was completely white. He was wearing a dark trench coat over charcoal pants and a pale-blue dress shirt.

"I should have called you as soon as I hit town," Elliot said, "but my need for coffee won out." He turned to me. "Kathleen, it's good to see you. It's been too long."

"You too," I said. "Is this just a quick visit or can you stay for a few days?"

"Maybe longer than a few days," Elliot said.

Behind us, Brady had just come in. "Elliot is here to help with Georgia's case," he said. He was dressed in worn jeans and a gray hoodie with the Minnesota Vikings team logo on the front.

"I heard about the case," Elliot said. "Thanks to a

last-minute plea deal I suddenly had an opening in my schedule. I was intrigued by what I'd read in the paper, plus it gives me a chance to come to town and see my son."

"And I accepted because I don't have a lot of experience in murder cases and Elliot does," Brady said.

Brady had practiced law in Chicago for a while, but Mayville Heights was home and eventually he gave in to the pull to come back and open an office here, although he still took cases in Minneapolis from time to time. He looked at Marcus. "This isn't going to be a problem, is it? Us on one side and you on the other?"

Marcus shook his head. "As far as I'm concerned, there's only one side, the truth. That's what we're all trying to find."

If anyone else had said the words they would have sounded hokey, but coming from him it was impossible to think they were anything but sincere.

"How's your father?" Elliot said to Brady. Behind him, Claire turned from a table where she was topping up a customer's coffee and raised one finger. I nodded.

"Good, aside from a small war he's waging with the squirrels."

Elliot laughed. "I'll call him. I can see we need to catch up."

Brady looked at me. "Do you have bail money or should I stop at an ATM?"

I made a dismissive gesture with one hand. "I have it covered."

Elliot shook his head. "We sang one song in the bar at the St. James, and for the record, the crowd loved us."

"It was more than one song," I said, "and you passed out in my truck."

"Dad passed out just inside the door and slept on the floor all night," Brady said. "Ever see another person's complexion actually turn green?"

I gave Elliot the side-eye. "Oh yeah," I said.

He looked at Marcus. "You could leap in and defend me anytime."

Marcus grinned and shook his head. "Can't do that, Dad," he said. "I was there. You really were green."

Elliot Gordon and Burtis Chapman had been friends since they were boys. Their loyalty to each other ran bone deep and their ability to get into trouble together seemed to be greater than the sum of how much havoc they could raise separately.

"I'm changing the subject," Elliot said, but he was smiling and I knew he didn't mind the good-natured teasing. "Brady and I need to go over some things right now, but can the three of us have breakfast in the morning?"

Marcus looked at me. "It's Friday, so I'm free," I said.

"Seven thirty?" Marcus said. "I'm not going to ask if that's too early."

Elliot smiled. "Seven thirty is fine."

Marcus looked at me. "Do you have your keys?" he asked. I nodded. He turned back to his father. "I'll give you my key and you can head out to the house when you're done."

Elliot shook his head. "I appreciate the offer, but under the circumstances I'm better at the St. James.

The appearance of impropriety . . ." He didn't need to finish the sentence.

Claire came out of the kitchen then, carrying a large brown paper bag. She caught my eye. "Go ahead and just pick a table when you're ready," she said.

I nodded as Brady excused himself and went to pay for his food.

"It's good to see you," Marcus said to his father.

Elliot smiled. "I'm glad I came. I don't see enough of you." They hugged again. Elliot put a hand on my arm. "Either of you," he added.

He'd been a mostly absent father, building his career, while Marcus and his sister, Hannah, were growing up. Elliot hadn't taken Marcus's decision to become a police officer well. To his credit, he had realized his mistake and worked hard to build a better relationship with his son. He could still be somewhat arrogant and judgmental on occasion, but I didn't doubt how much he loved either of his children.

"I'll see you in the morning," I said.

Marcus and I took a table near the front window. Brady raised a hand in good-bye as he and Elliot left.

"That was a surprise," I said. "A good one, though."

"Do you feel a little better about things now?" Marcus asked.

"I do," I said. "I don't doubt Brady's competence, but your dad brings experience to the case, and that's important, too."

Claire came over and we ordered. "Your timing is perfect," Claire said. "Eric just took a pan out of the oven."

The pudding cake was delicious, as usual. Marcus smiled as I licked chocolate sauce off the back of my spoon. "I forgot to ask if there's anything new with respect to the practical joker?" he said.

I shook my head. "The camera's up and working but if things go as they have in the past, it will be at least a couple of weeks until something else turns up in the gazebo."

"I'm amazed by the amount of work this person has done."

"Whoever it is has to have help," I said.

Marcus gestured with his spoon. "I thought the same thing. But then why haven't you heard even a whisper about who's been making these creations?"

"Lots of people can keep what they know to themselves," I said, wondering if ordering seconds was a bad idea. "If I had a secret, Maggie wouldn't tell. And I would keep hers."

"That's true," he said. Then he narrowed his gaze and gave me a thoughtful look. "Maybe Maggie's the practical joker and you're helping her. She's creative enough to come up with something like that half man, half horse, and you have the organizational skills to get everything in place and to circumvent Larry's cameras."

"And why are we doing this?"

"That's the part I haven't figured out yet."

"Okay," I said. "Get back to me when you do." I smiled at him across the table.

He set his spoon down. "Seriously, do you have any idea why your culprit is doing this?"

I shook my head. "I don't. Harry thinks it's just some stupid kids who think it's a big joke. Mary says it's someone looking for attention."

"What do you think?"

"I don't know." I looked at my bowl. Why was it almost empty? "I keep thinking I'm missing something."

"What kind of something?" he asked, picking up his spoon again.

I shrugged. "That's the problem. I don't know."

Hercules woke me in the morning by swatting/patting my face with a paw—no claws. I opened one eye to see him looming over me. "What do you want?" I said. I squinted at my clock. "I have fourteen more minutes to sleep."

He meowed loudly, which meant, I guessed, that what he wanted was breakfast. "You need to do something about your morning breath," I said. All that got for a response was an unblinking, green-eyed stare. Hercules was not a morning person.

I got up and got dressed. When I stepped into the kitchen Owen walked over to me and seemed to be checking out what I was wearing. Or maybe he was just wondering why I was taking so long to get his breakfast.

"Sometimes I forget that you and your brother aren't people," I said as I picked up their dishes. To my amusement they exchanged a look. Then Owen meowed at me, his furry gray head cocked to one side.

I smiled down at him. "To answer a question I'm

not even sure you asked, I am not wearing my sweatpants because I'm meeting Marcus and his father for
breakfast."

Hercules, who had been peering under the refrigerator—probably because once again he'd knocked
something underneath it—immediately lifted his
head and looked at me. He and Elliot had been buddies ever since the two of them teamed up to look for
me when I'd been left to die in an abandoned well in
the woods.

"I'm sure you'll get a chance to see your buddy. He's
come to help with Georgia's case, so he should be here
for a while."

The cat's gaze moved from me to my computer, sitting on the kitchen table.

"Yes, we have more work to do when I get back," I
said, which seemed to satisfy him.

Hercules and Owen had breakfast. I finished getting ready and headed out the door. Hercules came
out with me to sit on the bench in the sunporch.

"Please stay away from Fifi," I said, giving the top
of his head a scratch.

He made an annoyed huff and pointedly stared out
the window. I knew when I'd been dismissed. I drove
down to the hotel, where we were meeting Elliot.

Even though I was a bit early, Elliot was already at
a table.

He smiled when he caught sight of me and got to
his feet. "Good morning," he said.

I slipped off my jacket and sat down. "Good morning," I said. I looked around. "It looks so different in

here in the daytime." In the morning the hotel served breakfast in the bar. It was a beautiful place to start the day, with the sun shining in through the floor-to-ceiling wall of windows.

I gestured at the carafe in the center of the table. "Is that coffee?"

"It is," Elliot said. "And very good coffee."

I poured myself a cup and added cream and sugar. He was right. It was good coffee, not that I would have turned up my nose at it if it had only been mediocre.

I looked across the table at Elliot. In many ways he reminded me of Marcus, and not just physically. They both had the same sharp gaze that seemed to miss nothing. "I'm very glad you came," I said.

"You like Ms. Tepper," he said.

I nodded. "I do. I consider her a friend. With all the things that have happened to her—her parents both died when she was just in her twenties, then her husband died, *then* her in-laws tried to take her child—you wouldn't be surprised if she was a bitter person, but she isn't. She's kindhearted and generous even though she's had more than her share of bad things in her life."

"Life isn't always fair," Elliot said.

"I know that," I said. "But this time I want it to be. I want Georgia to get her happy ending."

"And you think I can make that happen."

"I'm counting on it. I know you have a very strong sense of fair play."

He smiled as though I'd said something funny. "Why do you say that?"

"One word: Marcus."

Elliot laughed. "My son has made me eat my own words more than once. Burtis says the apple doesn't fall far from the tree."

I smiled at him over my coffee cup. "Burtis Chapman is a very, very smart man."

Marcus arrived then. "I'm sorry I'm late," he said, taking the chair to my right. "Micah is continuing her streak of bringing me something dead to start the day." Marcus's cat might have been small, but she was a determined hunter, probably because of the time she'd spent at Wisteria Hill.

"What was it this time?" I asked.

"A vole on the hood of my car," he said, reaching for the coffee. He looked at his father. "My cat has been leaving me little surprises almost every day for the past couple of weeks."

"It's her way of saying she considers you to be her family," Elliot said.

Marcus nodded. "That's what Kathleen said. I just wish the surprises were a little less . . . gory."

"She could be doing what Hercules is doing," I said. "Stealing things from the Justasons' dog. So far a rubber toy and a half-chewed rawhide bone."

"I thought Fifi was afraid of cats," he said.

"He is." I turned to Elliot. "A little context. Fifi is male, not female, something the Justason boys didn't understand when they named him. Second, he's a very large and intimidating-looking dog of indeterminate parentage."

"And he's terrified of cats," Marcus finished.

"Why would Hercules steal a dog's toys?" Elliot

frowned. "Are you sure it's him? Did you actually see him take the toy or the bone?"

Marcus's lips twitched. "Kathleen, were you aware that Hercules had retained counsel?"

"I was not," I said, struggling and failing to keep a straight face.

Elliot shook his head and smiled. "All I'm saying is just because everything makes Hercules look guilty doesn't mean he is."

Marcus laughed. "Dad, are you trying to say that the dog is setting Hercules up? Because he's a pretty smart dog, but I don't think he's *that* smart."

The waiter was heading our way. "Saved by the breakfast menu," Elliot said.

"Have you talked to Hannah recently?" Marcus asked his dad once we had ordered.

Elliot nodded. "A couple of days ago. She seems to like New York."

Marcus's sister had a role in an off-off-Broadway play that was getting good buzz. According to my mother, who had a lot of contacts in the theater world, Hannah was the best thing in it.

"I talked to her as well," Marcus said. "She mentioned possibly coming for a visit after Christmas. Maybe we could all get together."

"Just tell me where and when," Elliot said.

We spent the rest of breakfast talking about what had been going on in town but carefully avoiding anything to do with Georgia's case. Elliot put everything on his tab. "I invited both of you," he said to forestall any argument.

"Thank you," I said, reaching for my jacket. "Will you have time to come out for supper while you're here?"

He smiled. "I'd like that. I just need to take a look at my schedule."

"I need to get to the station," Marcus said. He kissed my cheek and clapped his father on the back. Then he left.

"I need to go as well," Elliot said. "I'll call you about dinner?"

I nodded. "Please." I had tucked my travel mug into my bag and I went over to the bar for a cup of coffee to take with me so I didn't have to make it when I got home. If sardine crackers were the boys' vice—and they were, especially since Roma had stopped everyone from feeding them pizza—then coffee was mine.

When I got home, Hercules was sitting in the same spot in the sunporch. There were no dog toys or bones on the back step. A good sign.

He jumped down and trailed me into the kitchen.

"Let me get changed and we'll go online and see what we can find," I said. He made a little murp of happiness.

I changed into sweatpants and a T-shirt and we settled in at the table with the computer and my coffee. It was very easy to find the names of the people in the lawsuits involving Hugh Wyler. One was suing him; the other two were being sued.

"So now what do we do?" I asked Hercules. "We can't exactly call three complete strangers and ask if they made a secret trip to Mayville Heights to push Hugh Wyler's wife off an embankment."

He wrinkled his whiskers.

"Yes, I know how crazy that just sounded."

He swatted at the keyboard a couple of times and we were suddenly on the Twitter account of someone I'd never heard of. But that gave me an idea.

"We could take a look at the social media accounts for all three of those people. We may be able to find out where they were the night Margery died."

Very quickly I discovered that the lawsuit between Hugh Wyler's company and a competitor had been settled out of court just a few days before Mrs. Wyler's death, so I eliminated the company's owner from my list of suspects. .

The second lawsuit had been brought against a professor who had been part of a research project funded by Wyler's company. I was able to find a photo of the professor at a symposium at Harvard on the afternoon that the Wylers showed up at the library. I mentally crossed off her name as well. But Hercules and I hit a roadblock when it came to the former company executive who was suing Hugh Wyler. The man appeared to have no social media accounts or any other presence online.

Finally, I set Hercules on the floor and stood up, stretching my arms over my head. "I'm stuck," I said. "I had three long-shot suspects and I can eliminate one and two, I have no way to check up on number three, and I have no idea what to do now." Hugh Wyler might have an idea of why someone would want to kill his wife but there was no way he was going to talk to me.

I sighed with frustration. I had no way to contact any of Margery Wyler's friends, not that I even knew their names. I couldn't even figure out how to find the man I'd seen Mrs. Wyler with the night she died. I rubbed the space between my eyebrows with two fingers. "I don't think that there's any way that I can help Georgia," I said to Hercules. I wasn't a police officer like Marcus or a lawyer like Brady and Elliot. Just because people talked to me didn't mean I would somehow be better at figuring out who killed Mrs. Wyler.

He rubbed against my leg and I picked him up. "It'll be okay," I told him. He nuzzled my chin.

I decided if I couldn't be Trixie Belden, I could at least clean the house. I threw a load of towels in the washer and cleaned the bathroom. Scrubbing the bathtub was a great way of working off some of my frustration.

Once the bathroom was sparkling, I packed the last of the chicken soup and a slice of bread from Rebecca's second half loaf for my lunch. By then the towels were dry. I folded them and got ready for work.

I called good-bye to Owen, who responded from somewhere upstairs. "If your brother pushes all of my shoes out of the closet again there is going to be trouble," I said to Hercules. " 'Right here in River City, trouble with a capital T.' "

The cat looked blankly at me.

"*The Music Man*? Hugh Jackman?" His green eyes didn't even blink. If he was somehow using the computer when I wasn't around, it clearly wasn't to listen to the soundtracks of Broadway musicals.

Abigail was working the desk when I got to the library. "I heard Marcus's father came to join the case," she said.

"He's a very good lawyer," I said. "Between him and Brady they'll get Georgia cleared of this. If I were in trouble I'd want Elliot on my side. And it's not that I think Brady isn't a good lawyer."

She nodded. "I know. I looked Mr. Gordon up last night. He has a lot more experience than Brady does. He's won some pretty big cases."

Suddenly, something just beyond my left shoulder caught Abigail's attention. She sucked in a breath as her face paled.

I turned around to see what had caused such a strong reaction.

Hugh Wyler had just walked in.

11

I took a breath and let it out. Then I put a hand on Abigail's shoulder. "Go sort books," I said in a quiet voice. "I've got this."

"You sure?" she said.

I nodded. I might not be able to help any other way, but I could do this. I walked over to Hugh Wyler. He looked older and thinner somehow. An image of Margery Wyler's body lying on the rocks flashed before my eyes. It didn't matter how badly they had treated Georgia, it was impossible not to feel some compassion for the man. "Mr. Wyler," I said. "How may I help you?"

"Could we talk somewhere more private?" he asked.

I nodded. "Come upstairs to my office." I led the way up the steps, unlocked the door and set my messenger bag on the desk. "What did you want to talk to me about?"

He cleared his throat. "We got off on the wrong foot

when we met last week. The detective working on my wife's case explained that you were the one who spotted Margery's . . . body and climbed down to try to save her."

"Anyone would have done what I did."

"Nonetheless, you were the one who actually did do it and I appreciate that you tried to save her."

"I'm sorry for your loss," I said.

"Thank you," he said. "Now that Paige has been arrested, I can start to put this whole nightmare behind me."

"Will you be heading back to Chicago now?" I asked. The conversation was making me uncomfortable.

"Not until I have my granddaughter. Surely now you can see what kind of person my former daughter-in-law is?"

I knew I needed to choose my words carefully. "I don't think that Georgia is a subject that we should talk about," I said.

Hugh Wyler looked incredulous. "Don't tell me you still support Paige?" he said. I noticed how he made a point of calling Georgia by her former name. He shook his head. "Ms. Paulson, you have my sympathy since you have clearly been conned by an unscrupulous woman. Again, thank you for trying to help my wife. I can see myself out."

He left and I slumped against my desk. I reminded myself that Hugh Wyler had just lost his wife and was grieving, but the look in his eyes when he talked about Georgia troubled me. I still had time before my shift started because I almost always came in early on Fridays, so I decided to go for a walk to clear my head.

I put on my jacket and headed downstairs.

Abigail came over to me. She looked worried. "Are you all right?" she asked. "I saw Mr. Wyler leave."

"I'm fine," I said.

"What did he want?"

"He wanted to thank me for trying to help his wife. But more important than that, I learned that he's going to try to use Georgia's arrest to get Emmy."

Abigail shook her head. "I wish that surprised me."

"Me too," I said. "I'm going for a walk. I won't be long."

I decided to take the sidewalk. I didn't want to walk along the riverbank right now. I was still in sight of the library when I spotted someone walking ahead of me on the opposite side of the street. He looked vaguely familiar. When he turned his head, I realized it was the man I'd seen talking to Margery Wyler at the St. James the night she died. Without thinking it through, I started to follow him.

He walked at a brisk pace but not so fast that I couldn't keep an eye on him. He went into the bookstore and I had to wait for a break in traffic to dart across the street.

I stepped inside the store and looked around. It wasn't that big a space but I couldn't spot the man. I looked around, wondering where he'd disappeared. I was certain he'd come into the store and not gone into Eric's Place. Was I wrong?

Maybe he was at the back of the building, I decided.

I started in that direction, when the man came around the corner of a bookshelf and stepped in front of me.

"Why are you following me?" he said.

I automatically took a step back. Then I reminded myself that I was in a public place. "I followed you because I wanted to talk to you about Margery Wyler," I said.

He studied me for a moment. "Why?"

"Because I found her body."

His expression changed, became a little less guarded. "You're Kathleen Paulson."

"I am," I said. "How did you know?" Bridget hadn't used my name in the article in the paper.

"I was the Wylers' lawyer. I'm Richard Benson."

"Was?" I said.

He nodded. He gestured in the direction of the front door. "Why don't we step outside?" he said.

I followed him out onto the sidewalk. Richard Benson was maybe three inches or so taller than me, which made him about five foot ten or so. He wasn't overweight but he was a solid brick of a man. He wore a dark-green rolled-neck fisherman's sweater, jeans and a pair of rimless glasses. His pewter gray hair was cut short on the sides, longer on the top.

"You're not going to tell me why you're not the Wylers' lawyer anymore, are you?" I said.

"No, I'm not," he said, "other than I believed my ability to discharge my duties had been compromised."

"Why are you still in town if you're not working for them any longer?"

He shrugged. "I had a block of time set aside for their case. I decided to take it as vacation time. I haven't taken any time off in three years. My hobby is photography and there is some beautiful scenery in this area."

He gave me what I guessed passed for a smile with him. There was no warmth in it. "You're a friend of Georgia Tepper." He wasn't asking a question.

"I am," I said. He used Georgia's correct name, not Paige, I noticed.

"So you don't believe she killed Margery Wyler."

"I know she didn't."

"Aren't you going to ask me if I did?"

"Did you?" I said.

Benson shook his head. "No. I was in the bar at the hotel listening to the jazz trio that was playing. The saxophonist who joined them was very good. Ask the bartender. I tip well."

His expression became serious again. "I had no reason to kill Margery. I was the one who terminated our working relationship."

I leaned my head to one side and studied him. He was a hard man to read. "You argued the night she died. I saw the two of you."

"We had a *conversation* in which I told her I could no longer be her attorney. It wasn't an argument."

"It looked like a pretty heated *conversation* to me," I said.

"I don't know what you think you saw, Ms. Paulson, but as I said, we were not arguing and we parted on cordial terms."

I didn't believe him. Richard Benson was very skilled, it seemed, at skirting around the truth, but small things gave him away; the way he put his hands in his pockets and the way he made a point of looking me in the eye a bit too much, the way he tilted his head, trying to look personable.

"Do you know anyone who might have wanted Margery Wyler dead?" I asked. I didn't actually expect him to name names. I just wanted to watch his reaction to the question.

"Georgia Tepper has been arrested. She certainly had motive."

I smiled. "You're a lawyer, Mr. Benson. You know just because someone is arrested doesn't make them guilty."

He shrugged one shoulder. "Mrs. Wyler raised money for a lot of good causes. Why would anyone want to kill her?"

"We all have secrets," I said.

"The same can be said for your friend." He gave me that cold smile again. "I have somewhere I have to be," he said. "Have a nice afternoon, Ms. Paulson." He walked away and I had the sensation that I'd just been talking with a crocodile. I needed to look into Richard Benson. All the years I'd watched my mother and father create complex characters just out of words on a page had taught me a lot about subterfuge. In other words, I was good at spotting a liar. Richard Benson was lying about a lot of things. Maybe I could help Georgia after all.

I walked back to the library. My appetite had

returned. I ate lunch at my desk and found that I was hard-pressed at this point to pick a favorite between Rebecca's two bread recipes.

The afternoon was busy. I arbitrated a heated discussion between patrons as to whether Agatha Christie was the first female author of cozy mysteries. "She wasn't," I said, and pointed them to the works of American author Anna Katharine Green. I reorganized the magazine section and met with Harry to go over the changes for the computer room.

At the end of the day Abigail appeared at my office door. "Kathleen, do you have a minute?" she asked. Her expression was troubled.

"Of course," I said. "What's wrong?"

She twisted her birthstone ring around her right ring finger. "You know that Georgia and I are close. I always wanted a sister and she's kind of filled that role."

I nodded. "And you for her."

"I was so angry when I found out that the Wylers had come here and ambushed her. I uh . . . I did something I don't usually do. I had a drink. More than one actually. I was going to walk home because I knew I wasn't safe to drive, and I saw Margery Wyler coming toward me on the sidewalk."

My stomach sank.

"I knew it was her because I'd seen photographs of her online."

"Abigail, what did you do?" I asked.

She looked past me, not really focusing on anything. I waited.

Finally, she looked at me again. "See, I can understand a tiny bit of what Georgia has been going through, because my grandmother was subjected to a protracted custody battle as a child and uh . . . and we were very close."

"What did you do?" I said again.

She stared down at her feet. I'd never seen Abigail so upset. "I told Mrs. Wyler exactly what I thought of her, what a horrible person she was."

I put a hand on her arm. "You were drunk and upset. Don't beat yourself up about it."

She looked up at me, stricken. "That's the problem. I'm afraid I could have argued with her a second time. I rarely drink and I don't remember everything I did that night. What if I'm the one who pushed Margery Wyler?"

12

You didn't," I said, feeling a rush of relief.

"You don't know that," Abigail said. "*I* don't know that."

"Did Georgia kill her former mother-in-law?"

She looked confused. "No."

"How do you know?" I asked.

"Because I know Georgia."

I nodded. "Exactly. And I know you. Who used a lacrosse stick to get that bat that flew in out of here last spring? Mary tried to bring it down with a can of hair spray."

A smile pulled at the corners of her mouth. "I think I got it out because it was a little stunned from the hair spray," she said.

"It was lucky it wasn't asphyxiated from the hair spray," I said. "My point is you saved that bat. You didn't let anyone else hurt it. There's no way you could have pushed Margery Wyler. It's not in your nature." I smiled at her. "My guess is you told Mrs. Wyler what you thought of her and the horse she rode in on, went home, fell asleep and woke up in the morning feeling as though your mouth had been done over in shag carpeting and the entire percussion section of the school band had set up residence in your frontal lobe."

I took both of her hands in mine. "You didn't hurt anyone. Trust me. Please."

To my surprise she threw her arms around me. "Thank you," she whispered.

It was a quiet evening. Either everyone had all the books they needed or no one felt like reading. The sky was an inky blue dome shot with stars as I drove up Mountain Road. Marcus's SUV was already parked in the driveway. I pulled in behind him. Happily, there were no bones or dog toys on the back step. Maybe Hercules had gotten the message.

Marcus was in the kitchen making popcorn with two furry helpers, each sitting on a chair. "Hi," I said, kicking off my shoes and then standing on tiptoe to give him a kiss. I looked over at Owen and Hercules. "What are you doing?"

Their heads swiveled in Marcus's direction.

I shook my head. "No. Don't try to con me into believing he gave you permission."

Neither one of them twitched so much as a whisker. Marcus, on the other hand, gave me a sheepish look. "I did tell them they could help," he said. "And they couldn't see well from the floor."

"You didn't feed them any popcorn, did you?"

Marcus was very particular about what kernels

and seasonings he used and my kitchen already smelled amazing. He turned back to the counter, where he had taken out two pots and three bowls. His popcorn making also made a lot of dirty dishes. "No. I did not feed Owen or Hercules any popcorn."

I saw a look pass between him and the cats. "So what did you feed them? Specifically."

Owen suddenly began studying the floor while Hercules began to wash his right front paw.

"Just a few crackers," Marcus said. "The ones Roma's vet friend makes." He tipped his head in the general direction of the toaster. There was a small brown paper bag partially hidden behind it. "They're organic," he added, a tad self-righteously.

"You spoil them," I said sternly. Then I stood up on tiptoe and kissed his mouth.

He smiled and wrapped his arms around me. I felt the tensions of the day drain out of me.

I gave him another kiss and then gestured at the array of dishes on the counter. "How long before the popcorn is ready?"

"Give me about ten minutes," he said.

While Marcus went back to measuring and frowning at a package of butter, I headed upstairs to change. No cats followed me. Butter was more interesting than watching me wash my face and pull on a pair of leggings.

When I came back down the pot was on the stove and the aroma of popping corn filled the kitchen. I stood by the table and watched Marcus work. Some people were wine snobs or cheese snobs, he was a popcorn snob. Since Halloween was coming up soon, we were watching the 2016 version of *Ghostbusters*. Some of the location shots had been done in Boston and I liked watching for landmarks I knew.

"How was your day?" Marcus asked.

"Hugh Wyler came to see me," I said.

He shot a quick glance at me over his shoulder. "What for?"

"He wanted to thank me for trying to save his wife." I sighed. "I wish we'd been able to help her."

"I do, too," he said. "You saw the injury to her head. Even a doctor couldn't have helped her."

"I know. And I kept trying to remember she was Hugh Wyler's wife and he's grieving for her, but he's a hard man to feel compassion for."

Marcus frowned. "Did he say something to you?"

"He's just shocked that I still believe in Georgia. Maybe if I were in his position I'd feel the same way." My cell phone rang then. I picked it up. It was Roma.

"Bad time?" she asked.

"Nope. I'm just watching Marcus make popcorn," I said.

"Any chance one or both of you could feed the cats Monday morning? Eddie's going to be away for a charity hockey game and do you remember the dog I told you about? The golden retriever?"

"The rescue dog with the brain tumor?" After Roma had told Maggie and me about the dog, I'd gone online and made a donation to the fund-raiser.

"Oscar. Yes. They're more than a thousand dollars over their goal. The surgery is a go first thing Monday morning and I'm going to assist." I could hear the elation in her voice.

I grinned even though she couldn't see me and did a little dance that it was probably better she hadn't seen. "That is such good news. Yes, I can feed the cats."

"Thank you," she said. "I should be back Monday night but if there's any problem, I'll let you know."

"I'll be crossing my fingers for Oscar."

"Thanks for that, too. I'll talk to you when I get back."

I set my phone on the table.

"Was that Roma?" Marcus asked.

"It was. She needs me or us to feed the cats Monday morning." I rolled my neck from one side to the other. "Did I tell you about Oscar?"

He lifted the pot off the heat. "No. Who's Oscar?"

"A rescue dog with a brain tumor. The vets are donating their time and a fund-raiser came up with the money for the rest of the expenses, so the surgery is Monday morning."

"As far as I know I can come out with you," he said. His forehead was wrinkled in concentration as he sprinkled spoonfuls of something over the hot popcorn.

"Good," I said. I moved closer to the counter. "I don't know what that is but I can't wait to try it."

He put a protective arm in front of the bowl. "It's Italian Parmesan seasoning and I haven't finished tossing it yet."

I took a step back. There was no way I was going to

get even a single piece of popcorn before Marcus decided it was ready.

"Abigail called me about an hour before you got home," Marcus said.

My stomach gurgled and I wrapped my arms around my midsection. "I thought she might. You don't actually think she could have pushed Margery Wyler to her death, do you?" I asked.

He shrugged. "No, but I still have to check out her story. I should be able to find some sort of surveillance video somewhere along the way she would have walked home."

"Have you talked to Richard Benson?" I asked.

That got his full attention. "Yes," he said. "Have you?"

I nodded. "I met him on the street."

"And?"

"And I think he was hiding something. But right now, I can't think of what reason he would have had for killing Mrs. Wyler. He said he has an alibi for the time."

"He does," Marcus said.

I studied his face for some indication on what he thought about the Wylers' former lawyer. He wasn't giving anything away.

"Did you check it out?" I asked.

For a long moment he didn't say anything. Finally, he nodded. "I didn't but someone did."

"I knew it couldn't be that easy," I said.

"Do you have any other suspects?"

"I had three but I managed to eliminate two of them through their social media."

Marcus was still carefully tossing the popcorn. "What about number three?"

"I can't eliminate the Eptec executive who's suing Hugh Wyler and the company."

He looked up at me. "Don't waste your time on him."

"Why?" I said.

"Just don't." He gave the bowl a little shake and finally seemed satisfied.

The police had alibied the man I hadn't been able to. "Okay," I said.

Marcus picked up the popcorn and leaned over to kiss me. "Let the world turn without you for a little while," he said. "Let's go watch the movie."

We settled on the sofa with the bowl of popcorn between us and both cats at Marcus's feet happily eating a couple of tiny chicken-shaped cat crackers that I had pretended not to see him slip to them.

Saturday morning made up for the quiet Friday at the library. Susan draped herself dramatically over the circulation desk after I locked the door behind the last book-laden patron. "Where did all the people come from?" she said. "And why, why, *why* don't they wash their hands before they touch the books?"

One of the elementary school classes had made slime at school and a lot of books had come back with sticky gooey streaks all over them.

Levi was collecting all the books that had been left

in different places around the building. He came from the computer area with an armload of them and a rubber chicken. He set the chicken next to Susan. "Have you thought about staying open longer on Saturday?" he asked.

Susan lifted her head and glared at him. "Don't make me hit you with this chicken, Levi," she said.

I smiled at him. "It's a valid question. Yes, we've thought about it. We've tried it more than once. And what happens is if we're open all day on Saturday then we have fewer people come in than if we're just open until one o'clock. Maybe when people think they have all day they keep putting off coming in but when they know we'll be closing right after lunch it motivates them to get here early."

"Makes sense," Levi said.

It didn't take long for the three of us to put the building back to rights. Clouds had rolled in when we were ready to leave and it was starting to spit rain. "How about I drop you off?" Susan said to Levi.

He looked out the window at the darkening sky. "Yeah, that would be good, thanks," he said.

"Go ahead," I said to them. "I think I'll go back upstairs for my umbrella." I let them out and went up to my office. My black umbrella was hanging from a hook on the back of the door. It was big enough to keep two people dry.

I headed back downstairs. I was just locking the inside doors when someone in an oversized hoodie scrambled up the library steps, tried the outside door and then smacked a hand on it in frustration as it registered that the door was locked. As the person turned away, I realized it was Riley Hollister.

I tapped on the glass and she turned around. I held up a finger and undid the lock. "Hey, Riley, did you need something?" I asked.

She shook her head. "No. I just didn't realize it was after one o'clock. I wanted to get more books for Duncan but *he* kept me working."

He was Riley's grandfather, Gerald Hollister. It was the only way she ever referred to him. Duncan was her eight-year-old brother. Their mother, Bella Lawrence, had died almost a year ago in a car accident. Riley was fiercely protective of Duncan. Burtis had once called Gerald Hollister "a mean old cuss" and the description was pretty accurate from what I'd seen. His son Lonnie, the kids' father, wasn't much better. I'd never understood why Bella had stayed with Lonnie or even ever given him the time of day. I'd offered my help if she ever wanted to leave her living situation but she'd never taken me up on it. I watched both Duncan and Riley for any signs of abuse and while I hadn't seen any, I wasn't convinced they were being well loved, either.

Riley had her arms wrapped around her middle and I realized that she had books underneath her sweatshirt to protect them from the rain. "Come in," I said. She hesitated. I opened the door wider. "You're getting wet. Come on."

She stepped inside and I locked the door behind her, then turned off the alarm system and let us into the building.

Riley pulled the books out from under her baggy sweatshirt. I took them from her and set them on the front desk. She pushed her hood back from her face. Riley had the same thick dark hair as her mother but a month after the accident she had shaved her head and kept it that way ever since. "Umm, thanks," she said. "I didn't want the books to get wet."

Riley liked to read almost as much as her little brother did, but she didn't get much time to do it anymore, based on how few books I knew she'd borrowed in the last six months.

"I wish everyone took as good care of their library books as you and Duncan do," I said. I tipped my head in the direction of the children's department. "Go get him more books."

She looked uncertain, hands jammed in the pocket of her faded jeans. "Is that all right?" she asked.

I nodded. "It's all right."

She smiled then and I could see so much of Bella in her. "Thanks," she said. "Duncan gets into a lot less trouble when he has lots of books."

It took Riley less than five minutes to find six books for her brother. "I think we have a book you requested." I moved around the desk to get to the computer. I checked out Duncan's books and the book we'd had on hold for her and handed them and her card over to her. She had sorted a handful of paperclips that had been left on the counter into little piles—a Fibonacci sequence, I realized.

She smiled when she saw her book. It was a book of mathematical puzzles. "I've been waiting for this for two months," she said. "Thanks for letting me come in."

"You're welcome," I said. "We math fiends have to stick together." I shut off the computer and turned off the few lights I'd turned on.

"I like this place when it's dark and no one's here," Riley said. "Sometimes I like to pretend I live here with all the books. Weird, huh?"

I shook my head. "Not weird at all. Sometimes I do the same thing."

It was raining a little harder. "Riley, how did you get down here?" I asked.

She was already stuffing the books up inside her hoodie. "Oh, I rode my bike," she said.

"I'll give you a ride home," I said. "It's too wet for your bike."

She shook her head. "You can't do that," she said.

"It's not any trouble."

Her dark eyes met mine. Her face flushed but her gaze didn't waver. "*He* won't like it."

"So I'll take you close but not all the way. Deal?"

It took a moment but then she agreed. "Deal."

I grabbed her bike, pointed out the truck in the parking lot and we sprinted through the puddles, protected for the most part by my oversized umbrella.

"I didn't picture you as a truck person," Riley said once we were inside with her bike in the bed of the truck and a tarp pulled over it.

"What did you think I drove?" I asked. "Some kind of sensible, old lady librarian car?"

"No," she said. "I don't know. Something safe."

I grinned at her. "This truck will blast through snow up to my waist. It's safe all right."

Riley didn't say much on the drive out to the Hollisters'. "Are you coming to the Halloween party?" I finally asked. "It's not just for the younger ones."

She shook her head. "*He* thinks Halloween is stupid. He won't even let Duncan come."

I suddenly had the urge to find Gerald Hollister and whack him over the head with the atlas we kept in the reference department. "I'm sorry about that," I said.

Just before we got to the old Hollister homestead the rain suddenly let up. I pulled over to the side of the road and got Riley's bike out of the back. "Thanks for the books and the ride," she said.

I nodded. "Anytime. And if you or Duncan need anything—"

"—yeah, I know." She cut me off before I could finish the sentence, swung her right leg over the top of the bike and was gone.

I drove home trying to come up with some way to get around Gerald Hollister so Duncan and Riley could come to the party. By the time I pulled into my driveway I still didn't have any ideas.

I had a slightly soft tomato and a bit of chicken so I used Rebecca's bread to make a sandwich—one slice from each loaf. I discovered I did have a favorite bread but my preference between the two was slight.

There was no sign of Owen or Hercules. I pulled on a sweatshirt and a pair of jeans and headed across the backyard to see if Rebecca was home. I found her in her garden shed sorting her recycling with "help" from Hercules.

"I've made my decision," I said. I'd brought the plastic bag with me that had held my final choice.

Rebecca looked at Hercules and smiled. "I'm so glad," she said. "Like I said, Everett has been no help whatsoever." Her blue eyes sparkled. "So?"

I unrolled the bag as though it were a royal proclamation. "Ta-da!" I said. Rebecca had written a large letter B on a piece of tape she'd stuck to the bag.

She clapped her hands together. "You have very refined taste buds. That is my Italian cheese bread made with Parmigiano Reggiano cheese imported from the city of Parma in Italy."

I handed her the empty bag. "I'm not saying the other bread wasn't good. It's just that this one had something . . ." I wasn't sure how to describe what I had liked about loaf B.

"A little extra special?" Rebecca said.

I nodded. "Yes."

She smiled. "Thank you for being my guinea pig."

"It wasn't a hardship," I said.

Hercules took a couple of steps toward me, then stopped, shook a paw and gave me his "poor me" look.

"I think he got caught in that shower we had a little while ago," she said. "Somehow he managed to push open this door and get inside."

Or more likely he just walked through the door, but I didn't say that. I reached down and picked up the cat. Rebecca's mention of the rain made me think of Riley again.

"Rebecca, you know Gerald Hollister," I said.

She nodded. "He's not a very nice man, Kathleen. Don't have any dealings with him if you can avoid them."

"His grandson, Duncan, is in Reading Buddies."

"Bella's little boy."

"Yes. His sister, Riley, was at the library today and she told me Gerald isn't going to let either of them come to the Halloween party. I want to do something but I don't want to make things harder for those two. Do you have any suggestions?"

"Let me handle it." There was a gleam in her blue eyes that told me she already had a plan.

I made a face. "I don't know. You just said he isn't a very nice man."

"And I stand by that," she said. "But this is not my first rodeo. Will you trust me?"

I gave her a one-armed hug. "Just be careful."

She reached up and patted my cheek. "Don't worry about me. I may look like a sweet old lady on the outside but on the inside, I'm Wonder Woman."

I laughed. "I have always secretly suspected that," I said. I gave her another hug and Hercules and I headed home. The clouds overhead were getting dark again. I hoped that wasn't a bad omen.

13

It started to rain, hammering on the roof as I un-locked the back door.

"Good timing," I said to Hercules. "The key to a happy life."

I got out the slow cooker and started a pot of pea soup. Then I pulled out my laptop. I wanted to know a little more about Richard Benson.

"Want to help me see what I can find out about the Wylers' former lawyer?" I asked Hercules.

He yawned and headed for the living room. That was a no.

Just about everything I learned about Richard Benson in the next half hour came from various news-papers. He, too, had almost no social media presence other than his firm's website. Benson, it seemed, was a very private person, twice divorced with a daughter who was in her second year of law school at Stanford University. He'd been seen with several women since his second marriage ended almost five years ago but who he was currently involved with—if he was involved with anyone at all—was a closely kept secret.

Benson had worked on several high-profile divorce cases and custody battles. He had a reputation for getting what his clients wanted while still keeping the details private. Two different newspapers called the lawyer "Mr. Discretion." The only recent black mark on his winning record was a custody case he'd lost on behalf of a Fortune 500 executive. Rumor had it that the executive had expressed his frustration with the loss by using a baseball bat on Benson's BMW.

I wasn't sure if any of what I'd dug up was going to be helpful. I was still convinced that Richard Benson hadn't been honest with me. I just didn't know how to figure out what he had lied about.

Marcus and his father were playing poker—a last-minute invitation from Burtis. They, along with Brady, who was the designated driver for the night, stopped in on their way out to the game to bring me a basket of Honeycrisp apples from Burtis's trees.

"Please tell your father thank you," I said to Brady. "And tell him that a basket of apples is not going to distract me from the fact that I haven't been invited to the game because he's still smarting over all the times I've bested him at pinball."

"When did your father get a pinball machine?" Elliot said. He looked at me. "And you play pinball? And poker?"

Marcus put a hand on his father's shoulder. "That's a road you do not want to go down."

I smiled at Elliot. "Yes and yes. As a matter of fact, the petty cash for Reading Buddies is getting low. Maybe you should ask Burtis if you and I could play a game or two."

"I'm pretty good at pinball myself," Elliot said.

I raised an eyebrow. "Are you sure you want to play against me?"

Much to my amusement he gave a tilt of an imaginary cowboy hat. "Are you sure you want to play against *me*?"

"This is not good," Marcus said to Brady. He gestured at the door. "I'm just going to go sit in the car."

Brady smiled. "Since the pinball machine actually belongs to me, whichever one of you wins—assuming this hypothetical match actually happens—is buying my lunch."

"I'd be happy to buy your lunch," Elliot said. He was even more competitive than Burtis. I was going to like playing against Elliot.

I gave him a saccharine smile. "That's very generous of you, Elliot. But Brady said whichever one of us *wins*, not loses."

"And we're going," Marcus said, pushing his father toward the door. "Good night, Kathleen."

I caught Elliot's eye, made a gun with my right index finger and thumb and fired it at him. Then I blew the smoke from the imaginary muzzle.

He paused in the doorway long enough to mime catching the bullet in his teeth and then holding it up to the light.

I was definitely going to like playing against Elliot.

I had a movie to watch and two books I'd been look-ing forward to starting, but I felt restless. I couldn't stop thinking about Richard Benson. Marcus had said the lawyer had an alibi, but he hadn't been the one to check it. Denny had said he was working Friday and Saturday nights at the bar. I didn't know him well enough to ask questions, but Maggie did. I called her.

Owen, with his uncanny instinct for knowing when I was talking to Maggie, appeared out of nowhere (lit-erally) and jumped onto my lap. He adored Maggie.

"What are you doing?" I asked her when she an-swered.

"Working on a sketch for a new project," she said. "Which means staring at the paper and sighing a lot."

"Good," I said.

"How can that be good? I haven't accomplished a single thing in the last hour."

"Then you can come and help me with a project that might just help Georgia."

"I like the sound of that," she said. "Are we going undercover? Is Roma coming with us? Are the Three Musketeers going to ride again?"

"I don't know," I said. "I haven't called her yet."

"So what are we doing?" Maggie asked. I pictured her sitting on a stool in her studio, her fingers smudged with pencil.

Owen was squirming on my lap, trying to get to the phone. "Could you please say hello to Owen first? He's going to put my eye out with one of his paws."

"You didn't say Owen was there. Put him on the phone."

I held the phone up to the cat's ear. It wasn't the first time I'd done that but it still felt slightly ridiculous. He listened intently, murped a couple of times and then jumped back to the floor.

I got back on the phone. "Thank you," I said.

"So what are we doing?" Maggie asked again.

"We're going over to the hotel so you can ask the bartender questions that he probably wouldn't answer coming from me."

"Who's the bartender?"

I curled one leg up underneath me and leaned against the back of the chrome chair. "Denny Albrecht."

"From my yoga class?"

"Yes."

"Denny's a good guy," Maggie said. "He'll help you in any way that he can. Did you know he's studying to be a nurse?"

"He told me," I said. "I think he's going to be good at it. He seems like he's good with people." I looked around. Owen had disappeared, literally or figuratively. "So are you in?"

"I'm in."

I did a little fist pump. "I'm going to call Roma and then I'll come get you."

"I'll be down by the door," she said.

I ended our call and made one to Roma. She answered on the second ring. It sounded like she was inside an airplane hangar. "Where are you?" I asked.

"I'm at the rink being an adoring wife," she said.

"You're always an adoring wife. Why are you doing it at the rink?"

"Because Eddie is here practicing slapshots so he doesn't look like an out-of-shape has-been—his words not mine—at that charity game he's playing in. I'm here for . . . I don't know, moral support, I guess. Mostly I'm cold and crabby."

"So come sit in the nice warm bar at the hotel with Maggie and me."

"You're up to something," she said.

"I'm not up to anything. I'm just looking for a little information that might help Georgia. I'm driving and I'll buy you a drink with a little umbrella and you can pretend you're on a beach in the Caribbean."

"I'm in," she said.

I told her I'd be there in fifteen minutes maximum, and we said good-bye. I ran upstairs and replaced my paint-spattered sweatshirt with a black ribbed sweater, put on a little lipstick, grabbed my black-and-red-plaid jacket and went back downstairs. My favorite lace-up boots were in the living room closet.

"I'm going out," I called. "I'll be back in a little while."

I heard a faint meow from the living room and after a moment another from the basement.

It was raining lightly when I got to Eddie's hockey training center. Roma dashed over to the truck and jumped in. She was wearing a yellow slicker and black rubber boots with yellow happy faces all over them. I knew Rebecca had persuaded Roma to buy the whimsical footwear. She had a similar pair.

Roma buckled her seat belt and held her hands, in

fingerless black gloves, in front of the dashboard heating vent. "Is Maggie coming with us?" she asked.

I nodded. "Yes. She knows the guy who's the weekend bartender. He's in one of her yoga classes."

"And you think he might know something that could help Georgia."

I put on my turn signal and we headed for River-arts, where Maggie had her studio.

"I'm hoping he can confirm someone's alibi," I said. I glanced over at Roma.

"Confirm it, or tell you the person doesn't have one?" she asked.

I shrugged. "I'm not sure."

Maggie was at the back door of the old school watching for us. Roma slid over and Mags climbed in next to her, smiled and said, "The Three Musketeers ride again!" She was wearing jeans, brown boots very similar to my black ones and her cherry-red teddy bear coat.

As we drove over to the hotel, I shared what I knew about Richard Benson. "I'm not saying that I think he killed Margery Wyler, but I am certain he was lying to me about something. He claims he was in the bar all evening listening to the jazz trio. He specifically mentioned the saxophone player who joined them. *He* was a last-minute guest and there was nothing on the sign about him sitting in."

"So you're thinking he may have been in the bar for part of the night but not all of it," Roma said.

I nodded. "Exactly."

"So you want me to ask Denny if Mr. Benson was in the bar last Friday night?" Maggie said. "I'm guessing you don't want me to tell him we're checking to see if the man has an alibi for someone's murder."

There were no parking spots in front of the hotel so I turned up a side street. "I'd like to avoid that if we could," I said.

"Well that's easy," Roma said. "Just tell him that your friend is interested in this guy and you want to know if he was there when he said he was."

"That would work," I said. "And it's the truth. I *am* interested in Benson and I do want to know if he was there." I spotted a place to park so I pulled ahead and managed to back in on the first try.

We got out and walked down to the hotel. It was raining harder. I had remembered to bring my umbrella and it just covered the three of us. The bar was quieter than I had expected for a Saturday night, probably because of the rain. I hoped that meant it would be easier to talk to Denny. Luck continued to be on our side. There were two empty places at the end of the bar. There were two men who looked to be in their early thirties sitting next to them, deep in conversation about something, and then another empty seat.

"It would be easier if we were sitting at the bar instead of a table," Maggie whispered to me.

"So ask those guys to move down one space," Roma said. "I'm sure they wouldn't mind." She gave Maggie a nudge with her elbow. "If they say no, we'll go to plan B."

"Do you have a plan B?" I asked Roma.

She leaned her head close to mine. "I don't need one," she said. "First of all, I saw the one with the stubble notice her when we walked in and his friend spotted her about two seconds later. They'll move. They'll go out and start picking up branches in the parking lot to make her a coffee table if she asks them to."

Maggie was tall and pretty and she moved with confidence. Men always noticed her. She didn't always notice that.

Roma was right. The two men happily moved over and we sat down. Denny was at the other end of the bar. He spotted Maggie and she waved. He came right over. "What are you doing here?" he asked.

"It was raining and we heard the trio is pretty good." She gestured toward the other end of the room.

Denny nodded. "They are." He noticed me then. "Hi, Kathleen," he said. His gaze flicked to Roma. He frowned for a moment, then his expression cleared. "Roma, right? The time I came to tai chi you were helping Kathleen with something called Cloudy Hands."

"Cloud Hands," Roma said. She leaned forward. "We don't talk about Kathleen's Cloud Hands," she stage-whispered.

"Not ever," Maggie added solemnly.

Denny smiled. "Duly noted," he said. "What could I get you?"

Maggie ordered a craft beer I'd never heard of. Roma chose Irish coffee. "I'm still cold," she said.

"Just decaf for me," I said to Denny. "I'm driving." I made a circle with one finger taking in Maggie,

Roma and me to let him know I was buying the drinks. "Could I run a tab?"

"Of course," he said. "And since you're the designated driver your coffee is on the house."

I thanked him and he went to get our drinks. Maggie was talking football with the two men sitting next to her. I was afraid she'd be too engrossed in the conversation to question Denny when he got back with our order.

Roma stood up and slipped off her rain jacket. She turned to hang it on a nearby hook on the wall, when one of the men said something. Her dark eyes narrowed and she swung around. "Excuse me," she said, a challenge in her voice. "I know that the Vikings' offensive line has ranked in the bottom ten for the last five years, but you're ignoring the fact that their pass protection is worlds better than it was last season." That was all it took for her to be pulled into the conversation. Roma continued to stand there and make her point—although I wasn't sure what that was.

After a minute, Maggie slid over onto the stool next to me. "I didn't know Roma was so passionate about football," she said.

I looked over at Roma, gesturing with her hands as she talked. "I didn't know Roma knew that much about football," I said.

Denny came back with our drinks then. Richard Benson's photo was on my phone and I slipped it onto her lap. Maggie held out the phone. "Hey, Denny, was this guy here last Friday night?" she asked.

"Why are you asking?" he said.

She leaned in toward him. "My friend is interested in this guy and I want to know if he was here when he said he was."

"You don't trust him."

Maggie shrugged. "Let's say none of us know him well enough to trust him."

Denny looked at the photo again. "He came in sometime before nine. But I wasn't here the whole time." He held out his left hand. There was a small waterproof bandage on the back of his hand at the base of his thumb. "Knife slipped and the night manager took me to the emergency room. It was bleeding pretty bad so they took me right in. I got three stitches but I was gone at least an hour and a half, maybe a bit longer." He looked around. "Hang on a sec," he said. He caught the eye of one of the waitstaff and beckoned her over. "Show her the picture," Denny said to Maggie.

Maggie held out the phone.

"Kelsey, do you remember him?" Denny asked. "Last Friday night?"

She nodded. "Biggest tipper I had all weekend. Why?"

"Was he here all night?"

She looked at Maggie. "Guy trouble?"

"Maybe," Maggie said. "Was he here?"

"He paid his tab around ten thirty and left but he was back again before midnight. He said he changed his mind about doing paperwork. Does that help?"

Maggie nodded. "It does. Thanks."

She smiled and went back to work.

"Thank you," Maggie said to Denny.

"No problem," he said. He held up his left hand. "Makes me glad I'm married."

Denny went to take care of a customer at the other end of the bar. "Is that what you needed?" Maggie asked.

"It might be," I said. "Richard Benson had more than enough time to meet up with Mrs. Wyler, walk down beyond the library and push her over the embankment. The question is: Did he?"

14

We stayed for another hour and listened to the music. Denny was right. The musicians were good. Maggie sent the two guys sitting next to us out to The Brick. They were looking for somewhere a little *less* quiet.

"Since when do you know so much about the Vikings' offensive line?" I asked Roma.

She grinned. "Since I heard Eddie and Brady talking about it yesterday."

Maggie shook her head. "I knew you didn't know very much about pass protection."

"I don't know what pass protection is," Roma said. "And by the way, why do you?"

Maggie shrugged and reached for her beer. "Everyone in Brady's family is nuts about football. You spend time with them and it's hard not to learn things. Burtis can quote stats on I don't know how many teams."

"You're pretty good at subterfuge," I said to Roma.

"I had no idea you didn't know what you were talking about. Are you sure you don't have a secret life that the rest of us don't know about?"

"I do have a secret life," she said. "Unfortunately, I can't tell you all about it because it's secret." She put a finger to her lips and made a loud shushing sound.

"No more Irish coffee for Roma," I said.

I got Denny to bring her a cup of decaf but she was happily tipsy as we walked back to where we were parked. She kept bumping me with her hip, singing, "'Summertime and the livin' is easy,'" softly in my ear.

When we got to the truck, I helped Roma in and fastened her seat belt. "You're my best friend in the world," she whispered loudly to me. "Don't tell Maggie."

Maggie slid in next to her and Roma immediately laid her head on Maggie's shoulder. "You're my best friend in the world," she said. "Don't tell Kathleen."

Roma snored softly all the way out to Wisteria Hill. Eddie was home and up when we got there. She smiled up at him and said, "You are so handsome I could eat your face."

I drove Maggie home. "Thank you for coming with me," I said.

"It was fun," she said. "Especially Roma." Her expression became serious. "Do you think what you found out might help Georgia?"

"Maybe," I said. "I can at least tell Marcus that Mr. Benson doesn't have an alibi. It's a start."

Maggie gave me a hug and we said good night.

The rain had stopped by the time I got home. The sky had cleared and the stars gleaming overhead seemed almost close enough to touch. I should have felt happy. I had proof now that Richard Benson had lied to the police about where he'd been when Margery Wyler was killed. If nothing else it created reasonable doubt. But instead I felt a bit sad and a little guilty. We all wanted to find the killer because we wanted Georgia exonerated, not because we were looking for justice for Mrs. Wyler. And no matter what kind of person she was, Margery Wyler deserved justice.

I was awake early Sunday morning since Hercules decided that if he was up everyone should be up. It had rained again during the night and everything was dripping wet. I went looking for my rubber boots. I knew it would be muddy out at Wisteria Hill Monday morning. It wasn't until after I'd scoured the porch and taken everything off the floor of the living room closet that I remembered my boots were in my office at the library. I'd worn them tromping around outside with Harry making plans for what he was going to plant next spring.

Hercules had kept me company while I was searching. "Want to go to the library with me?" I asked. He gave an enthusiastic meow.

I pulled on my gray hoodie and an old pair of sneakers I usually saved for yard work. Then I grabbed my purse and keys. "Let's go," I said to the cat.

He made it as far as the back stoop and then stopped. "C'mon," I said.

He looked at me and then lifted a paw and shook it. There were a few spots of water pooled on the steps.

Hercules had very strong opinions about wet feet. I bent down and picked him up.

"I'm not giving you my speech about how spoiled you are, but I'm thinking it," I said. He licked the side of my chin.

As we drove down the hill, I told him what I'd learned the night before. When we got to the bottom of Mountain Road he looked right and gave me an expectant look. I turned left.

"You don't even know if Mr. Benson is up yet," I said. "Not everyone gets up with the chickens the way you do. Or he could be up and off taking photographs somewhere."

I took Hercules inside the library with me since I had no way to ensure he'd stay in the truck. I set him down once I'd unlocked the inside doors and shut off the alarm. He followed me up to my office, peering around just about everything. He'd been to the library many times but it wasn't often he was allowed to roam at will.

I found my boots, and after Hercules had checked all around the circulation desk we went back out to the truck. When I got to the corner, instead of heading up Mountain Road again I kept driving down Main Street.

"You're a bad influence," I told him.

When we got to the St. James, I managed to find a place to park in the lot behind the hotel in the last row of spaces. I shut off the truck and turned to Hercules. "Here's the thing. I can't take you in with me. I need you to stay here. Right here in the truck. Please don't go roaming around the parking lot." He looked at me without blinking. After all this time it should have been less disconcerting.

I got out, locked the truck and headed for the front entrance, leaving Hercules in the driver's seat, where I hoped he'd stay. I went to the front desk and asked them to call Mr. Benson's room and tell them Kathleen Paulson was here to see him. There was no answer.

"I'm sorry," the desk clerk said. "Mr. Benson doesn't seem to be answering. Would you like to leave him a message?"

"No thank you," I said. "I'll try him later." For a brief moment, walking through the lobby, I had the wild idea that I could stuff Hercules into one of the cloth grocery bags I kept in the car, go up to Benson's room—I had the number: There were advantages to being able to read upside down—and let Hercules go inside to see what he could find. I knew it was a bad idea. Breaking into Richard Benson's room was wrong, even if technically it would be my cat that was doing it.

I sighed and pulled a hand over the back of my neck. All I was doing was running into obstacles everywhere I turned. There wasn't any way I could help Georgia other than be her friend. There wasn't any way I could get justice for Margery Wyler, either. I was done.

I went back to the truck and opened the driver's-side door. Hercules was gone.

He wasn't on the seat. He wasn't on the floor on either side. He wasn't even in the truck bed. What had I been thinking coming to try to see Richard Benson when I had Hercules with me? I'd told him to stay in the truck when I knew how inquisitive he was.

I took a deep breath and blew it out. Okay, what I needed to do was find him. How far could one little black-and-white cat go in less than ten minutes?

I checked the rose bushes that grew along the fence. The grass was wet and I didn't think he would have ventured in that direction. I looked in the SUV parked to the right of my truck. There was no sign of Hercules in the front seat or the back. He wasn't in the small sports car next to the SUV, or in the silver Audi next to that. I felt a bubble of panic forming in my chest. What if he'd followed me and had gotten into the hotel somehow? What if someone tried to pet him or pick him up?

I'd discovered Hercules and Owen out at Wisteria Hill when they were kittens. They were both feral and even though they had adapted well to living with me they did not like to be touched by anyone but me. A visit to Roma meant bringing out a long Kevlar glove. I warned everyone who met the boys for the first time not to try to pet them. Some people had learned that the hard way.

I looked around the parking lot. Hercules had to be out here somewhere. If he had followed me inside someone would have noticed him and since I had been standing at the reception desk I would have noticed as well.

I worked my way down the rest of the line of cars, peering inside each one and calling Herc's name in a low voice. There was no sign of him. I started on the next row. I was trying to see inside a sleek gray sedan with tinted windows, when out of the corner of my eye I thought I saw movement in the car to my left. It was a vintage BMW, 1972, Fjord blue. The only reason I recognized the car was that my mother had once driven one just like it in a James Bond movie. I couldn't believe the owner had left the vehicle outside in a public parking lot in the rain. I also couldn't believe there was a small cat sitting in the right rear seat.

"Good morning, Ms. Paulson," a voice behind me said. "Are you trying to break into my car?"

I straightened up and turned to face Richard Benson. I smiled and hoped it looked sincere. "I didn't know it was yours," I said. "It's beautiful. 1972?"

"Yes." His eyes narrowed. "You're a vintage BMW fan?"

I glanced at the car again. I couldn't see Hercules anymore. "My mother is an actress. She drove a car just like yours in a movie. Fjord blue was the director's favorite color." I put one hand behind my back and made a "hurry up" motion, hoping Hercules would see it and climb out of the car without Benson seeing him.

I moved toward the hood of the car. "It's not the original finish, is it?"

He nodded. "It is. And the original interior. And because I'm sure you're wondering, no, I didn't leave the car out here all night."

"I'm very glad I got to see it," I said.

"Ms. Paulson, what are you doing here?" he said.

"Looking for you. I checked at the front desk but they said you weren't in your room."

"What do you want?"

What I suddenly *didn't* want was to tell him I knew his alibi had more holes than a leaky rowboat. "How did you know Georgia and Emmy were here in Mayville Heights? After all this time, how did you find them?"

I didn't think he was going to answer. But then he spoke. "I didn't. Someone told the Wylers they were here. A former girlfriend of their son, Scott, I think. Why?"

I shrugged. "I just wondered why they showed up now."

"Because they wanted what they've always wanted, to be part of their granddaughter's life."

"So they've said." I'd stalled as long as I could. I hoped Hercules wasn't in the BMW any longer. "Thank you for answering my question, Mr. Benson. You have a good day." I walked back over to the truck. My knees went weak with relief when I opened the driver's door and found Hercules sitting on the passenger side. Benson was watching me, and I didn't want him to see me have a conversation with a cat, so I started the truck, fastened my seat belt and pulled out of the parking lot. I drove around the corner onto a side street and pulled over. Hercules glanced out the window then looked over at me, seemingly curious about why we had stopped.

"Do you realize how close you came to getting caught in that car?" I said. "And how did you know that was Benson's car? I didn't know."

He blinked his green eyes at me and then spit out a scrap of paper and a tiny bit of fabric with several rhinestones attached to it.

I pulled both hands down over the back of my head. "What did you do?" I said.

He nudged the triangle of paper a bit closer to me and then made a face like he was trying to get the taste of something bad out of his mouth.

Gingerly, I picked up the paper scrap. It was crumpled and damp with cat saliva and it looked as though it had been torn from something. I had seen that pumpkin-colored background somewhere recently. The piece had been torn from a flyer advertising Halloween karaoke at The Brick. I'd seen one on a bulletin board at the grocery store. The bar had started having karaoke night a couple of times a month and Maggie had been trying to get me to give it a try. The fact that I couldn't carry a tune no matter how many buckets you gave me didn't seem to be an issue as far as she was concerned.

What was Richard Benson doing with a flyer from The Brick, or at least part of one? Maybe Hercules hadn't found the scrap in the BMW at all. Maybe he'd found it on the ground.

I picked up the bit of fabric. It seemed to be made of red satin with the rhinestones attached in two rows. They were precisely aligned and it seemed to me this was from something that had been custom made, not mass produced. I couldn't see Richard Benson wearing a rhinestone-encrusted, red satin shirt to court.

Hercules could have picked the piece of fabric up off the pavement as well. That's what made the most sense.

But . . .

This wasn't the first time Hercules or Owen had brought me a bit of paper or something similar. And every time whatever they had found had turned out to be important. Every. Time. So I was going to trust that this time wasn't any different. The paper came from a flyer advertising karaoke night and the square of fabric did look like it could be part of a costume or a persona someone put on to go to karaoke night. All I had to do was figure out how Benson was connected. And if that connection had anything to do with Margery Wyler's death.

How hard could that be?

Marcus showed up about eleven thirty. "How was the poker game?" I asked.

He grinned as he hung up his jacket. "I won forty-one dollars."

I kissed him. "That's because you have such a good poker face."

"It didn't hurt that my dad and Burtis had a little competitive thing going and they both started playing a little recklessly. How was your night?"

"Maggie and Roma and I went down to listen to the trio at the hotel," I said. "They were good." I handed him the napkins and place mats.

"What did you find out about Richard Benson's alibi?" he asked, in the same conversational tone he used when he'd asked about my night.

I felt my face get warm. "How did you know?"

He set one of the place mats on the table and slid it sideways so it was centered in front of the chair. Then he looked at me. "When I told you where Benson had been, you got that look on your face."

"I don't have a look."

He raised an eyebrow.

"Okay, even I heard how defensive that sounded," I said. "Let me try that again." I leaned against the counter. "I don't have a look," I repeated, lowering my voice and tossing my hair at the same time. All that resulted in was a clump of hair going in my mouth while I sounded like I was coming down with a cold.

Marcus laughed. He came around the table and put his hands on my shoulders. "I just meant I could tell you were thinking that maybe the person who checked Benson's alibi had missed something."

"I wouldn't have thought that if you had been the one doing the checking."

He kissed the top of my head. "Thank you for the vote of confidence." I handed him the two soup spoons and knives that were on the counter beside me. He set them on the table. "You know Benson wasn't at the bar the whole evening."

I nodded. "You know where he was."

"I do," he said.

"And it's something you can't share with me."

"No, I can't."

I set the salt and pepper shakers in the middle of the table.

"Can you just trust me and let this go?" he asked.

"I trust you," I said. What I didn't say was that I wasn't sure if I could let this go.

Marcus and I had the pea soup I'd made in the slow cooker for lunch. After that we went to prowl around a couple of flea markets in Red Wing. I was looking for a larger dresser for my spare room. I didn't find the dresser but I did find two sets of skull lights to add to the decorations at the library.

We went to Fern's for macaroni and cheese for supper since Marcus had that forty-one dollars burning a hole in his pocket. I lifted my first forkful in a toast. "To Elliot and Burtis and their competitive streaks," I said.

"Are you going to play pinball with my father?" Marcus asked.

"Yes," I said.

"He's really good."

" 'If there is nothing to lose, no sacrifice, then there is nothing to gain.' "

"Shakespeare?"

"Lieutenant Worf from *Star Trek*," I said.

We went back to Marcus's house to check on Micah. I headed home about nine thirty. Marcus was in court in the morning and I knew he wanted to go over his notes.

"I can go out to feed the cats by myself," I said.

He shook his head. "I'll pick you up at quarter after seven."

"Just like old times," I teased.

He smiled. "Except now I get to kiss you instead of just think about it."

As I drove home, I thought about the piece of paper Hercules had found. I knew from the poster I'd seen that karaoke was starting about now. I could go home or I could drive out to The Brick and see if I could figure out what Hercules had been trying to tell me. When I got to Mountain Road, instead of heading down the hill toward home I turned in the opposite direction. I told myself that when I got to The Brick maybe I'd discover it was as simple as Benson having a client that liked to sing karaoke and he'd been there to lend moral support.

When I got to the bar it turned out to be even simpler than that.

Richard Benson liked to sing karaoke himself, dressed like a lawman from the Old West but with way more rhinestones. He was a karaoke country star according to the woman standing next to me at the bar. "The guy's a distant descendant of Bat Masterson," she said. Benson sang Willie Nelson's "Mammas Don't Let Your Babies Grow Up to Be Cowboys" and Garth Brooks's "Friends in Low Places." And he was good. Very good. After he finished, I made my way over to the little stage. There was no way he could avoid me.

"Buy you a drink?" I asked.

He shrugged. "Why not?"

A couple was just leaving and we managed to grab their table. Several people stopped to tell Benson how good he was, including the waitress who took our order. I ordered ginger ale. Benson a beer. "And a glass, please," he said.

"You have a great voice," I said. "How did all this get started?" I gestured at the stage. The woman singing now sounded nowhere near as good as he had.

"A dare," he said. He took off his cowboy hat and smoothed a hand over his hair. "We were out of town taking depositions on a case—one of the partners and a couple of associates. Things had gone better than expected and we were celebrating. I had a little more to drink than I usually do. We didn't even know the place had karaoke. A man and woman were butchering the Johnny Cash/June Carter song 'Jackson.' I said something about being able to sing better than that and things just went from there."

The waitress came back with our drinks. Benson poured the beer slowly into his glass. I waited until he'd taken a drink.

"How did you get from a dare to this?" I asked.

"That first night, I realized how much fun I had and I couldn't remember the last time I felt that way. At first, I thought it was just the combination of a bit more alcohol than I usually drank and the success of the deposition."

"But it wasn't."

He shook his head. "No, it wasn't. It was the music. It was being on stage. It was seeing how much people like listening to me sing."

"Are you really related to Bat Masterson?"

Benson laughed. "I really am. I'm not sure how he'd

feel about one of his descendants being a karaoke star."

I smiled. "I think he'd like the clothes," I said.

He took another drink. "How did you figure it out?"

"You had a flyer about tonight," I said. "The corner got torn off somehow. I found it."

He tented one hand over the top of his glass. "When you were looking at my car this morning."

I nodded. "Yes. It was a long shot. I had no idea what I was going to find out here. I didn't even know for sure that piece of paper had anything to do with you." I gestured with one hand. "This was just luck."

" 'Luck is what happens when preparation meets opportunity.' "

"Seneca," I said. I knew my Roman philosophers.

"So are you going to tell everyone my secret?"

"No. None of this has anything to do with Margery Wyler's death. I'm guessing you were here, checking the place out the night she died."

"I was. Talk to the bartender."

"I am curious about why you're keeping this part of your life a secret."

Benson leaned forward. "Do you know what they call me, Ms. Paulson?"

"Mr. Discretion," I said.

He nodded. "Exactly. And how do you think my clients would react if Mr. Discretion were outed as a karaoke star?"

I gestured at the people around us. "But people post videos from this kind of event on social media all the time. I don't understand how you've managed to keep this part of your life secret."

"I don't use my real name, so it's not like anything would turn up in an Internet search," he said. "And the people I work with tend to shy away from social media. But if this made the news—that they'd know about." He shrugged and took a drink of his beer. "Maybe deep down inside I want to be found out. I don't know."

We didn't have anything more to talk about. I stood up to leave. Richard Benson put out a hand to stop me. "I will tell you one thing about Margery Wyler. I don't know if it will help you or not. For the last couple of months, she hasn't been herself. She's been scattered and emotional. It's very out of character. I don't know if it means anything."

"Thank you," I said. I hesitated for a moment. "I know it seems that all anyone here in town cares about is proving Georgia didn't kill Margery Wyler. But it's more than that. People do want justice for her. At least I do."

I stopped at the bar and talked to the bartender. Both he and one of the waitresses confirmed that Richard Benson had been there the night Margery Wyler died. He had asked a lot of questions about karaoke night and he was a good tipper. I thanked them and walked out to the truck. Once again, I seemed to be back at square one.

15

I was up before Hercules in the morning. I came out of the bathroom as he came out of the spare room. He yawned and then blinked a couple of times when he saw me.

"Good morning," I said. I'd slept funny and the whole right side of my hair was standing up, moving like my head was waving.

He gave me an indifferent murp. Hercules wasn't at his best before breakfast. Not that I could blame him. I wasn't at my best until I'd had my first cup of coffee.

He followed me down to the kitchen. I had brought a plant stand from Marcus's house. It was made of metal, with four legs and a round top. He wasn't using it and I was hoping it was big enough to hold a peace lily we had at the library. It was certainly big enough to hold one small, gray tabby cat.

"What are you doing?" I said.

Owen blinked his golden eyes at me.

I picked up the cats' dishes. "Get down from there," I said. I wasn't sure how he'd gotten up there in the first place. The top part of the stand, where a plant would sit, had sides close to eight inches high. It was a little like being in a circular cage.

Which Owen just seemed to be figuring out. He looked at me. He looked at the floor. He looked at me again. Then he meowed loudly and, just in case I didn't get the message, cocked his head to one side and looked cute.

"You got up there. You can get down," I said. It was maybe three feet to the kitchen floor. Owen could jump a lot farther than that. And I knew he was capable of getting out of a much tighter spot. I'd seen him do it.

I got their food and water ready. Hercules sniffed his own breakfast and gave Owen's a quick sideways glance. That was all it took. Owen sprang from his perch. He landed on all fours, flicking his tail at me to show his displeasure at having to get down by himself. He went directly to his food, using the side of his head to nudge his dish sideways, away from his brother just a little.

I made coffee and ate half a banana. I decided I'd have time for breakfast when I got back. I had my boots and my jacket on when Marcus pulled up. Roma's spare key was in my pocket.

I climbed into his SUV and leaned over to kiss him before fastening my seat belt. "Are you ready for court?" I asked.

"I think so," he said, backing onto the street. "It's a

pretty straightforward case. I don't think there will be any problems. What's your day look like?"

"I need to put some usage numbers together for an upcoming board meeting, and unless something has changed, Larry is coming to set up the headless horse/man out in front of the building." I had a pair of mittens in my jacket pocket and I pulled them out. My hands were cold.

"What?" Marcus said.

I turned to look at him. "What do you mean, 'what'?"

"You sighed."

"I keep thinking, what if Larry had set up the camera that Friday? We'd know who the practical joker is and we might know who killed Margery Wyler. If only that garbage truck hadn't overturned almost in front of the building. It smelled so foul I didn't want the loading dock door open. It was bad enough just with people coming in and out the main doors. And it wasn't fair to expect Larry to work outside in that stench." I pulled on my mittens and slid my fingers under my legs to get warm. "'For want of a nail,'" I said, quoting the beginning of the old proverb.

Marcus flicked on his turn signal. "In this case it would be for want of a squirrel crosswalk."

"Maybe my new mantra could be: For want of a squirrel crosswalk the garbage was lost."

Marcus laughed. "No offense, Kathleen, but that doesn't have the same ring as Benjamin Franklin's words."

I grinned. "Yeah, it's probably not something that's going to be quoted hundreds of years from now."

He glanced over at me again. "You know, even if the garbage truck hadn't overturned, it doesn't mean things would have ended up any different."

"Are you trying to say what happened was fate?"

"No. But it could have been raining and Larry wouldn't have set up the camera. He could have been on some kind of emergency call and not been able to get to the library. The camera could have been disabled by your practical joker. They've done that before." A smile pulled at the corners of his mouth. "Heck, a squirrel could have climbed up and stolen the camera. There is precedent for that." He was referring to the time two squirrels had stolen my coffee and managed to get away even with Susan and Harry giving chase.

I laughed at the image of those two very enterprising squirrels filching one of Larry's little cameras from above the loading dock door. They were pretty resourceful.

Marcus reached over and patted my leg. "Maybe if the cameras had been there they would have recorded something useful, or maybe not. I don't know. What I do know is that's not on you."

"I love you," I said.

He nodded. "I know. That's the best part."

"The best part of what?"

He slowed down for Roma and Eddie's driveway, smiling at me as we started up the long hill. "The best part of everything," he said.

We parked near the old carriage house and got out of the truck. I stretched my arms up over my head and took a deep breath. There was something about the air out at Wisteria Hill.

Jugs of water and food for the cats were in Roma's porch along with a note that said *Thank you*.

We put out the food and water and then backed away just like we'd done more times than I could remember. Marcus wrapped his arms around me and I leaned against his chest, watching and waiting for the cats to appear.

"I still have a soft spot for the old carriage house," I said, tipping my head in that direction. "Has Eddie said anything about what they're going to do with it?"

"Not a word," he said. "Roma hasn't said anything to you?"

I brushed a stray strand of hair off my face. "No. For sentimental reasons, I'm hoping they don't tear it down."

"Me too," he said, kissing the top of my head.

Lucy came out then, stretching and, to me, looking surprised when she saw it was Marcus and me and not Roma or Eddie. The little cat came across the grass, stopping about four feet away from us.

"Merow," she said.

I crouched down but didn't make any move to get any closer to her. "It's good to see you, too," I said. She studied me for a moment and then looked Marcus over. She seemed happy with what she saw and turned back to the feeding station.

One by one the other cats came out to eat. Smokey was last. It had been several weeks since I'd seen the cats and it seemed to me that the old cat was slowing down. No one knew how old Smokey was. Roma had talked about taking him to live full time at her clinic. He'd spent time down there and seemed happy, but Wisteria Hill was his home, as I'd reminded Roma when the cats had been moved to the new building.

"Was I wrong?" I said to Marcus. "Should Smokey go live at the clinic full time? He might live longer if he were there."

"Someone told me that this is Smokey's home," he said gently. "And this is where he needs to be."

The cats ate and we looked them over—from a distance—for any signs of illness or injury. Once they were finished, we cleaned up, put out more water and returned everything else to the porch.

Marcus dropped me at home and headed to the station. He had his suit in the SUV. Rebecca had left a note on the door to let me know she'd worked things out so Riley and Duncan could come to the Halloween festivities. I did a little happy dance and celebrated with a breakfast sandwich with an egg, a bit of cheddar, some spinach and a slice of bacon.

I drove down to the library thinking one of these mornings I should leave the truck at home and walk down the way I did before Harrison gifted me with the truck. Susan pulled into the parking lot behind me. Once we were inside, I showed her the skull lights I'd found at the flea market.

"What were you thinking of doing with them?" she asked.

"What about wrapping them around the front desk?" I said.

She grinned. "That's what I was thinking." The black cat on the end of the pencil poked into her updo seemed to nod in agreement.

Susan used tiny removable hooks to hang the lights around the front desk. The two strings were just long enough to make it all the way around. She stood back and surveyed her work. "Perfect," she said. "Spooky but not too scary. And speaking of scary, is Harry bringing our horse/man today?"

I nodded. "He and Larry should be here sometime this morning."

I was up in my office just starting to go over our usage numbers when Harry arrived with our horse/man. "Larry's running late, but as soon as he gets here we can unload this thing," he said.

"I can help you," Levi said. He was going to be with us all week, part of his work/study project at school. There were lots of small projects that needed to be done and I was looking forward to crossing some of them off my list. At the top of that list were four large bins of books that we had inherited from a patron who had gone to live with his daughter. Levi was going to sort through them. Some of the books would make it into our collection and some would end up in our book sale in the spring.

Harry and Levi made short work out of getting the horse/man off the trailer and setting him (it?) to the right of the stairs.

"Larry had to stop and get another clamp to hold the light in the neck," Harry said. "He says two aren't enough and he doesn't have one that's the right size."

He shook his head. "Which is hard to believe because I woulda sworn he has about a dozen of every clamp ever made in his shop. That and extension cords."

"Extension cords?" I said. "Larry's always getting on me about using them."

Harry grinned. "Oh, I know," he said. "He said the same thing to me about a dozen times. Then I was over there a week ago Friday looking for an Allen wrench—Larry wasn't there—and he had his dehumidifier plugged into an extension cord. He gave me all kinds of hassle when I did the same thing in my basement."

Harry was still talking but his words weren't registering anymore. All I could hear were three words: *Larry wasn't there.* He'd told me he'd been in his workshop all Friday night. He couldn't have killed Margery Wyler. Not deliberately. Not accidentally. And he would never have kept his mouth shut and let Georgia be arrested. But he had lied to me. Why?

I forced myself to focus on what Harry was saying to me. Was the horse/man too close to the building?

"I uh . . . I don't know."

"Back up a little more," Levi said.

I took several steps backward. "It looks great right where it is," I said. "But doesn't it need to be closer to the outside outlet so the light can be plugged in?"

Harry shook his head. "It's solar. Got a little panel that's going to sit on the grass. With a good charge it'll stay lit until midnight."

I walked back over to Harry and Levi. Harry patted the horse/man's flank. "You know, whoever put this together spent some time thinking about how it would all fit. When I got it out to the house, I realized it comes apart in four pieces. It wouldn't have been as hard as you'd think to move this thing. It's not heavy."

"It sounds to me like you're starting to have a little respect for this person's creativity," I said.

Harry shook his head but he couldn't quite hide a smile. "I think I'm just going to go with 'no comment,'" he said.

I thanked Levi, who went back in to sort more books.

"If you don't need me for anything else, I need to run over to Henderson Holdings to talk to Lita," Harry said. "I won't be long and Larry should be here anytime now."

"Go ahead," I said. "And thank you for all of this, for taking the horse/man home and now bringing it back."

"You're welcome," he said. "I think the kids are going to get a kick out of it."

He left and I went back inside. "Larry should be here soon," I said to Susan. "Will you let me know when he arrives?"

"I will," she said. She gestured toward the main doors. "How does it look?"

I smiled. "Good. Do you want to go take a peek?"

She shook her head. "Nope. I'm waiting until Larry gets the light in the neck. I want the full effect."

I went up to my office and dropped onto my desk chair. I propped my elbows on the desk and leaned my head on my hands. Larry had lied about where he was the night Margery Wyler had died. I couldn't think of one good reason for him to do that.

About fifteen minutes later Susan poked her head into my office. "Larry's here," she said.

"Thanks," I said. I took a deep breath, let it out and followed her downstairs.

Larry was standing on a small stepladder working on the neck of the horse/man. "Hey, Kathleen," he said. "I'm just getting the light set up in the neck. Did my big brother tell you we decided to use a solar panel instead of running an extension cord?"

I nodded. "He did." I cleared my throat. "There's something I need to talk to you about first."

"You think the light in the neck is too much?"

"No. It doesn't have anything to do with any of this." I gestured with one hand.

"Okay," he said, coming down the ladder. "What is it?"

I didn't see any point in beating around the bush. "You lied to me," I said. "You said you were in your workshop the night Margery Wyler died."

"I was." He managed to keep looking me in the eye but color flooded his face.

"All night?" I asked.

He didn't answer and this time he did look away.

I pressed my lips together and swallowed down my frustration. "You don't have any obligation to be straight with me," I said. "But if you're lying to the police it will come back to bite you."

I turned to go back inside but Larry caught my arm.

"Kathleen, wait," he said. I swung back around to face him. "It's not what you think."

"Did you lie to the police?"

He shifted uncomfortably from one foot to the other. "I told them the same thing I told you."

"So yes?"

"Yes."

For a moment I didn't know what to do with my hands. "You're a smart man, Larry. And lying to the police is really stupid."

"What was I supposed to do, Kathleen? Tell them that I was putting together a way that I could take Georgia and Emmy and run?"

I stared at him, dumbfounded. "You were going to leave town? Leave . . . everything?"

His chin came up. "I love Georgia. And Emmy? I couldn't love her more if she were mine." He tapped the left side of his chest with a loose fist. "As far as I'm concerned, she is mine. I would give up my life for her, for her happiness, her safety. So yes, I was going to leave."

"Does Brady know?" I asked.

Larry shook his head. "The only person who knows is you."

"Call Brady," I said. "Part of me loves that you care so much about Georgia and Emmy. And part of me knows that if the police find out what you were doing it could make things worse for Georgia. A prosecutor could argue that she was pushing Margery Wyler while you were putting together an escape plan." The color drained from his face. "Call Brady. I don't know the legal ramifications of coming clean now, but he will."

"I just wanted to keep them safe," he said.

I nodded. "I know."

Larry pulled out his cell phone and I went back inside. His protectiveness made me think about my brother and sister, Ethan and Sara. Because I was a teenager when they were born, I had always been very protective of them. I understood, a least a little, his need to keep Emmy safe. He'd done the right thing for the wrong reason. I hoped it didn't hurt him or Georgia.

16

The rest of the morning went even more downhill. Susan sat in one of the chairs we'd moved from the computer area to the circulation desk and the back fell off. She jumped up and the bottom half of the chair went skidding to one side.

"What the Fraggle Rock?" she exclaimed.

"Are you all right?" I asked.

She nodded. "I'm fine. I can't say the same for this chair."

We moved both parts into a corner of one of the meeting rooms. "I'll get Harry to take a look at it," I said. "Maybe it's an easy fix. In the meantime, we could bring a chair down from the workroom."

Levi and I managed to get the lightest chair we had in the workroom down the steps without dropping it. I pushed it over to the desk. Susan sat down, keeping one hand on the counter in front of her. "So far so good," she said. She leaned back very cautiously. Nothing happened. She sat up and smiled.

"Problem solved," I said. "At least for now. If that's the worst thing that goes wrong today, I'll be happy." I probably shouldn't have said that.

Just as the quilters were arriving for their meeting, one of the shelves in our new fiction section collapsed. The books crashed to the floor, knocking several more volumes off the shelf below. Luckily only one of the books was slightly damaged and it looked as though it would be an easy fix for Abigail. I set it aside to go up in the workroom.

I had just gotten the books and the shelf back to rights when the lights blinked three times. Susan looked at me. "Poltergeists," she said matter-of-factly.

Given the way things had been going, I was almost inclined to agree.

About ten thirty Levi came to find me in the stacks, a sober expression on his face. "I don't know if there's anything to be done to salvage this, but I didn't want to toss it before I asked," he said.

He handed over a copy of Maurice Sendak's *Where the Wild Things Are*. I looked inside. The title page had Sendak's signature and a sketch of a small, hairy creature. I flipped back to the copyright page. "This is a signed first edition," I said. "Do you have any idea how much money this could be worth at auction? Why were you going to toss it?"

"Keep going," Levi said.

I turned to the first page of the story. Someone had colored all over it with a purple crayon. The next page as well. Every page until the end of the book had purple crayon all over it.

I shook my head in frustration. "A signed first edition like this sold for twenty-five thousand dollars back in 2012. Minus the purple crayon, obviously."

"Yeah, I know," Levi said. "I looked it up. There isn't anything Abigail could do, is there?"

"Not with crayon. Once someone colors in a book it's there to stay. We could scrape away any excess and then use paper towels and a warm iron to get rid of some of the crayon, but it's not going to disappear."

He made a face. "My dad underlines things in books and that drives me crazy, but at least he uses pencil and he only does it to his own books."

"I know it's aggravating when a book gets damaged," I said. "But this was probably done by a two- or three-year-old. Most kids that age, if they get their hands on a crayon, they're going to color something. Or everything."

"Okay, that I can understand," Levi said, taking the book back from me. "But there's a ring from a coffee cup on the back cover. A three-year-old didn't do that."

I nodded in sympathy. "People don't always treat books well. You've seen the kind of things they use for bookmarks—mustard packets, used tissues, gum. I think it's just carelessness for the most part. I wouldn't call it deliberate destructiveness."

He rolled his eyes. "My dad uses toilet paper for a bookmark, which probably gives you a good idea about where he does a lot of his reading. What would you call that?"

I patted his shoulder. "A little more information than I needed to have."

* * *

By the time lunch rolled around I needed a break. I decided to eat outside in the gazebo. The sun was shining and there was no sign of any squirrels. It was so peaceful I wondered if maybe I could move my office outside for the afternoon. I was actually trying to decide if I could legitimately find a way to do a little work out there, when Abigail walked around the building.

"Kathleen, what are you doing out here?" she said. She was wearing a deep-green sweater the color of the grass around us.

"I'm hiding from the poltergeists and purple crayons," I said.

She looked at me, perplexed. "Since when do we have ghosts? Especially ones with crayons."

"The poltergeists and the crayons are two separate things," I said. "I think the former snuck in with the Halloween decorations or escaped from one of Mary's Halloween sweaters." I described the morning.

Abigail shook her head. "That is disappointing about the book. But why don't we try to auction it off for whatever we can get? A big Sendak fan might pay something for the signed title page with its little sketch."

I nodded slowly. "You're right. It's worth a try."

Abigail inclined her head in the direction of the building. "Do you have time for a walk before you head in?"

I checked my watch. I did have time. I'd taken less

time to eat than I realized. "Yes," I said. "It would be good to stretch my legs before I go back to the usage numbers."

We started in the general direction of the old warehouses. "You're here early today," I said.

She kicked a small rock and sent it bouncing over the grass. "I was feeling antsy at home." We walked a little farther in silence. The sun was warm on the back of my head. "I'm thinking about getting hypnotized," she suddenly blurted.

"Why?" I asked, even though I thought I knew.

"I want to know what I'm not remembering from the night Mrs. Wyler died." She stopped walking and faced me. "Kathleen, what if I was here?"

"I don't think you were," I said. "Marcus and I didn't see you and neither did anyone else."

"What about the practical joker? She or he was here and nobody saw them."

"Because they were trying *not* to be seen. And we don't know for sure that no one saw them. All we know is no one has *admitted* they saw them."

She looked down at her feet. "I don't like having a blank space in my memory."

I put a hand on her arm. "I wouldn't like it, either, but hypnosis isn't a reliable way to retrieve memories. And you know that even if you hadn't been drinking, memories are fallible. They aren't an exact record of what happened, like a photograph. Memories are our brain's reconstructions of that reality."

"I just keep thinking, what if I saw something and just ran off?"

I shook my head. "You are not that kind of person. I don't care how much you had to drink. It doesn't mean you had a personality transplant. And if you had run off that would have guaranteed someone saw you. You know you're not coordinated and you run like a wild turkey."

That made her smile. "I guess I just don't like the not knowing. I like to be in control."

"As one control . . . aficionado . . . to another, I know how you feel," I said. "But let's say you did get hypnotized and did remember something that helped Georgia. You'd never be able to testify. The first thing a lawyer would do would be to point out the fallibility of memory regained this way. The best way you can help Georgia is to be there for her and Emmy."

She didn't say anything for a moment. Then she nodded. "You're right. I hate that you're right, but you are."

"If it makes you feel better, I wish I wasn't," I said. "I wish you could just go get hypnotized, discover you saw Mrs. Wyler's killer and Georgia would be in the clear, but it doesn't work that way."

"Marcus is still investigating, isn't he?" she asked.

I nodded. "He is, and before you ask if he's found anything, if he has, he isn't sharing it with me." I stuffed my hands in my pockets. "Maybe Elliot will come up with something. He has a lot more experience with this kind of case."

"What about you?"

I knew she meant what had I come up with. I sighed. "So far all I can tell you is who didn't kill Margery Wyler. I still don't have any idea who did."

"Well, no offense to Marcus, his father or Brady, but I have faith in you."

"Well, umm . . . thank you," I said. What I thought but didn't say was it was beginning to look like having faith in me was a bad idea.

We walked a little farther, turning back before we got to the spot where Mrs. Wyler had fallen. The afternoon was busy for a Monday but nothing else broke and Levi found a couple of books that collectors might be interested in. At the end of the day we all trooped out and admired the horse/man with the light streaming up out of his neck. I thought I might come back after supper when it was nice and dark to get a better look, but even now I liked the spooky touch our horse/man gave the building. Larry had done a good job. I really hoped he'd gone to talk to Brady after he left.

I was almost at the truck when Georgia pulled into the parking lot. I waited as she walked over to me. She looked drawn and tired. Her hair needed to be combed and she was wearing jeans and an old T-shirt. She looked like she hadn't slept. "I was afraid I'd missed you," she said. "Could we talk? Do you have time?"

"Of course," I said. "Would you like to go inside? It's a little more private."

She nodded. "If that's okay."

I let us into the building, disabling the alarm. "What do you need?" I asked once we were inside.

"I need to talk to someone who won't judge me, and I know you won't do that," she said. She was picking at the side of her thumb with the nail of her middle finger. "I didn't tell the truth about the night Margery died."

I felt a bubble of panic suddenly pressing in my chest. "What did you lie about? I said.

"I saw Margery the night she died."

I remembered Marcus's witness who claimed they'd seen the two women arguing the night Margery Wyler died. I hadn't given the story much credence.

"She called about quarter to nine that night," Georgia continued. "She wanted me to meet her in about an hour. I decided I had nothing to lose by trying to talk to her, mother to mother." She looked down at the mosaic tile floor for a moment. Then her eyes met mine again. "It was a big mistake. Margery wasn't herself, not the person I remember."

I had one hand in my pocket, clenched so tightly around my keys they were cutting into my palm. "What do you mean?" I asked.

"She was very emotional and angry. Margery is . . . was . . . always cool, always in control, the way she'd been at the library. I thought . . . I thought maybe she'd been drinking even though she rarely had more than half a glass of wine when I knew her. And I noticed she was favoring her right arm and trying to hide that from me. I wondered if maybe she'd had too much to drink and bumped into something or even fallen." Georgia stopped picking at her thumb. She wrapped one arm around her midsection and pulled her free hand into a fist, tapping it repeatedly on her chest. "The strangest thing is she called me Georgia, not Paige, which she's never done before. I couldn't talk to her. She just seemed to want to tell me how much she

hated me and how I was going to get what I deserved."
She drew in a breath. "Finally, I just walked away."

"You did the right thing."

She shook her head. "You're just saying that because we both know I did the wrong thing. I didn't
push her. I swear. Not accidentally and not on purpose, but I could see that . . . that she wasn't herself
and I shouldn't have left her there. It . . . it *is* my fault
that Margery is dead."

She was shaking and I wrapped my arms around
her. "You didn't do the wrong thing," I said. "She
didn't want to work things out. Staying and arguing
wouldn't have accomplished anything. I think . . . I
think she wanted to hurt you."

"She blamed me for Scott's death and I don't think
that would ever have changed. She thought if Scott
hadn't married me he would have been living in their
neighborhood and he wouldn't have been on that road."

"Magical thinking," I said gently. "Not a whole lot
different from believing that if you'd stayed and kept
arguing with Margery, she'd still be alive." Georgia
stared down at her feet. "I know you didn't kill her.
Wishing she was dead didn't make it happen."

Georgia lifted her head. It was impossible to miss
the guilt in her expression. "I was just so tired. I've
never stopped looking over my shoulder. Never
stopped wondering, will this be the day they show
up? And then there they were. My nightmares come
to life. And when she was standing in front of me, just
for a moment, I wished she wasn't. I wished that she
was dead."

"But you didn't kill her. You just wished she were gone. If wishes were horses then beggars would ride."

"I shouldn't have lied about seeing her," Georgia said. A tear slid down her face and she swiped at her cheek with one hand. "I was afraid no one would believe I hadn't killed Margery if I admitted I'd been with her right before she died."

I wished she hadn't felt that way but I could understand why she had. Georgia had had to rely on herself for such a long time, I was guessing it was difficult for her to completely trust the connections she'd made since she'd come to Mayville Heights.

"I couldn't keep lying," she said in a small voice. "Everyone had faith in me even after I was arrested— Larry, Harrison, Abigail, you. I can't eat. I can't sleep. I had to tell someone the truth."

"I still believe in you," I said. "And so will everyone else." I could see that she was stressed and sleep deprived. I also knew how bad it would look when it came out that she had lied. I pulled out my phone. "I'm going to call Elliot if that's okay. I think you need to talk to him before you do anything else."

She nodded, wrapping her arms around herself again.

"I'm with Georgia at the library," I said when he answered his phone. "We need to talk to you."

He didn't ask any questions other than if I wanted him to come to us or us to him.

"We'll come to you," I said. He gave me his room number.

"Elliot's waiting for us," I told Georgia. I fished a Kleenex out of my pocket and handed it to her.

"I was stupid for not telling the truth in the first place," she said.

I gave her a small smile. "Hey, you were under a lot of stress. I could give you a whole explanation of what was likely going on in your brain, but I won't because you'd probably fall asleep."

Georgia managed a smile of her own. "I've been having trouble getting to sleep. Maybe that would help."

I locked the building again and we drove over to the St. James. Elliot was on the top floor in a suite with a beautiful view of the water. He had a sitting room that he had set up as an office, plus a separate bedroom.

"I know I can't be in the room while Georgia talks to you," I said to Elliot, "so I'll wait in the hall."

"Thank you," he said.

I gave Georgia a hug. "I'm not going anywhere." I gestured at Elliot. "You already know he's one of the good guys. Trust him."

Elliot smiled at Georgia. "No matter what you say you can't shock me because I promise I've heard worse."

I stood in the hallway across from the door to Elliot's suite and fished out a pen and a small pad of paper from my messenger bag. I tried to picture my mom's recipe for minestrone soup and started making a list of what I'd need to make it. I was trying to remember whether I had any canned tomatoes when I heard footsteps. I looked up and Hugh Wyler came around the corner. He was wearing a dark-gray suit and I wondered where he'd been that he was dressed that way.

"What are you doing here?" he said when he got sight of me. "I told you I don't want to talk to you."

"I'm not here to talk to you, Mr. Wyler," I said. "I'm waiting for a friend."

He looked at me like I was something his Italian leather shoes had picked up on the sidewalk. "I don't believe you," he said. "I'm going to call hotel security." He pulled his phone out of the pocket of his beautifully tailored suit jacket.

"It would probably be faster to just call the manager, because that's what security will do." I got my own cell phone out. "Do you want to make the call or would you like me to?"

His lips were pulled into a tight, thin line. "You're bluffing, Ms. Paulson," he said.

"What makes you think I came here to talk to you?" I asked. I was genuinely curious. "I know how you feel about Georgia, which means there would be no point in trying to have a conversation with you."

"She's the reason my wife is dead. They talked on the phone the night she died. That's the kind of person Margery was. She was reaching out to Paige, trying to find a reasonable solution to this circumstance we'd found ourselves in. Of course, she didn't get anywhere."

"She must have been upset," I said.

"Of course she was upset. Because of Paige we've missed years of Scott's child's life."

Scott's child. Hugh Wyler hadn't called Emmy by her name, not even by the name Georgia and Scott had first given their child.

"Margery was restless after that phone call. She paced around our suite. Finally, she decided to go for a walk," he said. "She said she wanted to think."

I nodded but didn't speak.

"I followed her downstairs. Then I turned around. I thought Margery just needed a little time to herself. I will always regret not going after her. She'd be alive if I had."

He put his phone away. "If you're here when I come back, I will call hotel security." He turned and walked in the direction of the elevator. The vehemence of his words didn't surprise me. He was angry and looking for revenge. Would I be any different if I'd lost someone I loved?

Elliot stepped out into the hallway then. "Thanks for waiting," he said. "Come in, please."

Georgia was curled in a wing chair holding a cup of tea. She seemed calmer. Less panicked.

"We have a plan," Elliot said. "Larry is coming to get Georgia and she's going to spend the night at his place."

"He's going to take Emmy to spend the night with Abigail," Georgia said.

"That'll be fun for both of them," I said.

Elliot turned to me. "I hope you don't mind. I said you would see that Abigail's shift is covered at the library tomorrow."

I nodded. "I'll take care of it."

Larry arrived just a couple of minutes later. Georgia hugged me. "I'm really glad we're friends," she whispered.

"Me too," I said.

"We'll talk in the morning," Elliot said.

Larry shook Elliot's hand and thanked him. He looked at me and mouthed "Thank you" over Georgia's head.

Elliot touched my arm. "Kathleen, could you stay for a minute?" he asked.

"Of course," I said.

Larry and Georgia left and after Elliot closed the door to the suite behind them, he turned to me. "Would you like a cup of tea or coffee?" he asked.

I shook my head. "No. Thank you."

"I'm not going to ask what you and Georgia talked about," Elliot said.

"It was a private conversation. I won't be talking about it with anyone unless I'm asked directly, in which case I won't lie."

Elliot's expression didn't change. I seemed to have given the right answer. "Thank you for calling me when Georgia came to you."

"It's all getting to her," I said. "She feels guilty about Mrs. Wyler's death and terrified that she'll somehow lose Emmy because of it. I knew that you would know how to protect her."

"I will do my best."

"Do you have any suspects?" I asked. "Anything that can raise even a little reasonable doubt?"

Elliot brushed a bit of lint from the front of his shirt. "That's probably not a subject we should talk about."

I nodded. "Fair enough. If you have Richard Benson on your suspect list, he has an alibi—one I know is valid."

"Thank you," he said.

I hesitated for a moment. Then I explained about Abigail's drinking and memory loss the night of the murder and her worry that she might have seen something she'd forgotten. "I know you must be looking at the footage from every security camera in the area," I said. "If you see Abigail, could you let me know, please?"

"I can't share anything that might compromise the case."

"I understand that," I said.

For a moment the silence hung between us. "We will prove Georgia's innocence," Elliot finally said.

"I hope so."

He raised an eyebrow but didn't say anything.

I pulled a hand back over my hair. It had been a long day and I was hungry and tired. "It's not that I don't think you're a good lawyer. I know you are. I know if anyone can get Georgia out of this mess, it's you."

"But."

"I think . . . we're missing something, or maybe I'm missing something and you have it all figured out, and I hope it's the latter."

"What do you mean?" he said.

I shrugged. "I don't really know. It's just from what I've been able to find out no one hated Margery Wyler enough to kill her. I'm not sure anyone other than her husband ever got very close to her. It makes no sense that she was killed to somehow hurt Hugh Wyler. He doesn't scare easily. Threaten him and he digs in."

Elliot nodded.

"Georgia didn't push Margery, and neither did Larry, who would be the next best suspect, or maybe Abigail." Frustration was creeping into my voice and I gestured with both hands. "Any other time I've been involved in something like this there have been suspects—someone, usually more than one person, who had a reason to want the victim dead. There isn't this time. The most likely person is Georgia, and I know one hundred percent it isn't her."

"I don't disagree, but for the sake of argument, explain to me why you're so certain," Elliot said.

"One word: Emmy. Emmy is the most important person in the world to Georgia. She wouldn't have pushed Margery, even in the heat of the moment, because she is never not thinking about her child. She wouldn't have done anything that even had the tiniest possibility of causing her to lose Emmy. If Margery had fallen by accident Georgia would have gotten help."

"The fact that the Wylers had found Georgia meant there was a chance that she *could* lose Emmy. Killing Margery was one way to stop that from happening."

I was shaking my head before Elliot finished speaking. "No. I don't think Georgia looked at it that way. She's what Burtis would call long-headed."

"She thinks things through."

"A lot more than a lot of people. Unless Georgia also had a plan to kill Hugh Wyler, there was no point in killing Margery. All her death did was give Hugh more ammunition to use against Georgia."

I couldn't read what Elliot was thinking just from his face. He seemed to be waiting for me to finish my thought. "I have no facts or logic to offer you," I said. "I just know I'm right. It probably sounds silly to you because you're a just-the-facts kind of person."

Elliot smiled. "Kathleen, I once followed your cat through the woods in the rain because I had a feeling. I know there's more than just facts and logic. I know how important instinct and intuition can be."

I didn't even try to hide my surprise. The time he'd followed Hercules was the time he helped rescue Marcus's former partner and me. We had been thrown in an abandoned well close to Roma and Eddie's property. That day he had been following a small black-and-white cat that seemed to know where he was going even though there was no logic and no facts to support that.

"I have a question for you," Elliot said. "Who benefits?"

I smiled. "That's what Marcus says."

"Maybe that's where the answers lie. Now that Margery Wyler is dead, who benefits?"

17

Elliot promised me he would check on Georgia in the morning. I told him if I learned anything I would let him know, and we said good night. I got in the truck and decided to drive back over to the library to see our headless horse/man in the dark. I needed something to make me forget, for a few minutes at least, about real bogeymen.

The centaur looked even better in the dark with light streaming out of its neck. I crossed my fingers that Saturday's Halloween party would be a success.

Mary came in the next morning to work for Abigail and brought a batch of her ginger cookies. I poured a cup of coffee and took a cookie from the pumpkin cookie tin. It was gone in three bites. "Did I mention you are my favorite staff member?" I said to Mary. She was wearing a black sweater with a skeleton on the back and dangling eyeball earrings. She looked like someone's sweet, cookie-baking grandmother.

Which she was. She did not look like the state kickboxing champion for her age group. Which she also was.

"Save your flattery for someone who hasn't been around the block as many times as I have," she said.

I reached for another cookie and she swatted my hand. "Other people work here, too."

"That can is full of cookies," I protested.

"You'll be full of cookies if you keep inhaling them the way you did the first one."

"It's not my fault you're such a good cook."

"Still not working," Mary said.

She turned to get the milk from the refrigerator and I took the opportunity to grab another cookie. All that kickboxing meant she had fast reflexes. She turned and caught me with the cookie halfway to my mouth. And out of nowhere I sneezed. All over the cookie.

She shook her head. "Go ahead and eat it. No one else is going to want that cookie now."

"I didn't do that on purpose," I said. "I swear." I took a bite. It was just as good as the first cookie had been. "And you really do make the best cookies."

"Go unlock the front doors before people start banging on them," she said. "It's time to open." She was trying not to smile and not quite succeeding.

I emptied the book drop and Mary started checking the contents back in. Levi had managed to go through all the bins of books on Monday so I set him to work looking for cookbooks for a Thanksgiving display I was planning for November. I went to turn on the computers, very grateful that in less than a month I should be able to stop both literally and figuratively holding my breath while I did it.

Marcus and I were supposed to have lunch together but he called at eleven thirty to cancel. "I'm sorry about this," he said. "This trial is taking longer than anyone expected. I have to testify again today." He promised he'd call me later and we said good-bye. At lunchtime I walked over to Eric's and got a turkey club sandwich. I also managed to snag another couple of Mary's cookies from the staff room.

Elliot called just before I left for the day. "Could I stop by after supper?" he asked. "I have something to show you." On and off, all day, I tried to think of someone who would have benefitted from Margery Wyler's death. From what I could infer from my research, the Wylers' wealth was tied up in trusts and holding companies and no organization benefited from her death. There was no whiff of any extramarital affairs, so it seemed unlikely a scorned or jealous lover had killed her. I needed to learn more about the Wylers' inner circle but I had no idea how. Maybe Elliot had found something that would help.

"I'm going to tai chi," I said. "Would after that work for you?"

"It would," he said. "I'm going to Fern's for Meatloaf Tuesday with Burtis."

I got to tai chi a little early and Maggie and I talked about the card-making workshop the artists' co-op was offering at the library in November. It was already full and I was wondering if we should offer a second session.

Roma dashed in at the last minute. Her hair was pulled back in a stubby ponytail and she had cat hair on her shoulder. I leaned over and brushed it away.

"How did the surgery go?" I asked as soon as we finished the form at the end of class.

Her dark eyes lit up. "It went really well. The surgeon got all the tumor. It had clean margins and Oscar's prognosis is good."

"I'm so glad to hear that," I said.

"A lot of people pulled together to make the surgery happen. Oscar is a retired service dog and his owner didn't have the money to pay for the treatment he needed. He was having trouble with his balance. He wasn't his usual easygoing self and he had lost his sense of smell, which meant he wasn't eating. It took a while to figure out what was wrong with him. Without the fund-raiser and so many people donating their time, he would have had to be put down."

Roma got a little choked up. She swallowed a couple of times. I hugged her. "I'm so glad to know you," I said.

Elliot arrived about twenty minutes after I'd gotten home.

"How was Meatloaf Tuesday?" I asked.

"Delicious," he said. "And Burtis said to tell you not to buy potatoes. He said that would make sense to you."

I smiled. "It does."

Elliot hadn't learned any more about Margery Wyler, but he had come up with security camera footage of Abigail walking home a couple of hours before Mrs. Wyler's death.

I watched the video and then handed his cell back to him. "Thank you," I said. "Abigail will be relieved."

He put the phone back in his pocket. "I have someone digging into the Wylers' inner circle. The only thing I've learned is they had continued their relationship with Scott's former girlfriend, Amber Hart, but so far there's nothing that suggests she would have had a reason to want Mrs. Wyler dead."

"So we keep digging," I said.

Elliot nodded. "To extend your metaphor, at some point I'm hoping we'll unearth some evidence to help point us toward the real killer."

"Is there anywhere you have to be?" I asked. "Do you have time for a cup of coffee? I have ginger cookies. Mary's cookies."

Elliot smiled. "Good company and Mary Lowe's cookies? How could I refuse?"

We sat at the table with Hercules at Elliot's feet. The cat seemed to think that the two of them were close friends, and given the way Elliot was talking to the cat it looked like he felt the same way. I told him more about Herc swiping the dog toys from Fifi next door.

"Do you need representation?" Elliot asked, looking down at the cat.

Hercules gave an emphatic meow.

"From now on don't talk to anyone without me present." Elliot looked at me with a smile playing on his face. "Kathleen, your case against my client is completely circumstantial. You have no proof that Hercules stole the toy or the bone."

The little tuxedo cat narrowed his green eyes at me as though he understood every word Elliot was saying. Which he probably did.

"The culprit could have been Owen," Elliot continued. "Someone could be trying to set Hercules up. A grackle, for instance."

"Merow!" Hercules said. His war with the grackle over who ruled the backyard had been going on for a long time.

"Until you can prove these accusations, I insist that you cease maligning my client's character."

"Duly noted," I said, struggling not to laugh.

"New client, Dad?" Marcus said from the doorway.

Elliot smiled. "Everyone is entitled to legal representation."

"So that's why you're here? To represent a cat?" Marcus glanced down at Hercules. "No offense."

"Mrrr," Hercules replied, his way, it seemed to me, of saying, "None taken."

"Actually, I've been telling Kathleen embarrassing stories about you," Elliot said.

Marcus groaned. "I really want to believe you're kidding but I'm afraid you're not." He came around the table and kissed the top of my head. "Don't believe anything he tells you," he said in a stage whisper. "I was a perfect child."

Elliot laughed. "Kathleen, thank you for the coffee and conversation. And please tell Mary her cookies were delicious. I do need to get going."

"Dad, you don't have to leave on my account," Marcus said.

"I have to go over a couple of things with Brady."

I gave Elliot a hug. "Thank you for the video. I'll call Abigail."

"I'll be in touch." He leaned around me. "Remember, don't talk to anyone if I'm not here," he said to Hercules.

The cat murped his agreement.

Elliot put on his jacket and turned to give Marcus a hug.

"We're still on for lunch tomorrow?" Marcus asked.

Elliot nodded. "Absolutely." He looked at me. "Could you join us?"

"I owe you for missing lunch today," Marcus added.

"I'd love to," I said, "but I have a meeting with Ruby to finalize the details of the party." I smiled at Elliot. "Could you come for dinner on the weekend? How about Sunday because the party is Saturday afternoon?"

"Please come, Dad," Marcus said.

Elliot smiled. "I would like that. Yes."

We said good night and Elliot left. Marcus put his arms around me and kissed me again. "What was my father doing here? Other than apparently telling embarrassing stories to you."

"He found surveillance footage that puts Abigail in the clear, not that anyone could think she pushed Mrs. Wyler. And it seems your father is Hercules's lawyer."

Marcus looked at the cat. "Why do you need a lawyer?"

Hercules pointedly looked away at the question.

I laughed. "Elliot did tell Hercules not to talk about what's been going on without him present. He seems to be taking that to heart." I picked up my phone. "I'm going to give Abigail a quick call."

"Sure. Go ahead," Marcus said.

I called but got Abigail's voice mail. I left a brief message saying she was in the clear.

While I was on the phone Marcus had started nosing around, looking for something to eat, it seemed. "There's pea soup left," I said. "Did you have any supper?"

He shrugged. "Kind of."

"Kind of yes or kind of no?"

"The second one."

I started for the refrigerator.

"You're not my maid," he said. He grabbed the last cookie, moved past me and got the soup out of the fridge.

I sat at the table while he ate and we talked about our days in general terms. "Are you working with my father?" Marcus suddenly asked.

I shook my head. "No, but we are on the same side." I wasn't sure if he knew yet that Georgia had lied about seeing Mrs. Wyler the night of the murder. I couldn't ask and I didn't like keeping the secret. It felt like the definition of between a rock and a hard place.

"So does that make me your opponent?"

I propped one foot on the seat of my chair and wrapped my arms around my knee. "No. We all want the same thing: the truth." I sighed. "This case is giving me a brain itch."

Marcus crumbled two crackers into his soup and added a chunk of cheese as well. "What's a brain itch?"

"You know that feeling you get that you're missing something but you don't know what?"

He nodded.

"That's a brain itch. I have that feeling I'm missing something obvious about Margery Wyler's death but I can't put my finger on what it is." I picked a bit of cat hair off of my leg. "I keep hoping the light will suddenly come on and I'll throw up my hands and say, 'Well, of course,' but so far it hasn't happened." I tapped the side of my head. "So far it's still dark in here."

I was just getting out of my truck in the library parking lot the next morning, when Abigail arrived. I walked over to her.

"I got your message," she said. "Thank you." Her smile was warmer and she seemed much less stressed. "And thank you for making sure my shift was covered. I had a lot of fun with Emmy, and Georgia seemed better after twenty-four hours with just Larry."

"I'm glad things are better." We walked toward the building.

"I remembered something," she said. "I think your message triggered a memory."

I pulled out my keys. Given that Abigail had been drinking, her memory was a little suspect.

"I remember that I sat on the gazebo steps after arguing with Mrs. Wyler."

I stopped, one hand on the wrought-iron railing.

"So you were here at the library when you argued with her."

A frown creased her forehead. "I think I must have been. I don't remember being anywhere else. Does it help?"

"I don't know. Maybe."

I let us inside and we went through the usual pre-opening routine: making the coffee, turning on the lights, double-checking what was scheduled for the day, but it wasn't until I was in my office looking at the wish list for Reading Buddies books that I had time to think about what Abigail had told me.

I decided to put aside what I knew about the fallibility of memory and start with the assumption that she remembered sitting on the gazebo steps because that's what she'd done. Marcus and I had found Mrs. Wyler's body sometime around eleven thirty. She had called Georgia at approximately eight forty-five. That left two hours and forty-five minutes I needed to account for.

According to the time stamp on the video Elliot had come up with, Abigail was close to home at nine forty-one. Working backward, and allowing for a few minutes for her to sit on the gazebo steps, it meant that Abigail's confrontation with Mrs. Wyler likely occurred between nine and nine fifteen, soon after the phone conversation between Georgia and her former mother-in-law.

I looked at the timeline I'd drawn on the pad of paper in front of me. Georgia said Margery had asked to meet her at the library at quarter to ten. They had argued and Georgia had walked away. I set my pen down, stood up and moved over to the window.

I looked out at the water. My best guess was that Mrs. Wyler had been dead an hour or less when Marcus and I found her body. She was still warm and I knew that body temperature remained stable for the first thirty minutes to an hour after death. That meant she had been pushed somewhere between ten thirty and eleven. That didn't leave a lot of time for her to have connected with her killer.

I rubbed the back of my neck with one hand. Had she arranged to meet her killer here, or was it just a chance encounter?

And then the light came on. I turned back around and picked up my timeline. Maybe someone *had* seen Mrs. Wyler with her killer. Abigail was sitting on the gazebo steps at about quarter after nine, according to my calculations. And there was no sign of our headless horse/man. By the time Marcus and I showed up, two plus hours later, it was here. That two-hour window was when the practical joker had to have been here setting up in the gazebo. That meant there was a chance he or she had *seen the killer.*

It was more important than ever to figure out who the practical joker was. For the first time I felt as though I was getting somewhere. I just hoped I ended up in the right place.

Ruby showed up for our lunchtime meeting with tiny, juicy tomatoes from the plants in her greenhouse window.

"These tomatoes are delicious," I said after my third one.

"The credit goes to Harry," Ruby said. "He built the plant shelves for my window and he gave me the seeds. I haven't had any kind of a garden in years." She speared one of the tomatoes with her fork. "I guess the kids and their gardening kind of inspired me." She grinned then. "You might say the library has inspired my Halloween costume."

"You're not going to tell me what it is, are you?" I said.

She shook her head. "Not a chance, but I promise you're going to love it."

We made quick work of finalizing the plans for Saturday's party.

"Thanks for letting me get involved with Reading Buddies," Ruby said, winding a long multicolored scarf that I recognized as being one of Ella's around her neck.

"I'm the one who should be thanking you," I said. "The kids love you and the program is better because you're part of it."

Ruby flipped one end of her scarf over her shoulder and smiled. "I think we should just agree we are both fabulous."

When I turned on my computer back in my office, I discovered that Roma had e-mailed me a photo of Oscar the dog. He had a bandage on his head and a plastic cone to protect it. *He's moving and eating,* she wrote.

I love a happy ending, I replied.

* * *

As I got out of the truck at the end of the day, Mike Justason walked over. "Hey, Kathleen," he said. "I um . . . I kind of owe you and Hercules an apology."

I smiled. "Okay. What for?"

He pulled out his phone. "Your cat hasn't been stealing Fifi's toys. The dog has been bringing stuff to him."

"I thought Fifi was afraid of cats," I said.

"He is," Mike said. He held out his phone. "Take a look at this. It's from my security camera. I think Fifi might be trying to make friends."

In the black-and-white video Hercules was sitting close to the edge of our driveway. Fifi had some kind of rubber toy in his mouth. It looked like a carrot. He crept closer to the cat, looking like he was ready to bolt at any moment. Maybe eight or nine feet away from Hercules the dog stopped, dropped the toy on the driveway and beat a rapid retreat. Hercules yawned, took a couple of passes at his face with one paw and then walked over to Fifi's gift. He poked it with the same paw he'd used to wash his face. Then he sniffed it carefully. Finally, he picked up the toy and carried it out of the frame, probably to the back step.

I looked up at Mike.

"I know," he said. "I wouldn't have believed it if I hadn't have seen this. Like I said, I'm sorry."

"You don't have to apologize. You were very nice when I said my cat was stealing your dog's things."

He reached into the pocket of his jacket and pulled

out a small blue rubber bone and a can of sardines. "From Fifi," he said. "I know cats like sardines and I thought . . . maybe Hercules might like to bat the bone around your kitchen. Fifi has one and the boys kind of play floor hockey with him."

"You didn't have to do that," I said.

"Take them, please," he said. "And would you be willing to see if Fifi can get a little closer to Hercules? It seems like he wants to."

I nodded. "I'd be happy to try it. I can't make any promises about Hercules."

Mike laughed. "It's worth a shot. Thanks, Kathleen."

Owen was waiting for me in the kitchen. "Where's your brother?" I asked as I hung up my jacket. He glanced at the back door.

"Let me guess," I said. "He's over at Rebecca's."

His answering murp might have been a *yes* or might have been *I don't know*.

I tried to surreptitiously put the sardines on the counter but Owen had laser sharp vision for that sort of thing. He meowed loudly.

"They belong to your brother," I said. "It's a long story." I went out onto the back step and looked around. I didn't see a sign of Hercules or Rebecca. I knew there was no point in calling Hercules. Unless he felt like coming home, he'd just ignore me.

I was cooking a chicken burger and talking to Owen about my Halloween costume when Hercules walked through the kitchen door. Literally, of course. I took the pan off the heat and crouched down in front of the cat. "I know you didn't steal those things from Fifi," I said. "I'm sorry I accused you."

He turned his head and looked at the refrigerator. He seemed to be taking Elliot's admonishment to heart. On the other hand, that wasn't really any weirder than me trying to get a cat to accept my apology.

I opened the can of sardines and gave him one. "These are from Fifi. He wants to be friends. That's why he brought you those . . . gifts." Hercules pushed the dish sideways with a paw so he could eat it without looking at me. I set the rubber toy down beside him. He continued to look away. I wasn't so sure this was him following Elliot's instructions. It felt more like him making me grovel a little.

He finished the sardine, licked his whiskers and then walked off holding the toy bone in his mouth. He was either making me grovel or he was just being a cat—which was pretty much the same thing.

I put my chicken burger back on to cook. Owen had finished his supper and since Hercules hadn't counted how many sardines were in the can—at least as far as I knew—I gave one to Owen.

I ate my chicken burger on a potato roll with salsa, lettuce and cheese. I picked up my phone and looked at the photo of Oscar the dog again. It made me happy to think the dog was getting a happy ending. It was nice to see something go right. I scrolled through the photos I'd taken of the horse/man. It did look good in the dark with the light coming out of its neck.

I looked at the photos of the various stunts the prankster had pulled. Owen leaped onto my lap. He had sardine breath. He kept pushing his face in to see the screen and then pawing at the bottom of the photos.

I held the phone up in the air, out of his reach. "Knock it off."

He glared at me.

"Fine," I said. "What do you want me to see?"

He looked over at my messenger bag hanging on the back of the chair next to us.

"You want to see these on the computer?"

"Mrrr," he said.

I wasn't sure if that was a yes or not. I wasn't sure if Owen was really interested in the photos. On the other hand, it couldn't hurt to look at a larger version of the pictures. It was more important than ever to me to figure out who the practical joker was. I set my phone on the table and reached for my bag.

Owen waited more or less patiently until I pulled up the first photograph. He put a paw on the screen near the bottom of the image and then the next one and the next one. I had to go back and forth between the photos before I realized what Owen seemed to want me to see.

There were flat river rocks in most of the pictures— one rock in the photos of the second and third pranks, none in the first one, and two rocks in the fourth. When I checked the photos of the fifth stunt, I counted three of the stones and there were five in the sixth.

"The rocks are a Fibonacci sequence," I said slowly. How had I missed that? I looked at Owen. "And since when did you know about Fibonacci sequences?"

He just blinked his golden eyes at me.

I stroked his fur. "I can't believe I didn't see that sooner."

"Mrrr," Owen said. It seemed he was surprised, too.

Fibonacci numbers formed a sequence. Each number was the sum of the two previous ones starting with zero and one, so zero, one, one, two, three, five, eight, thirteen and so on. Any math lover would know that.

Our practical joker was a math geek. Suddenly it was obvious.

I looked down at Owen. "It's Riley Hollister," I said.

18

I needed to talk to Riley. I couldn't just drive out to the Hollisters'. I didn't want to get her in trouble with Lonnie or her grandfather. Then I remembered that Rebecca had fixed things so both Riley and Duncan could be part of the Halloween celebrations. Levi and Harry's daughter, Mariah, were coming after supper on Thursday to help decorate the two meeting rooms for Saturday's party, along with Ruby and Rebecca. Ruby and I were taking the night off from tai chi. My part was pretty much restricted to ordering pizza and doing whatever task Ruby set for me. I wondered if when Rebecca said she'd convinced Lonnie and Gerald to let Riley be part of the festivities she meant the setup as well. It was easy enough to find out. I picked up my phone.

"Yes, Riley is joining us tomorrow night," Rebecca said. "I'm picking her up because I don't trust the old coot to keep his word. He's as slippery as a walleye."

"Good," I said. "I wanted to make sure I ordered enough pizza."

"How do you feel about things that glow in the dark?" Rebecca asked.

"As long as it's not due to radioactivity I don't have a problem," I said.

"Splendid!" I could picture her smiling on the other end of the phone. "I'll see you tomorrow night."

Rebecca arrived at the library at about five thirty Thursday night. Ruby and Riley were right behind her carrying a large, flat box.

"What is that?" I said. I had a feeling the contents had something to do with Rebecca's question about things that glow in the dark.

Rebecca patted my arm. "It will be so much more fun if it's a surprise."

Mariah arrived shortly after that. Levi finished his shift and joined us just as the pizza arrived. While we ate Ruby explained what was happening in the large meeting room. She had black curtains for the window to filter the light and "cobwebs" to drape over them. There were paper spiders and bats to attach to the ceiling, lots of twinkle lights and even a trio of ghosts made from fabric and three small mannequins I knew Ruby had scavenged from the landfill. Ruby put Riley and Levi to work hanging the spiders and bats. She sent Mariah into our smaller meeting room to help Rebecca with whatever had been in that box. My job was to hang the curtains and artfully arrange the cobwebs. Watching Riley work out a simple grid pattern for the placements of the bats and spiders told me I was right that she was the practical joker.

About twenty minutes after we'd started Ruby went next door. She came back almost immediately and sent Riley to work with Rebecca and Mariah. Then she came over to inspect my cobweb draping.

"Very nice," she said. She grabbed a box off the table behind us and handed it to me. It was full of very tiny three-dimensional paper spiders. I held one up. "Ruby, these are incredible," I said. "Did you make them?"

She shook her head. "Nic did."

I set the spider in the palm of my hand. "I'm trying to picture Nic's big hands making something so small and detailed."

Ruby smiled. "Yeah, I know. I thought the same thing."

"Why did Rebecca need Riley?" I asked.

Ruby continued to smile. "It's a surprise," she said. She mimed zippering her lips and walked away.

It was a few minutes after closing time before we were finished. Ruby had made a point of keeping me where she could see me, so I had no idea what Rebecca, Mariah and Riley were working on. Finally, Riley appeared in the doorway and gave Ruby a thumbs-up. Ruby nodded at Levi and grinned. So everyone knew what the "surprise" was but me. I was starting to think that I wasn't going to like whatever the surprise turned out to be.

We walked out into the main part of the library. Mary and Susan had been working and they came to join us. Someone had turned most of the lights out.

There was a large spider hanging at the top of the stairs. I hadn't known what to expect, but it wasn't this. Not a large, hairy and, yes, glow-in-the-dark spider that had to be at least four feet wide.

"Clap three times," Rebecca said.

"Okay," I said slowly. "But you should know that if something jumps out at me, I will scream."

Ruby poked me with her elbow. "Just clap, Kathleen."

I held out my hands and clapped loudly three times. The spider started to dance.

Ruby and Mary were grinning. Levi, Mariah and Riley were trying not to and totally failing. "What do you think?" Rebecca asked, a mischievous twinkle in her eyes.

"It's great!" I said, walking over to the foot of the stairs. The spider had blue eyes, long false lashes and a sweet smile. It wasn't scary at all.

Riley joined me. She was holding a small device about half the size of a cell phone. "You can disable the clapping feature anytime you want to."

I took the controller from her. "Thank you," I said.

"And you don't have to worry about it falling down," Mariah said. "We attached it to those bolts Dad put up there for the quilt show."

Ruby yawned and stretched. "Is there any pizza left?" she asked.

I shook my head. "We ate it all."

"I brought chocolate chip cookies," Rebecca said.

"Want me to show you how that works?" Riley asked, pointing at the controller.

"Please," I said. "But go get a cookie first." The spider

seemed to be doing something akin to the twist now. I put a hand on Rebecca's shoulder. "I need a few minutes with Riley," I said quietly.

She looked a little curious but all she did was nod and say, "All right."

Riley followed the others but she was right back with a cookie for her and one for me. She'd even set mine on an orange napkin. I saw a lot of Bella in her. We sat down on the steps and Riley went through the various features of the remote control.

"Thank you for coming to help tonight," I said.

"You got Mrs. Henderson to ask *him*, didn't you?" she said.

There was no point in lying. "I asked for her help, yes."

Riley smiled. "Thank you. Duncan wants to come so bad on Saturday."

"I'm glad Rebecca was able to make it work out." Suddenly I didn't want to confront her with what I knew. I wanted to forget what I'd figured out. But I couldn't. "You did a good job with the headless horse/man," I said. "And I like the play on words. Horse. Man. The Grim Sweeper is my favorite, though."

"I don't know what you're talking about," she said. She didn't look away but she swallowed a couple of times and played with the cord bracelet on her wrist. I was relieved that she didn't lie easily. She was more her mother's child than she was a Hollister.

"I can't believe it took me so long to figure out it was you," I continued, as though she hadn't just denied she was the practical joker. "You're smart, you're creative, you're resourceful. And it took me until yesterday to notice the Fibonacci sequence. I don't know how I missed that."

Riley rubbed the bottom of her sneaker back and forth over the edge of the step. "I figured you'd catch on way sooner," she said in a low voice, staring down at her feet. "I never thought the math would give me away."

I shrugged. "It might not have except that the other day when you were here, I saw you arrange the paperclips that were on the circulation desk into a Fibonacci sequence. I don't think you even knew you were doing it."

"My mother said the Fibonacci sequence was the fingerprint of God." She was still staring at the floor. "She said you can see it in things like pinecones and flower petals."

"So it's your signature," I said. "The way an artist signs a painting."

"I never thought of it like that," she said, "but yeah, I guess so."

"So why have you been doing this?" I gestured at the front door. I could see the light from the horse/ man through the window.

She looked at me then. She was still twisting her bracelet around her arm. It had left a red mark on her skin. "I guess because I could. Because *he* says I'm stupid. Mostly because it was a way to take things from him without him knowing. Please? Don't tell him."

"I won't," I said. I could guess how Gerald Hollister

would react if he found out what Riley had been doing. "Was trying to spite your grandfather the only
reason you did all this?"

Riley shrugged. "Mostly. It all would have made
my mother laugh and sometimes I think I'm forget-
ting what that sounded like. I don't know."

It all seemed to come back to Bella. "Why the library?" I asked.

"Because it was easy to get stuff here without being
seen. I mean, you put up one camera and it was so
obvious. And by the way, I spotted the new camera
and the fake decoy one the day they got put up."

"How did you get everything here without anyone
knowing what you were doing?"

"Who says no one knew?" she said. "Even if you
have no hair, if you're a girl you can get guys to help
you do stuff." She ran a hand over her stubbled head.

"So everything came from the farm?"

She smiled. "What do you think? There's so much
junk out there. There's old buildings piled full of crap.
He never knew. I even took his old truck a couple of
times but I was afraid *he'd* figure it out so the last two
times I took Lonnie's." She laughed. "When he's been
drinking, he never remembers where he leaves it. I
take his keys all the time so he won't drive and he
never remembers. I could park it sideways on the middle of the highway and Lonnie wouldn't know he
didn't do it."

"You don't have a driver's license," I said.

"I'm a better driver than lots of people that do."
There was a hint of defiance in her voice.

"The night you were here, setting up the horse/man, did you see the woman who went over the embankment?"

Riley took a long time to answer. "Am I going to get in trouble?"

"For the driving part, if you do it again, absolutely. For whatever you saw that night, no."

"I saw her," Riley said.

My heart was suddenly tap-dancing in my chest. "She was acting crazy." She held up her hands. "Sorry. She was acting like she was mentally ill. I can show you." She pulled out her phone and scrolled through several screens. Then she turned it toward me.

The video was dark but I could clearly make out the back half of the horse/man lying on the grass somewhere just behind the gazebo. And in the background, I saw Margery Wyler. I recognized her hair and her clothing. She seemed to be talking to herself. There was no one else around.

"Did you see anyone else?" I asked.

Riley shook her head. "Just her, talking to herself and looking at a piece of paper."

"Wait a minute," I said. "What piece of paper?"

"Watch at the very beginning. She puts it in her pocket." She started the video again and I saw that she was right. Margery Wyler looked at a small piece of paper and then put it in her pocket. Could that have been the piece of paper I found?

"Could you send me that video?" I asked.

She nodded. "Are you going to tell on me?"

"I don't know," I said. "The police need to see this

video. I promise I won't give them your name unless I have to. And I want *your* word that you won't drive anymore."

Her mouth twisted to one side. "All right. I won't drive," she said, just as the silence was becoming uncomfortable. "I promise."

"And no more surprises in the gazebo."

"Fine." She wasn't looking at me anymore.

"And when you're here for the party on Saturday, you will show me where you think those outside cameras should go."

That got her attention. "Why do I have to do that?" she asked.

"Because you're the one who told me how easy it was to spot the one that's out there now."

"Not everyone is as smart as I am," she said.

I nodded. "I know. That's why I want to know where you would put the cameras."

She almost smiled.

We joined the others. Rebecca had saved two cookies for Riley. "One for you and one for Duncan," she said.

"Thank you," Riley said, sticking them carefully in her pocket before she went to join Ruby, who was walking around the room staring up at the ceiling.

Rebecca joined me. "Did your conversation go all right?" she asked.

I nodded. "It did. Thank you for giving me the time."

Rebecca looked over at Riley, who, based on the way she was gesturing, seemed to be explaining how she'd worked out the pattern for the ceiling decorations to

Ruby. "Do you think Riley and Duncan would be better away from Gerald and Lonnie?" she asked.

"I haven't seen any sign that they're being abused, but I don't think they're well taken care of, either," I said. "I guess the best answer I can give you is maybe."

She eyed me thoughtfully. "You don't like Gerald." The words weren't framed as a question.

"I don't like the way he treated Bella. I don't like the way he treats Riley and Duncan. And I don't like the way he makes it easy for Lonnie to walk away from his responsibilities."

"He doesn't seem to like you, either."

"Do you remember when Child Protective Services paid a visit to the farm not long after Bella died?"

Rebecca nodded. "They didn't find any reason to take the children away, but Gerald didn't like people poking around in what he saw as his family, his business."

"Well, he thought I'd made an anonymous call and reported him."

Rebecca's gaze narrowed. "But you didn't."

"No," I said. "He showed up here the day after CPS showed up at the farm. He wanted me to admit I was the one who had made the call. I told him it wasn't me, and if he didn't have anything to hide then why did it matter who called?" I paused. "I shouldn't have said that last part."

Susan was waving us over. Mary seemed to be showing her and Levi and Mariah some kind of kickboxing move.

"I didn't know Gerald had behaved that way. I'm

sorry," Rebecca said. She gave my arm a squeeze. "I don't know where he got the idea it was an anonymous call. I gave them my name."

We put the empty boxes upstairs in the workroom, which looked more like someone's storage room this time of year. Ruby offered Levi and Mariah a ride home. Rebecca took Riley. I was happy to see Mariah and Riley exchange phone numbers. The two of them had a lot in common.

I closed the building and drove up the hill, wondering what I should do with what I'd learned. I didn't want Riley arrested. I wasn't sure I wanted anyone to know she was the practical joker. I certainly didn't think it would be a good thing if her father and grandfather found out.

There was no sign of Hercules when I got home, a pretty good indication that he was still mad at me. There was no sign of Owen, either, but he appeared—on one of the kitchen chairs—when I started the toaster. I was hungry and in a little need of comfort food. Owen knew the sound of the toaster generally meant toast with peanut butter, and he was always fishing to have a bite.

I gave him a cracker instead. Marcus had stopped in to give them both supper before hockey practice. "How many crackers have you already had?" I said. Owen started sniffing the one I'd just set in front of him and very wisely ignored the question.

I made a cup of hot chocolate and slathered lots of peanut butter on my toast. Then I sat at the table and told Owen everything I'd learned from Riley. I hoped that hearing myself say it all out loud would help me make sense of everything.

Owen ate his cracker, washed his face and then, no surprise, jumped onto my lap. Why sit on the floor when he could sprawl across me? Roma had sent me another photo of Oscar. There was something about that dog that caught my attention. I think it was his kind eyes and the friendly expression he seemed to have on his face. Even with the cone on, the dog seemed to be smiling.

Owen leaned sideways to look at the phone. "That's Oscar," I said. "Remember how we donated to his fund-raiser?" Maybe the reason I was so invested in the dog's story was because it made me feel good. With all the things around me that weren't going right, this was something that was. A few days ago, the dog hadn't been able to move around because two of his legs weren't working right. He wasn't eating because he had no sense of smell and he wasn't the calm, even-tempered animal he'd been in the past.

The dog had no sense of smell.

"Margery Wyler didn't smell the garbage truck," I said to Owen.

He made a face, his whiskers twitching. He knew the word "garbage."

I started stroking his fur. "Georgia said Mrs. Wyler was emotional, not her usual cool, collected self. She was favoring her arm." Margery Wyler's actions seemed to have a lot in common with Oscar's symptoms. "Am I crazy?" I said to Owen.

He seemed to stop and think about the question, then he licked my chin and jumped down to the floor.

I looked at the photo of Oscar again. If . . . *if* Margery Wyler had had a brain tumor, how did that fit into her death? Or did it even matter? It could explain why she'd been talking to herself in the video Riley had shown me. I'd noticed that right away and so, it seemed, had Riley. When I'd asked if she'd seen anyone else, she'd said, "Just her, talking to herself and looking at a piece of paper."

That piece of paper. I remembered that I had taken a photograph of it before I'd given it to Marcus. I pulled it up and took a look at it. There was some sort of calculation at the top and two columns of numbers below. Instead of trying to figure out what it all meant, I just looked at the numbers. And then I realized I'd seen something similar: those three boys who had been in the library trying to learn about kinetic energy. This was a calculation of force of impact: kinetic energy divided by distance.

My stomach rolled over and I pressed a hand to my mouth. I knew who had killed Margery Wyler and I knew why.

19

I felt sick but I couldn't see any flaw in my reasoning. I tried Marcus, but all I got was his voice mail. Then I remembered. He was at hockey practice. I knew I wouldn't be able to sleep until someone had told me whether I was onto something or that my leap in logic was the equivalent of jumping off the roof with a bath towel as a cape.

I decided to drive down to the Sweeney Center and wait for him. I put on a hoodie and my shoes, stuffed my wallet in my pocket and grabbed my keys. Hercules was in the porch looking out the window. "I'll be back," I said. One ear twitched but it was the only acknowledgment I got.

I was halfway to the truck when I realized that Hercules was following me. I stopped and turned around. "You can't come with me," I said.

He walked past me as though I hadn't spoken, heading purposefully for the truck. Then he jumped up on the hood and walked through the windshield.

I pressed my fingers to my temples and closed my eyes for a moment. When I opened them again Hercules was sitting on the passenger side looking at me, head cocked quizzically to one side. I opened the driver's door. "Out," I said.

He blinked his green eyes at me. He didn't move.

I knew if I tried to grab him, he'd be under the seat before I could reach across it. I put one hand on my hip and glared at him. "Fine. I don't have time to have a war with you so you can come, but you stay in the truck, and if you wander off like you did the last time, I *will* leave you behind." I knew it was an inadequate threat and so did he.

Marcus wasn't at the Sweeney Center. There was only one car in the parking lot and it wasn't his. I tried his phone again and got his voice mail again. I got out of the truck and Hercules followed me. I decided having the same old conversation about staying in the truck was tiresome and let him come. The building was locked. A couple of times they'd gone to Fern's after practice when they had something to celebrate. Maybe that's where they were.

Instead of going back to the truck I picked my way down to the water, Hercules grumbling behind me. He hated wet feet. "You didn't have to come with me," I said. He flicked his tail at me.

I walked along the shoreline a short distance. Hercules perched on a rock and watched me. The embankment looked much steeper from this angle. Nothing I saw changed my mind about my reasoning.

I walked back to Hercules, picked him up and

made my way back to the truck. We started for home but instead of turning up Mountain Road I kept going.

Hercules gave a questioning murp. "We're so close to the hotel I thought I'd drive over and see if Elliot is there."

I found a place to park in the hotel lot. I turned to Hercules, who gave me a guileless green-eyed look. I narrowed my own eyes at him. "That innocent look doesn't work on me," I said. "Do not get caught breaking into peoples' cars or you really will need Elliot to be your lawyer." I pointed at him for emphasis. Sometimes when I talked to the cats, I was convinced that they understood every word I said. Other times I was certain all they heard was "blah, blah, blah."

I locked the truck, which felt a little silly because Hercules would probably be in the Range Rover I was parked next to before I got to the front door of the hotel. I walked in and spotted Richard Benson at the reception desk. I didn't want to talk to him right now, so I headed for the elevators next to the ballroom.

I turned the corner and had to put out a hand to steady myself. Hercules was sitting there waiting, it seemed, for an elevator. By some miracle there was no one around. "Hercules," I hissed. "Come here. Now!"

His ear twitched but that was the only indication I got that he'd heard me.

How on earth had he gotten inside the hotel? I looked around. He must have come in the side emergency exit. I pointed at the door. "Go back to the truck," I said.

He continued to look at the elevator doors as the

numbers counted down to this floor. I crossed the space between us and grabbed him before he decided to go exploring and not wait for the elevator. I was about to leave when simultaneously I heard people coming in our direction and the elevator pinged that the door right in front of us was about to open.

I didn't think. I stuffed Hercules inside my hoodie. "Not. A. Sound," I whispered.

The elevator doors opened. There was one elderly man inside. I stepped inside and pushed the button for the second floor. Being on the elevator was the best method of escape since one of the voices I'd heard approaching was Richard Benson's. I would just go up a floor, get off and come down via the stairs.

Hercules was blessedly still and quiet but I knew he could poke his head out through the front of my hoodie anytime he wanted to. It would be just like the movie *Alien*. Did that make me Sigourney Weaver? Her character in the movie did have a cat. I was tired and stressed and for some reason the idea made me grin. The older man moved a little closer to the wall. I wondered how he would feel if he knew I had a cat under my hoodie, and I almost laughed out loud.

I got off on the second floor. Luckily it was late enough that most people were settled in their rooms for the evening. Hercules was wriggling and I opened the zipper of my hoodie a couple of inches. "Knock it off if you ever want to eat sardines in this hemisphere again," I said.

I was pretty sure I remembered where the stairs were. I turned down a corridor to the left and saw the exit sign at the end. There were two men halfway down the long hallway. One of them was Elliot, I realized. I was about to call out to him when I recognized that Hugh Wyler was the other. They were walking close together. Like they were friends.

The hairs rose on the back of my neck. I slowed down a little. Hugh Wyler's left hand was on Elliot's back. I could see the other hand pressing something I was almost sure was a knife to Elliot's right side. I could hear Elliot's voice, calm and even, talking to Wyler, but I couldn't make out what he was saying. Where were they going? My best guess was either to Wyler's room or the stairs. They turned left. So not the stairs. Not out of the building. If Mr. Wyler got Elliot into his room things could get very ugly.

I carefully slid down the zipper of my hoodie and set Hercules on the carpeted floor, pressing my index finger to my lips. He was the only backup I had. I was afraid that if I pulled out my phone to call for help Hugh Wyler might realize that someone was behind him. If I hung back long enough to make a call, I might not see where he took Elliot. I remembered how I'd felt when I'd seen Elliot coming to my rescue through the woods in the rain. Now it was my turn.

I hoped Hercules could create a distraction if I needed one. I gestured for him to stay behind me, close to the wall, and he seemed to understand. Hugh Wyler had stopped. It was now or never, do or die, backs against the wall and all the other clichés.

I straightened up, squared my shoulders and

walked toward Wyler and Elliot with a confidence I did not feel. Wyler had a keycard out. "Elliot," I called out.

Hugh Wyler looked over his shoulder. I saw him shoot Elliot a warning look. "Go away, Ms. Paulson," he said.

"I need to talk to Mr. Gordon," I said. "It's important."

"You can talk to him in the morning."

"I can't wait until the morning." My knees were shaking, but luckily my voice wasn't.

Elliot gave me a warning look. "Now isn't a good time, Kathleen," he said.

Hugh Wyler's face was tight and angry looking. "I can call hotel security," he said.

I smiled, hoping I looked more like the crocodile that had been Captain Hook's nemesis than a librarian with a small cat for backup. "I think that would be an excellent idea."

Wyler swiped his card and opened the door. He looked directly at me. "Step inside, Ms. Paulson, or I will be forced to stick this expensive French steak knife with its very nice olivewood handle into Mr. Gordon's liver."

Elliot was already shaking his head. "Don't," he said.

Something in Hugh Wyler's expression told me he would do exactly what he'd said he would do. I walked through the door. He pushed Elliot into the room ahead of him, not trying to hide the knife any longer.

"I should have had you arrested for harassing me the first time I saw you in this hotel," he said.

I ignored the comment. "Your wife had a brain

tumor," I said. "That must have been agonizing for you. You two had been together most of your lives." I tried to feel some compassion for him, but it was difficult with that knife pressed to Elliot's side. Out of the corner of my eye I saw Elliot's eyes narrow. He hadn't known.

"Margery was a good woman," Wyler said. "Don't pretend to have sympathy for me. I am not easily played, Ms. Paulson."

"I don't have any sympathy for you," I said. "But I do have it for your wife. She lost her only child and she was starting to lose parts of herself." He wouldn't look at me. "She loved you."

His jaw tightened. "You know nothing about the two of us."

I needed to keep him talking. "Mrs. Wyler wanted you to have a relationship with your granddaughter. She wanted to give you that. She was dying anyway."

The flash of surprise on Elliot's face told me that he didn't know that detail, either.

"She decided to kill herself and set up the scenario to make it look like Georgia murdered her. That's why you came to the library, wasn't it?"

Wyler's disdainful expression didn't change.

"You needed witnesses to the animosity between the two of you and Georgia. It was also when she took Georgia's scarf. I don't know if that was planned or she just took advantage of the opportunity. She had periods of time when she was lucid and sharp. The argument on the street with Georgia later that evening—your wife orchestrated that, too. When she got to the riverbank it turned out the embankment wasn't quite high enough to be certain the fall would kill her—I know she had the calculations—so she climbed on top of a nearby rock and stepped backward."

"I think you've missed your calling, Ms. Paulson," Wyler said. "You shouldn't be working in a library. You should be writing fiction. Fantasy, to be specific." His shoulders were rigid, knuckles white on the hand holding the knife against Elliot. I had hit a nerve.

I put one hand behind my back, clenching my fingers into a tight fist. I was struggling to keep the panic out of my voice. "Because of that brain tumor she wasn't thinking clearly. But you were. You helped her set up Georgia. I figured it out. The police will, too, if they haven't already."

"Paige is not the person you think she is. She's selfish. We could have given our granddaughter a wonderful life—the kind of life Scott had—with the best schools, with piano and ballet, with the chance to make the right connections." He gestured with his free hand. "Look where she ended up."

I had ended up in Mayville Heights. It was a wonderful place to live. I had connections all over town just the way Georgia and Emmy did, and they were all just right.

Over Wyler's shoulder I saw movement. Hercules was in the room. The two of us had gotten out of worse situations than this, and having an ally, even a furry black-and-white one, was better than doing this alone.

"The truth will come out one way or another," I said.

He raised an eyebrow. "Is this where you tell me if I hurt the two of you everything I've done so far will be for nothing and then we go to a commercial break?"

Elliot, who had stayed remarkably calm so far, turned his head to look at Hugh Wyler. "Everything *you've* done?" he said.

I knew it was difficult to comprehend that Margery Wyler had decided to kill herself and frame Georgia for her death and that Hugh Wyler had helped his wife.

Wyler poked him with the knife and Elliot winced.

There was a lamp to my left with a heavy blue ceramic base. I edged slightly closer to it while Hugh was looking at Elliot. I needed to draw Wyler's attention away from Elliot. I could see the tension in every inch of his body, from the hand that held that knife against Elliot's side to his clenched jawline.

"I only helped Margery because I didn't want her to suffer and I knew she would go ahead with her plan no matter what I said. She wanted a good death. She wanted her death to have meaning. And for it to be fast."

I didn't see anything good or fast about going over the side of that embankment.

"The problem was that even with the extra elevation the fall wasn't far enough to guarantee Margery would be killed," Elliot said. "And she wasn't." He looked at me and his gaze flicked to the door behind me. He was going to do something, try to create some kind of distraction, and he expected me to run.

Behind the two men, Hercules had climbed on top of a table. He jumped from there to the back of a leather parsons chair. I had to do something now before Elliot got hurt. I was *not* running out on him.

"How did you know?" I said to him.

"My medical examiner looked at Mrs. Wyler's autopsy results and felt the injuries to her head weren't consistent with the distance she fell. He believes someone else was there and they smashed her head with a rock to end her life."

I put my hand to the right side of my head, near the back. "Right here," I said. I focused on Hugh Wyler again. "She wasn't dead. So you made sure she was. You hit her with a rock and then threw the evidence into the water."

"Margery wasn't in her right mind and everything that happened was because of Paige," he said. "She doesn't deserve to go on with her life after she ruined ours. We loved our son and all we ever wanted was what was best for him. That wasn't Paige. Scott would be alive if he hadn't married her. He wouldn't have been on that road where he was killed. He would have married his college girlfriend. They would have had several grandchildren for us by now and everything would be fine." His voice was icy cold and logical and I could see he believed what he was saying.

Elliot's eyes flicked to the door again. I gave my head an almost imperceptible shake. Everything that happened next seemed to happen all at once. Elliot brought his right arm up to hit Hugh Wyler in the face.

Somehow Wyler had anticipated this and he dodged

the worst of the blow. He stabbed the knife into Elliot's side. Elliot sucked in a ragged breath and doubled over. At the same time Hercules let out a hair-raising yowl and launched himself from the back of the leather chair, ears back, claws out, onto Hugh Wyler's back. I lunged for the lamp, yanked the cord out of the wall and hit Wyler over the head with every bit of my strength. His eyes rolled back and his legs buckled as though they had been kicked out from under him—which I might have done if I'd thought of it.

Hercules jumped down beside me. Elliot's legs sagged and he slid down to the carpet, his back against a chair. I grabbed a couple of napkins from the table. Elliot's face was ashen, his forehead beaded with sweat, eyes closed. He was clutching his side with one hand and blood was leaking through his fingers.

"Stay with me, Elliot," I said. I eased his hand and his sweater up just enough to get the folded napkins over the wound. Then I put my hand over his. "You have to help me. Press hard." Under my own hand I felt his press down.

Hercules stood by Elliot's shoulder, his fur disheveled. "Good job," I said to him. He made an answering "Mrrr" but didn't take his eyes off Elliot.

"You were supposed to run," Elliot said.

I wiped his forehead with the edge of my hoodie. "I'm not so good at doing what I'm supposed to do," I said. "Just ask your son."

I gave his free hand a squeeze and then put it on top of the one pressing on the napkins. "Keep that pressure on."

"I have a confession to make," he said. His color was ghastly. I wondered how deep the gash in his side went.

"What is it?"

"I don't do well with blood when it's my own."

So maybe it was squeamishness that made him look like he was about to pass out. "I was a teenager with two baby siblings," I said. "I can handle any bodily fluid you throw at me—even literally."

He smiled.

I dug out my phone and called 911. Then I pulled the cord off the broken lamp and lashed Wyler's feet together. I took the string from the hood of my sweatshirt and used it to tie his hands together. Finally, I opened the door and dropped back down beside Elliot. I put my hand over his and pressed down hard. He sucked in a sharp breath.

"I'm sorry," I said. "Help is coming." As I said the words, I heard the wail of sirens.

"Kathleen, is Hercules here or am I hallucinating?" Elliot suddenly asked.

The cat leaned over and meowed softly at him.

"He's here."

Blood had soaked into Elliot's sweater underneath our hands, but the sirens were louder and closer. Help was almost here. It was over.

20

After that, things were a bit of a blur. The paramedics arrived, and I was happy to see it was Ric Holm and his partner. Ric had taken care of me more than once and I knew he would take good care of Elliot. Stephen Keller was the police officer right behind them. He was ex-military, serious and more than capable of handling whatever he walked into. He gave me a brief nod of recognition.

"Hey, Kathleen, what's going on?" Ric asked as he crouched down next to Elliot.

"He was stabbed," I said. I looked at Officer Keller. "The knife is over there." I gestured toward the far end of the room. I had kicked it away as hard as I could.

Ric lifted Elliot's hands and checked my makeshift napkin compress. "Ric, this is Elliot Gordon, Marcus's father," I said.

"Mr. Gordon, I'm going to get an IV going and take a closer look at your side," Ric said.

Hugh Wyler was conscious and angry, trying to get someone to untie him, trying to get Officer Keller to arrest me. I had used a necktie I'd found discarded on a chair as a gag because he wouldn't stop threatening me when he regained consciousness, but Ric's partner had removed it.

Hercules was still standing guard over Elliot. I picked him up and got to my feet. "We're going to get out of your way," I said.

I was talking to Stephen Keller when Marcus came striding down the hallway a minute or so later. He seemed to sag a little with relief when he caught sight of me in the doorway. "Are you all right?" he said, putting a hand on my arm.

I put my hand over his. "I'm fine. But your father's hurt. Hugh Wyler stabbed him." I gestured over my shoulder. Ric and his partner had just placed Elliot on the stretcher.

Marcus raked a hand through his hair. "Give me a minute," he said.

He made his way over to Elliot. I couldn't make out what they were saying, but I told myself that Elliot's color was a little better. I shivered, suddenly noticing how cold the room was. My crumpled hoodie was on the floor where Elliot had been lying.

"Are you all right?" Officer Keller asked.

I nodded. "I'm fine. It's just a little cool in here."

He pulled off his jacket and wrapped it around my shoulders.

"Thank you," I said, pulling the jacket close around

me. Hercules poked his head out the front. "But I'm going to get cat hair on it."

He smiled. "Don't worry. That jacket's had a lot worse on it."

They had put Elliot on the stretcher partly sitting up. As he passed me he reached for my hand. I gave his hand a squeeze. "Thank you," he said.

"We'll be right behind the ambulance," I said.

They headed for the elevator. Another police officer was working on untying the lamp cord I had used to restrain Hugh Wyler's feet. "How many knots are on this thing?" I heard him say.

I glanced over my shoulder at him. "Every one I know," I said.

Marcus talked to the two police officers and hotel security. Finally, he came over to me. "Are you ready to go?" he asked. I nodded and slipped out of Officer Keller's jacket. I set it over the arm of a nearby chair and mouthed "Thank you" in his direction.

"I'm going to take you and Hercules home and then go to the hospital," Marcus said as we walked toward the elevators.

"I'm going with you."

I thought he was going to argue with me but all he said was, "Okay."

We dropped off Hercules. I carried him around the house, unlocked the back door and set him on the kitchen floor, giving him a kiss on the top of his head before I put him down.

"Tell me what happened," Marcus said as we headed to the hospital.

My head was against the back of my seat, one hand resting on his leg. "Margery Wyler had a brain tumor," I said.

"How did you know?" His eyes didn't leave the road.

He wasn't surprised. "Oscar."

He shot a quick glance my way. "The dog Roma helped operate on."

"Uh-huh. I realized Mrs. Wyler had the same symptoms the dog did." I explained about Riley's video. "I think she was working up her nerve," I said. "I kept thinking about what you say: Who benefits? And I realized if she was going to die anyway, the person who benefited the most from Margery Wyler's death was Margery Wyler."

"I'm not following."

"She wanted to hurt Georgia. Her death did that." My hands were cold and I pulled them up into my sleeves. "Look at the evidence. You said you had a witness that heard the two of them arguing. Mrs. Wyler called Georgia by name."

Marcus nodded.

"I didn't catch it at first, either," I said. "She called her Georgia. The Wylers never did that. They always referred to Georgia as Paige. I heard them. She hated that. Margery wanted anyone who heard them arguing to know exactly who she was talking to. And the scarf she was holding on to? She took it when they were at the library. Something else I missed. Georgia was wearing that scarf when she got to the library. Ruby took a photo of the two of us. Georgia took a surreptitious picture of the Wylers with her phone. Her coat is on a hook in the background but her scarf isn't there."

"Mrs. Wyler dropped her driver's license so someone would look for her."

"I think so. And left her watch at the hotel."

"How did you figure out that it was Hugh that was actually responsible for her death?" We were almost at the hospital.

"Remember I told you I had brain itch?"

He nodded. "I remember."

"I kept thinking about that night. Thinking about her body lying on the rocks when I first saw it, before we tried to save her. I realized she had two injuries to her head. One was on the back of her head but one was more to the side. I could see the second one. That's what didn't make sense, although I didn't recognize that at the time. How could I see that wound so well if it had happened when she hit the rocks? There were no other indications that she'd moved her head or any other part of her body."

"So you figured someone had to have killed her."

"Nothing else made sense. And Hugh Wyler was the only person I could think of who would have done that. I think it was partly out of love for his wife, who was suffering, and partly that their desire for revenge against Georgia had warped their thinking."

"So how did my father get involved?"

"I went to the rink to talk to you but you'd already left."

He sighed. "We went to Fern's."

I squeezed his leg. "I decided to stop and talk over what I'd figured out with Elliot. Hercules was with me—long story. He ended up inside the hotel—also long story. Your dad's medical examiner had a problem with the head wounds just like I did. He went to talk to Mr. Wyler to see if he could get him to agree to a second look at his wife's body. Elliot believed someone had hit Margery but didn't realize it was Hugh Wyler himself. I think Wyler felt the walls closing in on him and he grabbed a steak knife from a room service cart."

"Ric said he didn't think the knife hit any major organs," Marcus said, his expression grim.

"He'll be all right," I said. I refused to even think about any other possibility.

We turned into the hospital driveway. "He tried to save me, you know," I said.

He frowned. "What do you mean?"

"He signaled to me to run and then he hit Wyler in the face."

"My father doesn't know you very well if he thought that would work." Marcus pulled up by the emergency room entrance and turned down the visor so his police placard was displayed and we wouldn't get towed.

"He didn't know I had Hercules as backup."

Marcus shook his head. "Kathleen, a cat is not backup."

"That cat helped me build a flour bomb. I'll take him over a lot of people, thank you very much," I said.

Ric was right, and Elliot was lucky. The French

steak knife with its olivewood handle hadn't hit Elliot's liver or his kidney. They stitched him up in the ER and admitted him for observation overnight. Elliot was released the next morning and we took him back to Marcus's house over his objections that he would be fine at the St. James.

"Don't go there with me," Marcus said, giving his father a look. They also argued over whether they were going to call Marcus's mother, who was in Norway at a symposium on polar bears. At one point I had an attack of the giggles that then led to a secondary attack of hiccups because, as his father, Elliot forbade Marcus from making the call.

"You didn't really think that would work, did you?" I said to Elliot after Marcus had gone to the kitchen for some privacy to call his mother.

"He's acting like I'm a helpless old man," Elliot said, full of haughty indignation.

I patted his arm and hiccupped. "He doesn't think you're a helpless old man. He loves you."

Elliot shook his head. "Now, how am I supposed to argue with that?"

I smiled and hiccupped again. "You're not," I said. "That's why I used it."

Georgia and Larry, along with Emmy, showed up mid-morning on Friday with the cupcakes for Saturday's Halloween party. Marcus was fussing over Elliot so I answered the back door when I heard the knock.

"Cupcake delivery," Emmy said, giving me a big smile.

I smiled back at her. "Perfect timing."

"Is Marcus's dad up for visitors?" Larry asked.

"Yes," I said. "Elliot will be happy to see you. He's not very good at taking it easy. I was afraid Marcus was going to tie him to a chair a little while ago." I raised one eyebrow. "He may yet."

Georgia hadn't said a word. I smiled at her.

"Kathleen, I'm sorry," she blurted.

I shook my head. "You have absolutely nothing to apologize for."

She swallowed before she said anything else. "That's really nice of you, given what happened."

"None of which was caused by you."

Larry looked down at Emmy. He was carrying four large boxes that I guessed held the cupcakes. She had a fifth plus a smaller box. "Hey, kiddo, we should put these cupcakes on Marcus's kitchen table before I lose control and eat one," he said.

Emmy rolled her eyes. "I'm not six. Why don't you just say we need to give my mom and Kathleen some privacy?"

Larry nudged her with his elbow. "Okay," he said. "Then get moving."

I stepped out onto the back deck and the two of them made their way into the kitchen.

"Elliot really is all right?" Georgia asked.

"He is. If he'd had his way we would have taken him to see the prosecuting attorney on the way home from the hospital."

"I don't know how to thank either one of you. You gave me my life back."

"That's easy," I said. "Just be happy. Love Emmy, love Larry, spend time with your friends, make cupcakes, bring some of those cupcakes to the library."

She smiled. "I like the sound of all of that."

"That's good, because it's your life now."

She nodded, then her smile faded. "I knew that Hugh and Margery were extremely manipulative but I'm having trouble getting my mind around the idea that they tried to set me up for murder. What makes someone that way?"

I shrugged. "I've been asking myself that same question, and I just don't know."

"Scott would be so ashamed of them if he were alive," she said in a low voice. She stared out across Marcus's backyard. One tear slid down her cheek and she swiped it away. "It's hard to believe after all this time it's finally over."

"It's probably going to take some time to sink in," I said, "but you have lots of that."

Georgia gave me a shy smile. "Larry asked me to marry him and I said yes. I guess happy endings don't just happen in books."

"You and Emmy deserve yours," I said, wrapping her in a hug.

We went inside to find Emmy showing Elliot the cupcakes, Marcus hovering and Larry watching the scene with a happy smile and a cup of coffee. Seeing Elliot deep in conversation with Emmy seemed to set Georgia's mind at ease. She and Elliot stepped into the living room for a brief conversation while Marcus introduced Emmy to Micah.

I leaned against the counter next to Larry and watched as Marcus showed the child how to hold a cat.

"'Thank you' seems way too inadequate," Larry said.

I smiled at him. "I'll tell you what I told Georgia, and yes, I know it sounds a bit hokey—be happy. That's the only thank-you I need."

"Doesn't sound hokey to me," Larry said, raising his coffee mug in a toast. "Sounds pretty much perfect.

Elliot and Georgia rejoined us and she and Larry shared their engagement news with everyone else.

"Promise you'll come back for the wedding," Georgia said to Elliot.

"I wouldn't miss it," he said.

By Friday afternoon I'd finally decided what I was going to do now that I knew Riley was the prankster. I believed she'd keep her promise not to pull any more stunts but I wanted to help her and I wanted to find some way to channel her creativity.

Nic Sutton, who worked at Eric's Place, was also a found metal artist. He and Maggie and Ruby Blackthorne had teamed up on a secret project for the town's upcoming Winterfest celebrations. They would be happy to have an extra set of hands Maggie had said when I called her about Riley working with them. I didn't tell Mags that Riley had been behind the pranks at the library but I was pretty sure she'd figured it out and I knew she'd keep whatever she'd guessed to herself.

And every Friday after school Riley was going to

spend a couple of hours at Roma's clinic doing things like cleaning cages and looking after the various cats and dogs. Roma always needed help and she had been quick to say yes when I asked. Riley needed the chance to be loved just for her and I was hoping the dogs and cats would fill that need.

"If this stuff is supposed to be my punishment, then you suck at it because I don't think either one sounds that bad," Riley had said when I explained her two new volunteer jobs.

"You're not being punished," I'd replied. "This is a chance for you to figure out what you want and who you are."

She'd pulled one hand down over her stubbled head. "You're the only person I've ever met who talks like that." Then, to my surprise, she'd given me a quick, hard hug before she was out the library doors. I hoped she'd get a happy ending, too.

By Saturday morning Elliot was a restless, cranky patient. "He ate three eggs for breakfast," Marcus said on the phone. "Which he was frying at five to six this morning. Three eggs. I can only imagine what his cholesterol is like."

"My cholesterol is fine," I heard Elliot call out in the background.

There seemed to be some kind of issue with the phone then. For a moment I thought Marcus had dropped it in the sink. Then Elliot came on the line. "Kathleen, please come and collect my son for the Halloween party this afternoon. He's hovering."

"I heard that," Marcus said. From the sounds in the background, he was making oatmeal.

"You were supposed to hear that," Elliot retorted.

"I will take Marcus to the party," I said. "And you will give me your word that you won't do anything stupid while we're gone."

"Done," he said.

Since I knew Elliot's skills as a lawyer, after I hung up, I called Brady to see if he and Burtis were free. The two of them had just arrived when I got to Marcus's house. I noticed Burtis had a deck of cards.

"I thought we had an agreement," Elliot said when I walked in. He glared at me but I could see the tiniest hint of a smile.

"We did," I said. "I said I'd take Marcus to the Halloween party and you agreed not to do anything stupid. I didn't say I wasn't going to need proof of the latter."

Burtis laughed. "She's got you there, Elly Mae," he said.

Elliot narrowed his dark eyes at me. "Are you sure you didn't go to law school?" he said.

I reached up and patted his cheek. "Even better," I said. "I'm a librarian."

The party was a huge success. The kids devoured Georgia's cupcakes and a fair amount of cucumbers, carrots and snow peas. I thought I was seeing things when Lonnie Hollister dropped off Riley and Duncan. Lonnie was clean-shaven and he'd had a haircut. He looked . . . sober and a little shaky.

Duncan's left arm was in a cast. He'd fallen out of an old tree house at the farm. He was covered from head to toe with bandages that looked like they'd been made from a couple of torn sheets. "I'm a mummy," he told me with a grin before he ran off to join the other kids.

"Nice job," I said to Riley.

"Whatever," she said with a shrug, but I caught a glimpse of the tiniest hint of a smile. She looked around. "Mrs. Henderson says I should help with food."

"In the big meeting room," I said. "Mariah's already there." I spotted Rebecca, tying the shoe of a very tiny pumpkin and walked over to join her.

She smiled at me. "Wonderful Pippi Longstocking costume," she said, taking in my droopy sweater, the long striped scarf wound around my neck, my sagging socks and the red wig with two pigtails that curved up in big loops on either side of my head thanks to a couple of lengths of picture-hanging wire.

"Thank you," I said. "Everyone else thinks I'm Anne of Green Gables. You make a wonderful Mary Poppins."

Rebecca laughed. "And everyone thinks I'm Mother Goose."

"I saw Lonnie bring the kids," I said. "I know you had something to do with that."

"All I did was remind him of the time, years ago, when he broke his own arm. He was just a year older than Duncan and his mother was too drunk to take him to the hospital. I found him walking on the side of the road with duct tape on his arm."

She shook her head. "Gail Hollister was my friend but for a long time she was a drunk, too. The state even took Lonnie away from her for a little while. I reminded him of how that felt." She gave me a wry smile. "He asked me if I was the one who called CPS about Riley and Duncan after Bella died. I said yes but I wouldn't have to do it this time. The ER staff had already called the police because he was clearly intoxicated when he showed up at the hospital with Duncan. Riley told me they talked to her. Don't worry. I didn't tell Lonnie that." She paused for a moment. "He cried."

I put a hand on her shoulder.

"He needs help. More than he can get here," she went on. "Lita is family because she's family to the entire town in one way or the other so Duncan and Riley are going to stay with her and the rest of us will step in to help."

I nodded. "Do you think this will work?"

Rebecca shook her head. "I don't know. But it doesn't hurt to have hope."

I gave her a hug, which managed to send my wig off sideways in one direction and her black flower-trimmed boater in the other. We laughed and adjusted each other's headwear. I promised I'd help with Riley and Duncan in any way I could.

When I went outside, I discovered that Mary had taught the kids a variation on the game of tag that was a big hit. Whoever was it went and hid and the others searched for him or her. If you found the person you both had to squeeze into their hiding place. And so on for the next person and the next person. The game continued until there was one person left but in reality, it usually ended with a tangle of laughing kids falling out from behind a tree or clump of bushes. I was about to join in on the next game when the kids starting grinning and pushing each other, looking at something behind me. I turned around to see what it was. Ruby was coming across the grass. She wore tailored wool trousers and a blue sweater. There were no wild colors in her hair, which was pulled back in a sleek knot. She was carrying a reference book on grammar and a take-out cup from Eric's. *She was me.*

It got even better. Susan came out of the building and walked over to us. "The book drop is jammed again," she said, totally straight-faced to Ruby. "Could you come take a look at it, Kathleen?"

The kids elbowed each other and hooted with laughter but I think I laughed the hardest. It was a good feeling.

About an hour later, just as we were about to wrap things up, Riley appeared with two tombstone cookies and a cup of coffee. "Mrs. Henderson said to bring these to you," she said.

"Thank you," I said. The coffee was nice and hot and Georgia's cookies, of course, were delicious.

Riley's hands were jammed in the pockets of her black jeans. "You probably heard Lonnie is going to rehab," she said.

"I did," I said. "And I'm glad."

"It probably won't work."

"You mean like putting a blow-up pool full of Jell-O in the gazebo without getting caught won't work?"

Riley rolled her eyes. "He's a crappy dad. I'm not forgiving him."

I broke my remaining cookie in half and offered her a piece. She took it with a mumbled "Thank you."

"You don't have to forgive him," I said. "Maybe he'll stop drinking. Maybe he won't. That's up to your father. Not you."

She shrugged. "I guess."

I smiled. "Now come show me where you think we should put the cameras."

After the party Marcus and I drove back to his house. Brady had won both his dad's and Elliot's money. He was taking them to Fern's for supper.

"You're doing too much," Marcus said. "You just got stabbed."

Elliot looked at his side. "It was just a little nick. Ask Kathleen."

I held up both hands. "Oh no. Do *not* try to rope me into this."

"I appreciate your concern," Elliot said. "I won't overdo it. I'm just going to eat a nice steak and talk football with Burtis."

Marcus did his hand-hair thing. "Right. Because that never gets out of hand."

Burtis patted him on the back. "Don't worry. I'll take care of Elly Mae."

"No offense," Marcus said, "but that doesn't fill me with confidence."

I leaned against him and rested one hand on his shoulder. "Have a little faith," I said.

To his credit, Marcus knew when he'd been beaten. "I'll keep an eye on both of them," I heard Brady say as they left.

I needed to check on Owen and Hercules and get out of my costume, so Marcus and I headed to my house. "Why don't we just stay here and eat?" I said as we pulled into the driveway. "I have spaghetti sauce."

"That sounds good," he said.

I got out of the SUV and as I closed the car door, I caught sight of Micah sitting on the backseat.

"Small problem," I said.

"Define small." Marcus eyed me over the hood of the car.

"Cat-sized."

"Micah?"

"She's in the back."

He looked in the backseat. "Let's just do it," he said.

"You mean introduce the three of them? Now?"

"C'mon, how long have we been talking about this? Let's just get it over with."

"We haven't done any of the things Roma said to do."

"Those things aren't going to work," Marcus said. "How do you keep two cats that can disappear and one that can walk through walls separated?"

I folded one arm up over my head. "What if they fight?"

"What if they don't? They're not exactly three typical cats, so their reaction to each other may not be typical."

He was right that we'd been putting this off, just the way I'd put off telling him the truth about the boys and Micah in the first place.

"Okay," I said.

Micah walked into the kitchen, curious and full of confidence. Owen was getting a drink and he looked up in surprise at this interloper. Hercules came in from the living room and stopped uncertainly in the doorway. I hovered.

Marcus put one arm around my shoulders and pulled me against him. "They're fine," he said. "Have a little faith."

"Where did you hear a cliché like that?" I asked.

He kissed the top of my head. "From a very smart and very beautiful woman."

I went over to Hercules. "This is Micah," I told him, feeling a little foolish for introducing three cats to one another. "She's family. She comes from Wisteria Hill."

Owen was watching us. I turned my attention to him. "Be nice," I said firmly.

I straightened up and looked at Micah. The little ginger cat tipped her head quizzically to one side. "Hercules. Owen," I said, pointing.

The three cats eyed one another. Owen looked a bit skeptical, Hercules was anxious and Micah just seemed curious. The small rubber dog bone that had been the present from Fifi was on the floor near the basement door. It caught Micah's attention. She made her way over to it, leaning over to sniff the toy. Hercules looked pointedly at me, meowing softly.

"She's not going to take your toy," I said.

He didn't seem convinced.

"What is that thing?" Marcus asked.

"It was a gift from Fifi," I said. "Remember I told you that Mike thinks she wants to be friends with Hercules?"

"Yeah, I remember," he said. "But isn't that a *dog* bone?"

I nodded. "Technically, yes, but Hercules and I try not to classify things by species."

He grinned. "I'll remind you that you said that the next time you tell me turkey bacon is *people* food, not cat food."

Micah was still checking out the blue dog bone and Hercules seemed to be getting more stressed. He was making little noises and standing up and sitting down again. He didn't share well under the best of circumstances and here was a strange cat in his house touching his things.

Owen looked from his brother to Micah and then headed down the basement stairs. He returned in a moment with a yellow catnip chicken, which he set down in front of Micah. They looked at each other and seemed to be doing that silent communication thing that Owen and Hercules sometimes did. Or maybe they were just giving each other the hairy eyeball.

After a moment Micah picked up Fred the Funky Chicken and Owen pushed the rubber bone across the kitchen floor to Hercules, who immediately put one paw on it. Owen looked expectantly at me. He thought he should be rewarded for his good deed.

I gave each of the cats three sardine crackers. I also

gave Owen a scratch on the head. "You're a good brother," I whispered. "You're also a little mercenary.

"Everything is fine," I told Hercules as I gave him his treat. He kept one paw firmly on the dog bone nonetheless.

"Don't think I don't know that you stowed away on purpose just to force this meeting," I said to Micah. The cat gave me a guileless look in return, but as she bent her head over the crackers, it seemed to me that she was smiling.

I went back over to Marcus. I leaned against him and he wrapped his arms around me. "See, it all worked out," he said.

"It did," I agreed. "In fact, it worked out so well I'm going to buy Micah a couple of catnip chickens because she clearly likes them, just the way you buy them for Owen. You might want to think about getting a better vacuum cleaner. The catnip from one chicken can make a big mess." I shifted in his arms so I could reach up and pat his cheek. "In case you hadn't noticed, karma is just finishing her coffee and she'll be right with you," I said. And then I laughed. Who knew introducing the cats was going to be so much fun?

I put the water on to boil while Marcus set the table and shredded a large apple and two carrots for a simple salad. I saw him check his phone a couple of times. "Your father's fine," I said after the second check.

"Two days ago, he was stabbed, Kathleen." Anger sharpened his voice. "No one, including my father, seems to be taking that seriously. If that knife had gone in just a little higher or lower . . ."

I turned to look at him. "I know," I said. "I was there."

He closed his eyes for a moment, took a deep breath. "I'm sorry. I've been trying not to think about what might have happened if you hadn't been there, or what could have because you *were*."

"But none of those bad things you're trying not to think about actually happened. And a lot of good things did. Your father is all right. He really is. Georgia and Larry are getting married. Lonnie Hollister is going to rehab. And if that's not some kind of miracle I don't know what is." I closed the distance between us and laid my palm against his cheek. "You don't always get to choose, but when you do, choose happy."

He smiled and wrapped his arms around me. "I think that's what I did when I chose you."

"You are so lucky flattery works on me," I said, and I kissed him.

We had supper and made plans for picking up Marcus's mother at the airport in the morning. "I think Dad is planning on going to get her himself," Marcus said.

I shook my head as I speared a meatball. "I don't think that's a good idea."

Marcus leaned back in his chair. "And you can tell him that. He at least listens to you."

I smiled. "That's because you're so like him. That's why the two of you bang heads."

"We bang heads because he's stubborn and opinionated and thinks whatever he wants to do is the best way to approach something."

"And he has a very strong sense of what's right and wrong," I added.

"Exactly!"

"You do get that you just described yourself?" I said.

"I am not stubborn and I don't think my way is the best way," Marcus said hotly, gesturing with his fork. "I'm very easygoing."

I laughed and almost choked on my spaghetti. "The gentleman doth protest too much, methinks," I said when I could talk again.

Marcus shook his head. "I'm a cliché. I've turned into my father."

"It's not a bad thing," I said. "For instance, that strong sense of right and wrong is why you asked him to help Brady, wasn't it?"

"I should have told you," he said. "I'm sorry."

"It's okay," I said. "I figured it out a long time ago."

We were still at the table with the three cats spread around the kitchen when Elliot and Burtis showed up.

"I just came to tell you that your mother got an earlier flight," Elliot said. "She'll be here in a couple of hours. Burtis is taking me to the airport to pick her up."

"Don't worry, I'll do all the driving," Burtis said.

I pointed a finger at him. "Straight there. Straight back. No side trips."

"Yes, ma'am," he said.

"I'll see you back at the house then, Dad," Marcus

said. If he had any objections to this road trip—and
I was pretty sure he did—he was keeping them to
himself.

Elliot nodded. "Your mother will be happy to see
you." He looked at me. "Kathleen, you saved my life.
I know I said thank you but it's nowhere near ade-
quate."

I felt the prickle of tears and blinked them away. "I
was just returning the favor."

Elliot reached into the pocket of his jacket and
handed me a faded brown leather ring box. Then he
looked at Marcus. "Don't screw this up," he said. He
turned to Burtis. "Let's roll."

I stood in the middle of the kitchen holding on to
the box without a clue about what to do next. I knew
I had to be holding some kind of heirloom, an engagement ring that might have been in Marcus's family for
generations.

We hadn't even talked about getting married. Elliot
was stubborn, opinionated and had a strong sense of
right and wrong. He also wasn't subtle.

I offered the box to Marcus. "You don't have to do
anything," I said.

He smiled. "It's not what you think," he said. "Just
open the box."

When I did, to my surprise it contained a man's
gold signet ring. The ring Elliot always wore. It wasn't
what I was expecting.

"My grandfather was injured in the Second World
War," Marcus said. "He was burned." He ran one
hand down over his shoulder and the left side of his

body. "My grandmother had promised to marry him but he released her from that promise because of his scars. So *she* proposed to *him* with the ring you're holding. When Dad met my mother, my grandfather gave his ring to *her* to propose."

And now Elliot had given it to me, his way of offering us his blessing.

My eyes filled with tears.

"You don't have to do anything," Marcus said, repeating my own words back to me.

There wasn't anything I wanted to do more, I realized. All three cats were sitting by the table, watching us, Owen and Hercules flanking Micah. It was the perfect moment.

I dropped down on one knee and took Marcus's hand. "Marcus Gordon, I love you," I said. "You make me laugh, you make me crazy. I want to spend the rest of my life with you and it won't be anywhere near enough time." I held up the ring. "Will you marry me?"

All three cats turned to look at him. For a moment it felt as though time had stopped. And then all my tomorrows began. Because then he said, "Yes."

ACKNOWLEDGMENTS

The fact that the Magical Cats Mysteries are still around is due in no small part to the enthusiasm of so many booksellers. Thank you all. Thanks as well to my editor, Jessica Wade, who has championed Kathleen, Hercules and Owen from the beginning. My agent, Kim Lionetti, is the kind of person every writer deserves to have in their corner. I'm very grateful she's in mine. Artist Tristan Elwell outdoes himself with every cover. Thanks, Tristan, for bringing Owen and Hercules to life so beautifully.

And last but never least, thank you to Patrick and Lauren, who always have my back and my heart.

If you love Sofie Kelly's
Magical Cats Mysteries, read on for an
excerpt of the first book in Sofie Ryan's
New York Times bestselling
Second Chance Cat Mysteries . . .

THE WHOLE CAT AND CABOODLE

Available wherever books are sold.

E lvis was sitting in the middle of my desk when I opened the door to my office. The cat, not the King of Rock and Roll, although the cat had an air of entitlement about him sometimes, as though he thought he was royalty. He had one jet-black paw on top of a small cardboard box—my new business cards, I was hoping.

"How did you get in here?" I asked.

His ears twitched but he didn't look at me. His green eyes were fixed on the vintage Wonder Woman lunch box in my hand. I was having an early lunch, and Elvis seemed to want one as well.

"No," I said firmly. I dropped onto the retro red womb chair I'd brought up from the shop downstairs, kicked off my sneakers, and propped my feet on the matching footstool. The chair was so comfortable. To me, the round shape was like being cupped in a soft, warm giant hand. I knew the chair had to go back down to the shop, but I was still trying to figure out a way to keep it for myself.

Before I could get my sandwich out of the yellow vinyl lunch box, the big black cat landed on my lap. He wiggled his back end, curled his tail around his feet and looked from the bag to me.

"No," I said again. Like that was going to stop him.

He tipped his head to one side and gave me a pitiful look made all the sadder because he had a fairly awesome scar cutting across the bridge of his nose.

I took my sandwich out of the lunch can. It was roast beef on a hard roll with mustard, tomatoes and dill pickles. The cat's whiskers quivered. "One bite," I said sternly. "Cats eat cat food. People eat people food. Do you want to end up looking like the real Elvis in his chunky days?"

He shook his head, as if to say, "Don't be ridiculous."

I pulled a tiny bit of meat out of the roll and held it out. Elvis ate it from my hand, licked two of my fingers and then made a rumbly noise in his throat that sounded a lot like a sigh of satisfaction. He jumped over to the footstool, settled himself next to my feet and began to wash his face. After a couple of passes over his fur with one paw he paused and looked at me, eyes narrowed—his way of saying, "Are you going to eat that or what?"

I ate.

By the time I'd finished my sandwich Elvis had finished his meticulous grooming of his face, paws and chest. I patted my legs. "C'mon over," I said.

He swiped a paw at my jeans. There was no way he was going to hop onto my lap if he thought he might get a crumb on his inky black fur. I made an elaborate show of brushing off both legs. "Better?" I asked.

Elvis meowed his approval and walked his way up my legs, poking my thighs with his front paws—no claws, thankfully—and wiggling his back end until he was comfortable.

I reached for the box on my desk, keeping one hand on the cat. I'd guessed correctly. My new business cards were inside. I pulled one out and Elvis leaned sideways for a look. The cards were thick brown recycled card stock, with SECOND CHANCE, THE REPURPOSE SHOP, angled across the top in heavy red letters, and SARAH GRAYSON and my contact information, all in black, in the bottom right corner.

Second Chance was a cross between an antiques store and a thrift shop. We sold furniture and housewares—many things repurposed from their original use, like the tub chair that in its previous life had actually been a tub. As for the name, the business was sort of a second chance—for the cat and for me. We'd been open only a few months and I was amazed at how busy we already were.

The shop was in a redbrick building from the late 1800s on Mill Street, in downtown North Harbor, Maine, just where the street curved and began to climb uphill. We were about a twenty-minute walk from the harbor front and easily accessed from the highway—the best of both worlds. My grandmother held the mortgage on the property and I wanted to pay her back as quickly as I could.

"What do you think?" I said, scratching behind

Elvis's right ear. He made a murping sound, cat-speak for "good," and lifted his chin. I switched to stroking the fur on his chest.

He started to purr, eyes closed. It sounded a lot like there was a gas-powered generator running in the room.

"Mac and I went to look at the Harrington house," I said to him. "I have to put together an offer, but there are some pieces I want to buy, and you're definitely going with me next time." Eighty-year-old Mabel Harrington was on a cruise with her new beau, a ninety-one-year-old retired doctor with a bad toupee and lots of money. They were moving to Florida when the cruise was over.

One green eye winked open and fixed on my face. Elvis's unofficial job at Second Chance was rodent wrangler.

"Given all the squeaks and scrambling sounds I heard when I poked my head through the trapdoor to the attic, I'm pretty sure the place is the hotel for some kind of mouse convention."

Elvis straightened up, opened his other eye, and licked his lips. Chasing mice, birds, bats and the occasional bug was his idea of a very good time.

I'd had Elvis for about four months. As far as I could find out, the cat had spent several weeks on his own, scrounging around downtown North Harbor.

The town sits on the midcoast of Maine. "Where the hills touch the sea" is the way it's been described for the past 250 years. North Harbor stretches from the Swift Hills in the north to the Atlantic Ocean in the south. It was settled by Alexander Swift in the late 1760s. It's full of beautiful historic buildings, award-winning restaurants and quirky little shops. Where else could you buy a blueberry muffin, a rare book and fishing gear all on the same street?

The town's population is about thirteen thousand, but that more than triples in the summer with tourists and summer residents. It grew by one black cat one evening in late May. Elvis just appeared at The Black Bear. Sam, who owns the pub, and his pickup band, The Hairy Bananas—long story on the name—were doing their Elvis Presley medley when Sam noticed a black cat sitting just inside the front door. He swore the cat stayed put through the entire set and left only when they launched into their version of the Stones' "Satisfaction."

The cat was back the next morning, in the narrow alley beside the shop, watching Sam as he took a pile of cardboard boxes to the recycling bin. "Hey, Elvis. Want some breakfast?" Sam had asked after tossing the last flattened box in the bin. To his surprise, the cat walked up to him and meowed a loud yes.

He showed up at the pub about every third day for the next couple of weeks. The cat clearly wasn't wild—he didn't run from people—but no one seemed to know whom Elvis (the name had stuck) belonged to. The scar on his nose wasn't new; neither were a couple of others on his back, hidden by his fur. Then someone remembered a guy in a van who had stayed two nights at the campgrounds up on Mount Batten. He'd had a cat with him. It was black. Or black and white. Or possibly gray. But it definitely had had a scar on its nose. Or it had been missing an ear. Or maybe part of its tail.

Elvis was still perched on my lap, staring off into space, thinking about stalking rodents out at the old Harrington house, I was guessing.

I glanced over at the carton sitting on the walnut sideboard that I used for storage in the office. The fact that it was still there meant that Arthur Fenety hadn't come in while Mac and I had been gone. I was glad. I was hoping I'd be at the shop when Fenety came back for the silver tea service that was packed in the box.

A couple of days prior he had brought the tea set into my shop. Fenety had a charming story about the ornate pieces that he said had belonged to his mother. A bit too charming for my taste, like the man himself. Arthur Fenety was somewhere in his seventies, tall with a full head of white hair, a matching mustache and an engaging smile to go with his polished demeanor. He could have gotten a lot more for the tea set at an antiques store or an auction. Something about the whole transaction felt off.

Elvis had been sitting on the counter by the cash register and Fenety had reached over to stroke his fur. The cat didn't so much as twitch a whisker, but his ears had flattened and he'd looked at the older man with his green eyes half-lidded, pupils narrowed. He was the picture of skepticism.

The day after he'd brought the pieces in, Fenety had called to ask if he could buy them back. The more I thought about it, the more suspicious the whole thing felt. The tea set hadn't been on the list of stolen items from the most recent police update, but I still had a niggling feeling about it and Arthur Fenety.

"Time to do some work," I said to Elvis. "Let's go downstairs and see what's happening in the store."

The cat jumped down to the floor and shook himself, and then he had to pause and pass a paw over his face. Elvis knew *store* meant "people," especially tourists, and *tourists* meant "new people who would generally take one look at the scar on his face and be overcome with the urge to stroke his fur and tell him what a sweet kitty he was."

I put on some lipstick and gave my head a shake. I'd gotten my thick, dark brown hair from my father and my dark eyes from my mom. I'd just cut my hair in long layers to my shoulders a couple of weeks previous. If we were moving furniture or I was going for a run I could still pull it back in a ponytail. Otherwise I could pretty much shake my head and my hair looked okay.

One of my part-time staff members, Avery, was by the cash register downstairs, nestling three mismatched soup bowls that had gotten a second life as herb planters into a box half-filled with shredded paper. Her hair was the color of cranberry sauce, and she'd shown up that morning with elaborate henna tattoos covering the backs of both hands. They were beautiful. (She claimed the look was all part of her "rebellious teenager" phase.) Avery worked afternoons in the store—her progressive private school had only morning classes—and full days when there was no school, like today.

I'd had a few rebellious moments myself as a teenager, so Avery's style didn't bother me. She was smart and hardworking, and even though one of the main reasons I'd hired her was because she was the granddaughter of one of my gram's closest friends, I kept her because she did a good job. And my customers seemed to like her.

Mac, the store's resident jack-of-all-trades, was showing a customer a tall metal postman's desk that we'd reclaimed from the basement of a house near the harbor. We'd had to cut the desk apart to get it up the narrow, cramped steps and through the door to the kitchen. Mac had banged out all the dents, put everything back together and then painted the piece a deep sky blue, even though I'd voted for basic black. I watched him hand the customer a tape measure, then give me a knowing smile across the room.

I could see the muscles in his arms move under his long-sleeved gray T-shirt. He was tall and fit with close-cropped black hair and light brown skin. Avery had given Mac the nickname Wall Street. He'd been a financial planner but had ditched his high-powered life to come to Maine and sail. In his free time he crewed for pretty much anyone who asked. There were eight windjammer schooners based in North Harbor, along with dozens of other sailing vessels. Mac was looking for space where he could build his own boat. He worked for me because he said he liked fixing things.

Second Chance had been open for a little less than four months. The main floor was one big open area, with some storage behind the staircase to the second floor. My office was under the eaves on the second floor. There was also a minuscule staff room and one other large space that was being used for storage.

Some things we offered in the shop were vintage kitsch, like my yellow vinyl Wonder Woman lunch box—with matching thermos. Some things were like Elvis—working on a new incarnation, like the electric blue shelving unit that used to be a floor-model TV console. Everything in the store was on its second or sometimes third life.

Our stock came from lots of different places: flea markets, yard sales, people looking to downsize. Mac had even trash-picked a metal bed frame that we'd sold for a very nice profit. A couple of Dumpster divers had been stopping by fairly regularly and in the last month I'd bought items from the estates of three different people. So far, rummaging around in boxes and closets I'd found half a dozen wills, a diamond ring, a set of false teeth, a stuffed armadillo and a box of ashes that thankfully were the remains of some-one's long-ago love letters and not, well, the remains of someone.

We sold some items in the store on consignment. Others, like the post office desk, we'd buy outright and refurbish. Mac could repair just about anything, and I was pretty good at coming up with new ways to use old things. And if I ran out of ideas, I could just call my mom, who was a master at giving new life to other people's discards.

Elvis had headed for a couple that was browsing near the guitars on the back wall. The young woman crouched down, stroking his fur and making sympathetic noises about his nose. The young man moved a couple of steps sideways to take a closer look at a Washburn mandolin from the '70s, with a spruce top and ebony fingerboard.

Avery had finished with the customer at the counter. She walked over and lifted the mandolin down from its place on the wall and handed it to the young man. "Why don't you give it a try?" she said. I knew as soon as he had it in his hands he'd be sold.

Avery glanced down at Elvis. He tipped his furry head to one side, leaning into the hand of the young woman who was scratching the top of his head, commanding all her attention, and it almost looked as though he winked at Avery.

A musical instrument was the reason I'd ended up with Elvis—that and his slightly devious nature. I'd taken a guitar down to Sam for a second opinion on what it was worth. Sam Newman and my dad had grown up together. I could play, and I knew a little about some of the older models, but Sam knew more about guitars than anyone I'd ever met. I'd found him sitting in one of the back booths with a cup of coffee and a pile of sheet music. The cat was on the opposite banquette, eating what looked suspiciously to me like scrambled eggs and salami.

Sam had moved his mug and the music out of the way, and I'd set the guitar case on the table. Elvis studied me for a moment and then went back to his breakfast.

"Who's your friend?" I asked, tipping my head toward the cat.

"That's Elvis," Sam said, flipping open the latches on the battered Tolex case with his long fingers. He was tall and lean, his shaggy hair a mix of blond and white.

"Really?" I said. "The King of Rock and Roll was reincarnated as a cat?"

Sam looked at me over the top of his dollar-store reading glasses. "Ha, ha. You're so funny."

I made a face at him. Elvis was watching me again. "Move over." I gestured with one hand. To my surprise the cat obligingly scooted around to the other side of the plate. "Thank you," I said, sliding onto the burgundy vinyl. He dipped his head, almost as though he were saying, "You're welcome," and went back to his scrambled eggs. They were definitely Sam's specialty. I could smell the salami.

"Is this the cat I've been hearing about?" I asked.

Sam was engrossed in examining the vintage Fender. "What? Oh yeah, it is."

Elvis's ears twitched, as though he knew we were talking about him.

"Why Elvis?"

Sam shrugged. "He doesn't seem to like the Stones, so naming him Mick was kinda out of the question." He waved a hand in the direction of the bar. "There's coffee."

That was Sam's way of telling me to stop talking so he could focus his full attention on the candy apple red Stratocaster. I got up and went behind the bar for the coffee, careful to keep the mug well out of the way of the old guitar when I brought it back to the table. Elvis had finished eating and was washing his face.

"What do you think?" I asked after a couple of minutes of silence. Sam's head was bent over the neck of the guitar, examining the fret board.

"Gimme a second," he said.

I waited, and after another minute or so he straightened up, pulling a hand over the back of his neck. "So, tell me what you think," he said, setting his glasses on the table.

I put my coffee cup on the floor beside my feet before I answered. "Based on what the homeowner told me it's a 1966. It belonged to her husband. It's not mint, but it's in good shape. There's some buckle wear on the back, but overall it's been taken care of. I think it's the real thing and I think it could bring twelve to fifteen thousand."

Beside me Elvis gave a loud meow.

"The cat agrees," I said.

"That makes three of us, then," Sam said.

I grinned at him across the table. "Thanks."

When I got up to leave, Elvis jumped down and followed me. "I think you made a friend," Sam said. He walked me out to my truck, set the guitar carefully on the passenger's side, and then wrapped me in a bear hug. He smelled like coffee and Old Spice. "Come by Saturday night, if you're free," he said. "I think you'll like the band."

"Old stuff?" I asked, pulling my keys out of the pocket of my jeans.

"Hey, it's gotta be rock-and-roll music if you wanna dance with me," he said, raising his eyebrows and giving me a sly smile. He looked down at Elvis, who had been sitting by the truck, watching us. "C'mon, you. You're gonna get turned into roadkill if you stay here." He reached for the cat, who jumped up onto the front seat.

"Hey, get down from there," I said.

Elvis ignored me, made his way along the black vinyl seat and settled himself on the passenger's side, next to the guitar case.

"No, no, no, you can't come with me." I leaned into the truck to grab him, but he slipped off the seat, onto the floor mat. With the guitar there I couldn't reach him.

Behind me, I could hear Sam laughing.

I blew my hair out of my face, backed out of the truck and glared at Sam. "Your cat's in my truck. Do something!"

He folded his arms over his chest. "He's not my cat. I'm pretty sure he's your cat now."

"I don't want a cat."

"Tell him that," Sam said with a shrug.

I stuck my head back through the open driver's door. "I don't want a cat," I said.

Ensconced out of my reach in the little lean-to made by the guitar case, Elvis looked up from washing his face—again—and meowed once and went back to it.

"I have a dog," I warned. "A big, mean one with big, mean teeth." The cat's whiskers didn't so much as quiver.

Sam leaned over my shoulder. "No, she doesn't," he said.

I elbowed him. "You're not helping."

He laughed. "Look, the cat likes you." He rolled his eyes. "Lord knows why. Take him. Do you want him to just keep living on the street?"

"No," I mumbled. I glanced in the truck again. Elvis, with some kind of uncanny timing, chose that moment to tip his head to one side and look up at me with his big green eyes. With his scarred nose he looked . . . lonely.

"What am I going to do with a cat?" I said, bouncing the keys in my right hand.

Sam shrugged. "Feed him. Talk to him. Scratch under his chin. He likes that."

I glanced at the cat again. He still had that lonely, slightly pathetic look going.

"You two will make a great team," Sam said. "Like Lennon and McCartney or Jagger and Richards."

"SpongeBob and Patrick," I muttered.

"Exactly," Sam said.

I was pretty sure I was being conned, but, like it or not, I had a cat.

I looked over now toward the end wall of the store. My cat had apparently helped sell a mandolin. The young man was headed to the cash register with it. Elvis made his way over to me.

I leaned over to stroke the top of his head. "Nice

work," I whispered. I wasn't imagining the cat smile he gave me.

The woman who had been looking at the post office desk was headed for the door, but there was a certain smugness to Mac's expression that told me he'd made the sale. I walked over to him. "Go ahead, say 'I told you so,'" I said.

He folded his arms over his chest. "I can't. I'm fairly certain she's going to buy it. She just wishes it were black."

I laughed. "I guess black really is the new black," I said. "I'm about ready to leave. I have to pick up Charlotte, and Avery is going to get her grandmother. Do you need anything before I go?"

I was doing a workshop on color-washing furniture for a group of seniors over at Legacy Place. North Harbor was full of beautiful old buildings. It was part of the town's charm. The top floors of the old chocolate factory had been converted into seniors' apartments. There were a couple of community rooms on the main level, where the residents had various classes like French and yoga and got together to socialize. We were using one of them for the workshop since many of the class participants lived in the building. Eventually I wanted to renovate part of the old garage next to the Second Chance building for workshops; for now, when I did classes for the general public, I had to settle for renting space at the high school. Luckily the hourly rate was pretty good. This workshop was a freebie my gram had nudged me into doing.

Mac shook his head. "I've got everything covered." He narrowed his brown eyes at me. "Are you sure it's a good idea to make Avery go with you?"

"Actually she volunteered."

"Avery volunteered to help you teach a workshop for a bunch of senior citizens?" One eyebrow shot up. "Seriously?"

"Seriously. She's good with older people. They'll be feeding her cookies and exclaiming over her hair color, and before you know it she'll have wangled an invitation to go prowl around someone's attic." Avery had a thing for vintage jewelry, and thanks to her grandmother Liz's friends, was building a nice collection.

I pressed my hands into the small of my back and stretched. I was still kinked from crawling around that old house all morning. "You know, I used to hang around with some of those same women when I was Avery's age." I'd spent my summers in North Harbor with my grandmother as far back as I could remember. The rest of the time I'd lived first in upstate New York and then in New Hampshire. "Liz taught me how to wax my legs and put on false eyelashes."

"I could have gone the rest of my life not knowing that," Mac said dryly.

"And I know the secret to Charlotte's potpie," I teased.

"You're not going to say it's love, are you?"

I shook my head and grinned. "Nope. Actually it's bacon fat."

My father had been an only child and so was my mother, so I didn't have a gaggle of cousins to hang out with in the summer. My grandmother's friends, Charlotte, Liz and Rose had become a kind of surrogate extended family, a trio of indulgent aunts. When I'd decided to open Second Chance, they'd been almost as pleased as my grandmother, and Charlotte and Rose had come to work for me part-time. Now with Gram out of town on her honeymoon, the three women fed me, gently nagged me about working too much and pointed out every single man between twenty-five and, well, death. When Gram had asked me to offer one of my workshops to her friends, how could I say no?

I glanced at my watch. "I don't expect to be more than a couple of hours," I said. "And I have my cell."

"Elvis and I can hold down the fort," Mac said. "Are you going to take another look at that SUV?"

I'd been thinking about replacing the aging truck we used to move furniture with an SUV, if I could get it for the right price. "I might," I said.

"Well, take your time," Mac said. "It's Monday afternoon. Nothing ever happens in this town on a Monday."

Of course he was wrong.

Sofie Kelly is a *New York Times* bestselling author and mixed-media artist who lives on the East Coast with her husband and daughter. She writes the *New York Times* bestselling Magical Cats Mysteries (*Whiskers and Lies*, *Hooked on a Feline*, and *A Case of Cat and Mouse*) and, as Sofie Ryan, writes the *New York Times* bestselling Second Chance Cat Mysteries (*Scaredy Cat*, *Totally Pawstruck*, and *Undercover Kitty*).

CONNECT ONLINE

SofieKelly.com